THE UNWEA

THE
UNWEAVING

A NOVEL

CHERYL PARISIEN

TIDEWATER
PRESS

Published by Tidewater Press
New Westminster, BC, Canada
tidewaterpress.ca

978-1-990160-40-0 (print)
978-1-990160-41-7 (e-book)

LIBRARY AND ARCHIVES CANADA CATALOGUING IN PUBLICATION
Title: The unweaving : a novel / Cheryl Parisien.
Names: Parisien, Cheryl, author.
Identifiers: Canadiana 20240461029 | ISBN 9781990160400 (softcover)
Subjects: LCGFT: Historical fiction.
Classification: LCC PS8631.A7468 U59 2024 | DDC C813/.6—dc23

Canada

Tidewater Press gratefully acknowledges the support of the Government of Canada.

For my family, especially my great-great-great uncle,
Norbert Parisien.

Author's Note

This is a work of fiction. However, many of the people and events are real. My own ancestors lived on river lots in St. Norbert and I always wondered how they ended up where they did when their beginnings were so different. This novel is my attempt to answer that question. I have amalgamated some historical figures, altered some of the historical events, and compressed timelines to suit the story. Any factual errors are mine.

Fredie
St. Norbert, Red River, May 1869

Fredie crouched in the tall grass by the side of the road where the tufts whispered just above his head. Hidden, he held his breath. He was not the baby of the Rougeau family, he was aen rinaar, a fox stalking his prey.

Fredie was eight now, maybe getting too big to play like this—at least that's what Suzette said. His sister was four years older and thought she knew everything. The bucket he was supposed to be filling with water from the well lay in the grass beside him as he sniffed the air, ready to pounce on voles. He narrowed his eyes and tilted his ear to the ground. He imagined the scratching of mice underground, burrowing deep to stay safe from his claws and hungry mouth.

The late afternoon sun gave everything a yellow glow and cast lanky shadows on the ground. It was pleasantly warm on his skin, not like earlier in the day. It had been too hot to play fox in the grass then. Instead, he'd stayed under the broad trees by the riverbank, even though he wasn't supposed to play too close to the water. The river was high after the spring flood and flowing faster than usual. His Papaa said that was because of the drought last summer. "You stay away from the shore, Fredie. If you fall in, you'll be all the way to Lake Winnipeg before anyone knows you are gone." But the swirling water drew Fredie and he couldn't stay away.

Tiny spotted frogs lived in the pools left behind after the flood. The pools were drying up but were still big enough to make a nice habitat. Fredie squished his hands in the mud at the edge of one, watching the water fill his handprint. The mud was cool. Fredie liked listening to the croaking frogs at night. He wondered how such small things could fill the air with so much sound. Their part of the river had a bend that swirled in on itself and seemed like a little pond. He liked to stand at the riverbed to watch the light dance on water.

As a breeze blew up, the grass brushed his face. A ball of cotton-wood fluff drifted by and tickled his nose. He swatted it away. Fredie saw a cloud of dust in the distance, moving closer. He stood up so he could see better and saw it was a man on a horse racing toward him.

The houses of St. Norbert were staggered on their lots. Most of them hugged the river but some, like Fredie's, sat farther away from shore. The rutted road cut through the midpoint of the lots, separating the hay lands from the homesteads. The rider didn't glance at any of the houses as he barrelled past. Fredie's house was the last in the settlement, next to a series of empty lots, but soon there would be new neighbours to the south—he could tell from the stakes in the ground. He'd heard his father say some people from Quebec were going to settle there.

The dust cloud stretched long and thin behind the rider and, as he got closer, Fredie felt the ground shake. He wondered if that was what the buffalo sounded like. His father and uncles loved to talk about the big buffalo hunts from their younger days. Fredie couldn't remember them going on a hunt. That was because the buffalo were fewer and farther away, at least that's what his father said. Fredie wished he could go on a hunt sometime; maybe he could be in charge of one of the lines that tied the Red River carts together, like Julien had done. Fredie envied his older brother. It was an important job—if the carts got loose, they could end up following in the same track as the cart ahead and get stuck in the prairie sod. Tying them one behind the other but slightly off to the side kept everything moving and in place. The sod stayed flat and the dust stayed down. Fredie puffed up thinking about it.

The man turned his horse into Fredie's lot, still riding fast. He blew past Fredie, who jumped out of the grass and followed him toward the house. The man leaped off the horse smoothly, patted its flank, and tied it to the post. The horse drank from the water barrel, its dark hide shining in the sun.

The big man was dressed in a fitted hide coat and matching trousers. The fringes on his sleeves swished as he moved. The back of his coat was decorated in a floral beadwork pattern, the red flowers and green stems snaked in a scalloped V-shape on the coat's yoke. Beads ran along the fringed outer seams of his trousers, and his moccasins were also heavily beaded, all in the same matching floral pattern. The man was tall and barrel-chested, yet he looked lean and elegant in his clothes. They moved with him, unrestricted. Fredie didn't think he'd seen this man before but wasn't sure. There were lots of men on the hunts or cart trips that he hadn't met yet. He could tell this man was important.

Fredie retrieved the bucket and went to the well. If he filled it quickly, he could get inside and hear what was going on. The pulley creaked as he yanked on the rope. It reminded him of a crow's squawk. Crows were tricksters, so he was wary of them. He looked up to see if any were in the trees, watching him. He didn't see any, but that didn't mean they weren't there. Crows brought change too, and change could be tricky. Fredie looked at the empty lot next to theirs. He could see the small stakes poking up from the ground like something growing. Erupting.

Water spilled on his moccasins as he transferred the water into his carrying bucket. He shook them, trying to shake off the wet. When he stamped his feet, a small frog hopped out from its hiding place by the well and froze under Fredie's gaze. It wasn't a vole, but aen rinaar pounced anyway, and chased the frog into the grass.

CHAPTER 1

Julien

May 1869

Julien shouted and spurred his horse into a gallop.

"We'll see who makes it to old Norbert-from-St.-Norbert first, eh?" he said to Henri, who grinned at him from his own horse. He nodded his head toward Norbert, who stood by the dead tree they used as a marker for the finish line.

Norbert-from-St.-Norbert raised his hand above his head. "Go!" he shouted, his voice faint from the distance.

Julien and Henri took off. Julien kicked his horse, urging it to go faster. He couldn't let Henri win, not after their last race. His friend had won by a head and rubbed Julien's face in the loss. Julien could laugh off losing to others, but not to Henri Lambert. They'd competed in everything since they were children. Henri's mother joked that even learning to walk was a race for them.

"You'll be swallowing my dust for dinner!" he shouted to Henri.

Julien leaned forward, enjoying the feel of the wind in his long hair. When he raced, he never tied his hair back—it was a superstition. It had to be free to whip around his face if he was to win. He breathed deep and felt his pulse slow down. He focused on the moment only, on the horizon, nothing else. He wished he could exist in that place all the time; where he felt no restlessness, only intense calm.

He could see the dead tree just ahead. He broke his concentration and turned to see Henri half a horse-length behind him.

"Bah!" he scoffed.

"I'm coming for you!" Henri said and laughed.

Julien surged ahead, giving it all he had. He passed the tree and pulled his horse to a stop.

"It's Julien, by a hair!" shouted Norbert-from-St.-Norbert.

Henri pulled up beside Julien and smiled at him. "Next time, it'll be me. Right, Norbert?"

Norbert nodded. "Could have gone either way. Henri is going to be better than you, Julien. Soon."

Julien felt his anger flare, but it faded when he looked at Norbert's smiling face. Norbert Parisien lived in St. Norbert too, in a small house with his mother and six younger sisters, all still unmarried. Everyone called him Norbert-from-St.-Norbert. He was twenty-six, eight years older than Julien and Henri, and his pleasant nature and easy ways made him liked by all. He worked as a labourer on nearby farms and at Fort Garry, picking up any odd job he could. He especially liked caring for animals but was best known as a woodcutter—he could split a cord of logs in half the time of anyone else. He swung his axe in a perfect arc, splitting logs and setting up a new one to cut, all in one motion. Watching him had a soothing, hypnotic effect.

Norbert patted the flank of Julien's horse. "This one's a beauty, Julien. Make sure you keep her. You should give her a name already."

"Bah!" Julien scoffed. "My Papaa says it is foolish to name horses, since they just get traded away anyway. He said horses are currency, and it isn't good to get attached."

"That's old-timer talk," said Henri. "No one uses the horse currency anymore."

Norbert shook his head. "Some still do. A horse trade still comes in handy. It's good to remember that. But still, Julien, you should name this horse."

Julien laughed. "I suppose you're right. But we've only ever called her Julien's Horse. I don't think she can learn a new name."

"Call her Julienne, then," Norbert said, as he smoothed the ribbons that decorated the saddle. "She won't know the difference."

They all laughed, but Julien liked the suggestion. Norbert had a subtle mind. He listened to whatever Norbert had to say—there was wisdom in it.

"I should get home," Henri said, looking in the direction of his house, which was a speck in the distance. "I won't hear the end of it if I don't help with the chores."

Julien looked the opposite way, toward his house, which wasn't visible from where they stood. "You're right. I'll probably catch hell too. Even though Fredie is old enough to be doing some of my chores now. At that age I was already in charge of the carts on the buffalo hunt. I was practically a man! Fredie is spoiled."

"I need to go too," Norbert said. "I'm watching the Hamelin place while they're out on the hunt. I'm going to have to fetch their cow; she likes to wander."

They clapped each other's shoulders and went off in different directions. Julien cantered along the trail. He knew he looked good on his horse, with its beaded blanket and saddle with trailing ribbons. He didn't need to dress his horse up just to race against Henri, but looking good was a point of pride. The reason to go anywhere was to be seen, so he liked to look his best. You never knew who you might meet.

St. Norbert was one of the parishes that made up Red River. There were several of them, some French, some English, all hugging the shores of the two rivers that had made the area a meeting place for millennia: the Assiniboine and the Red. The lots stretched out from the riverbank in long strips like floorboards, extending out for two miles. Everyone had access to the water, and neighbours were close. It was nice.

Some of the houses he passed were hidden by trees, some lots had almost no trees left. Julien was glad his family had been one of the ones to travel to the eastern forests to get the timber for their house instead of cutting down all their trees. It was important to keep some on the land.

When they'd gone for the timber, he'd been seven or eight, his sister Charlotte five, and Suzette just a toddler. Fredie wasn't even born yet. Even though he had been too young to lift the logs, he helped saw off the branches and strip some of the bark. A bear had wandered into their camp on that trip, and his Uncle Pierre killed it with one shot. It happened so fast, Julien hadn't had time to be scared. Julien had helped to skin and butcher the bear and his father let him keep one of its teeth. He still had the yellowed tooth, stashed away with his clothes. He liked to rub it for luck. They came home with a nice fur, meat, and a good supply of bear grease in addition to the timber, and his father built their house, with the help of Uncle Pierre.

The sun warmed his face, and he turned it up to the sky, enjoying the feel of it. Summer was on its way and would bring clouds of mosquitoes, too, after the wet spring. The meadow grasses sweetened the air. The rhythmic thud of the horse's steps added to the calm feeling he had. He breathed deep. He felt like the world was open and he could do anything. Opportunity was everywhere, like the freighting trip that was coming up to St. Paul. He loved those trips, dozens of carts rumbling across the prairie, their ungreased wheels screeching for miles. Maybe his future lay in Minnesota. St. Paul had so much more to offer: a railway, a bustling city with more merchants and trade goods than anywhere else nearby. And so much cheaper. That's why his father and almost every other man he knew traded their furs and whatever other goods they could scrounge up in St. Paul. They brought back household items, tools, and even fabric sometimes, which they then sold in St. Norbert and the other parishes. The Hudson's Bay Company and English merchants called it smuggling, but they hired the carters anyway. Everyone got their piece.

Julien wanted his piece, too. On this trip, he was going to ask if he could do some of the talking, to make his own connections.

He passed the Pelletier lot, with its neatly tilled garden and single-storey log house. He could see Madame Pelletier examining the garden spouts with her hands on her hips. She looked up at Julien as he rode past and waved. He waved back, flashing a big smile.

"That garden is going to be your biggest yet," he called. "My mamaa will be full of envy. Better keep an eye on it!"

She laughed and dismissed him with a wave. "As if Marienne Rougeau would ever admit to being jealous of anyone."

"True enough. Still though…" Julien laughed and rode off.

The trail curved and his house came into view, farther back from shore than some of the others. His mother wanted to be closer to the river, since they used it for transport, but his father didn't want their house and garden flooding every spring, so he built it further back.

Their house was one of the few in the area to have an upstairs. Because his mother wanted to settle down and his father didn't really want to yet, his compromise had been to build a home that would stand out, something he could be proud of.

Julien turned onto the lane and saw Fredie waddling to the door carrying a full water bucket that looked as if it was about to tip over. He considered shouting to startle Fredie and make him spill the water, then noticed the sleek brown horse tied to the post near the house. He thought he recognized the beadwork on the blanket and saddle: those clusters of red flowers were favoured by the Dubeau family who lived in the neighbouring parish of St. Vital. Julien knew the eldest son, Florian, from the cart trail. Could he be the visitor? He tied his horse next to the visitor's and hurried inside. If it was Florian, Julien wanted to hear any news he was bringing.

CHAPTER 2

Marienne

May 1869

"Suzette! Quit dreaming and help me like I asked," Marienne shouted. She was carrying a large pot of stew from the wood stove to the table. It was bubbling over and she didn't want it making a mess on the floor. "Get the trivet mat and put it on the table."

Her younger daughter looked confused. "Trivet?"

"Ah ben! Don't play ignorant with me now. You wove the mat last winter. Made one for Aunt Denise and Madame Pelletier, too."

"Ohhh!" Suzette ran to the cupboard and retrieved the mat and slapped it down on the table.

Charlotte was setting biscuits on a plate on the other side of the kitchen. "Weaving those mats is the only thing you're good at. You'd think you'd know what they're called!" she said.

"Bah, Charlotte, leave her alone. We're going to eat right away."

Marienne's brown hair was braided and coiled in a low, tidy knot. Even in the heat, no stray hairs wisped about her face. She wore a long calico dress that swished around her legs as she moved. Her summer moccasins made no noise as she moved about the kitchen, her steps as light and dainty as the deer they were made from. She set the pot on the trivet with a thud and shook her head. Suzette had been useless lately, distracted all the time. She narrowed her eyes. Perhaps Suzette's blood was starting; she was twelve years old, the right age. Marienne had been twelve when hers first came, and her sister Denise had been thirteen. She softened at the realization. Let Suzette be distracted, then. She'd get used to it soon enough.

There was a knock at the door. "Come in," she called. "Clément! Someone's here!"

Her husband entered the kitchen as their visitor stepped in.

"Florian! It's good to see you." Clément clapped him on the back in greeting.

"Clément, it's been too long!"

Fredie slipped in after Florian, struggling with the water bucket. He bumped into the guest, who looked down at him and grinned.

"You must be young Fredie," he said, taking the bucket from him as if it weighed nothing and setting it down out of the way. "Soon enough you'll be carting with us men, eh?"

Fredie looked as if he didn't know whether to be afraid of the large man or curl up in his lap. Marienne put her arm around her baby and pushed him toward the small bedroom just off the kitchen. "Go tell Mare it's time to eat. She should be done resting by now."

She smiled at Florian. "We have some stew that's just ready—let's get you a bowl. Suzette, serve our guest before it gets cold."

Suzette looked at the steaming pot that had been simmering all afternoon and gave her another confused look. Marienne could sense Suzette was holding back an eye-roll; she had no patience for adolescent antics.

"Sit, sit!" Marienne said to Florian.

He pulled a kitchen chair back, and the wicker seat heaved under his bulk when he sank into it. It was like a doll's chair under him, yet he seemed comfortable, at ease.

"So, what news?" Clément asked.

Florian ran his hand over his hair and sighed.

"The Boucher brothers came back from Petite Pointe des Chênes about a week ago," Florian said. "They said they saw the Dawson Road crew there with surveyors right near the town, measuring strange rectangles with their chains and marking them with stakes."

"Isn't that just part of the road building?" asked Marienne. She nodded to Suzette to start ladling out the stew.

Florian shook his head. "This is different. They were marking up land on people's farms as if the farms weren't there. One of Boucher's cousins was doing some work for that crew— clearing land, the real heavy work—and those Ontario men were talking like the claims they marked out would be secured." Florian spooned the stew into his mouth without blowing on it first to cool it and gulped it down without flinching.

"But why at Petite Pointe des Chênes?" Clément asked. "There are already people there. Do they want to join the town? We heard we might get new neighbours here from Quebec. The stakes are already there."

"This is something different," Florian said. "That crew is not just building a road. Boucher's cousin wasn't paid the same as the Ontario workers. He didn't get paid in money but in chits, redeemable only at John Schultz's store."

"Schultz!" Clément said. "That Canadian Party fool. His newspaper has been harping about joining Canada and filling Red River with English settlers. He's been getting people riled up."

Marienne refilled his bowl. "Why would they want to settle in Petite Pointe des Chênes? They should rather be around their own people, more like. It makes no sense."

"Nothing about Schultz and his type makes sense." Florian paused to eat more stew. "The road will make it easier for people to come from the east. They're building it for a reason, and not for us. I think the same thing is going to happen here, too."

Charlotte set the biscuits on the table. She stood there as if waiting for someone to pull a chair out for her. No one did, so she sat and folded her hands neatly on the table. Suzette sat next to her.

"Why would settlers come here? Why not Selkirk or Kildonan?" asked Charlotte.

"Just watch," Florian said, pointing for emphasis. "They're going to mark up the land and parcel it away. Once there's a road, a railway will be next."

"That won't happen." Clément waved his hand in dismissal. "You're worrying over nothing. The land is ours. We have patent from the Company. It's all settled. Let them survey if they want. If they're busy laying down and counting chains, they can't cause any other trouble. Besides, it's only one crew. Let them have their road and railway. Nothing will come of it."

They fell quiet. Marienne looked from her husband to Florian. Clément had that head-in-the-sand expression he got when he was worried but didn't want to show it. She tensed when he got that look, because it meant he would gloss over and dismiss anything he didn't like. His habit of pretending problems weren't problems was why she'd insisted on them settling on this river lot in the first place. She had to be the one to make him see reality.

"It was the Company that wanted us all to settle on these lots, once the pemmican trade started to dry up," she said. "We've been here for years, and some of these lots have been settled for decades."

"The pemmican trade's not dried up yet!" Clément said.

"Well, it won't be around for long," Marienne huffed.

The door banged open as Julien came in. A slow smile spread across his face as he looked at everyone around the table. "Florian! I thought that was your horse. It's good to see you. You here to talk about the next cart trip? We're looking forward to it, eh Papaa?"

"He's here about something else," Clément said. "Sit down and eat and hear what he has to say."

Marienne filled a bowl and set it in front of Julien, who sat next to Suzette.

Florian rubbed his thick beard. His frizzy brown hair glowed in the light from the window and stuck out from his face in a nimbus, like in the paintings of angels and saints at church.

"The men have been talking," Florian said. "I'm getting a small group to ride out there to see what is happening. I came here to ask you to join us."

"Go where?" Julien asked. He didn't touch his stew but sat straight in his chair, alert. Marienne thought she could see his ears swivel forward like a dog's.

"Some surveyors have been marking up the town in Petite Pointe des Chênes," Clément said. "Florian wants to see what's going on, but I think it's a bunch of nothing. We'll miss too much time on the cart trail if we go east now when we should be heading south to St. Paul. "

"You may be right, Clément. It could be there is nothing to worry about. But we should know what is going on. And we should be ready."

Clément nodded. The air felt flatter, subdued. Florian clapped his hands on his tree-trunk thighs and stood up to leave. The chair legs screeched against the floorboards as, without a word, Suzette rose and cleared his bowl away. Clément stood and walked Florian outside. Clément was tall, but seemed tiny next to Florian, who had to duck his head as he passed through the doorway. Marienne could hear them talking in low tones and strained to make out what they said. Fredie returned from the bedroom without Mare.

"Mare said she wanted to rest some more and will eat later," he said.

"Hmm," Marienne said, sounding dubious. "I think you stayed in there extra long so you could eavesdrop with Mare. I'll bring her something in a while. Now, Frédéric, I know you were out there playing when you should have been fetching the water." She ruffled his hair. "Aen rinaar, you need to finish your chores before playing fox. Now sit and eat."

She handed him a bowl and smiled, so he'd know he wasn't in trouble.

"Mamaa, do you think we need to be worried about the surveyors?" Suzette asked.

"I don't know, ma fiyl. Maybe."

Julien stood up. "I'm going to talk to Papaa about this. Maybe I could go with Florian." He rushed out before Marienne could respond.

Charlotte scoffed. "I think they're worried over nothing. Having new people here is a good thing. They'll bring new life and opportunities with them. Do you really think the railway will come here?"

Marienne sighed. "If more people do come, let's hope the opportunities they bring are for everyone, not just themselves. A railway will bring more people here, but it will also take them away."

"Isn't that the point?" Charlotte said.

CHAPTER 3

Clément

May 1869

Clément brushed his horse down. He liked the steady, repetitive motion. Everything else fell away when he did that. Even as a child, he had found comfort in routine. His brother, Pierre, teased him about it still, but he didn't care. Everyone had different ways to calm the mind and doing chores was hardly unusual. If anything, his calm acceptance and pleasure in doing routine tasks had garnered him praise when he was young. Clément paused in his brushing—maybe that's why Pierre teased him. He hadn't put it together until just now. He resumed brushing with more vigour.

Clément wanted to know what Pierre thought of all this talk of surveyors. Ever since Florian Dubeau had shown up at his house raising the alarm, Clément had been considering what the younger man said. His words snagged onto Clément's thoughts like burrs and wouldn't let go.

"What do you think, eh?" He whispered to the horse and patted its neck. It blinked slowly at him, those long eyelashes sweeping his thoughts in—a perfect listener. "A whole lot of noise over nothing."

The horse snorted and stamped its foot. The other three horses in the barn stirred, too. Clément shushed them. The horse next to his was Julien's, which his son was now calling Julienne. Clément wondered if he should name his horse, too, but decided against it, even though he would probably keep it because of its endurance and calm temperament. He ran his hand along Julienne's flank. It was warm and smooth under his hand.

He returned to his own horse and continued grooming. He was ambivalent about the other two horses; they'd only had them for a couple of years. He might trade one of them after this carting trip to St. Paul. Old Man Boucher in St. Boniface had been asking around, looking to add another horse to his barn. Horses moved around from family to family like game pieces on a board. Sometimes he thought it was wrong to trade them, but those thoughts didn't linger. Didn't snag. A horse was a being from the spirit realm, with calm wisdom in its rolling eyes, but it was also a practical tool. He could live with that duality and had no problem using his horses to pull his cart, to race, to trade.

He was looking forward to the St. Paul trip. He liked having time on the road with Julien. At eighteen, his elder son was a man eager to strike out on his own, but Clément wasn't ready to let him go. It was helpful to have him around to share chores and the trips were even more important. Lately, though, Julien seemed more interested in racing horses and showing off like a prairie chicken rather than helping out at home. This trip was coming at a good time—it would keep Julien out of trouble.

He wanted to bring Fredie along, too, but when he'd told Marienne about it that morning, she objected. "Fredie is too young. It isn't safe on the road for him," she'd said.

He'd lost his temper. "Ever since you were pregnant with Fredie, you see threats everywhere. You refused to go on the hunt, and we had to scrape by that winter trapping meagre furs. We almost didn't make it that year!"

"You remember how hard Suzette's birth was! I was never the same after that. I couldn't do it again, jostling for weeks in a cart with a heavy belly. Remember how your cousin Nancy gave birth right when we finally found the herd and the slaughter began? That wasn't going to be me. Nor was I going to walk all the way home with a newborn in a cradleboard again. Never mind all the butchering, rendering, and making the pemmican. It's easy when you can ride on a horse. You've never had to walk behind a loaded cart while carrying a load of your own."

Clément had looked away then and was quiet for a few minutes. "What happened to the young woman who could jump on a horse and shoot as straight as any hunter? We'd talk all night by the fire on those hunts. I miss those days, when a thousand carts would roll across the land."

"You never see things as they are. You're either in the past or in some ideal present. Just open your eyes and look around sometimes." Her voice had softened, and she gave his arm a gentle squeeze.

The conversation had stayed with him all morning and was the reason the horses were getting such good attention now.

He felt bad that Fredie wouldn't get to experience the hunt. The boy always asked for stories about those days and seemed desperate to go. That's why he wanted Fredie to come along to St. Paul, to get a taste of it, at least. Plus he could get the boy away from that young priest, Father Courchene, who was too friendly with Fredie, filling his head with big ideas about going to school in Montreal and joining the seminary. The schooling he was getting in St. Norbert was good enough, even if the Métis weren't taught to read and write like the English kids. Maybe he should pull Fredie out of class. All he learned was French, catechism, animal husbandry, and numbers. The girls were taught the same, only they learned embroidery instead of animal care. Clément didn't see the point. Julien had only gone for a couple of years. Children could learn everything they needed to know travelling on the open plain. Movement was freedom, and travelling from place to place, sleeping under the stars and talking around a nighttime fire were what made life worth living.

Clément dressed his horse in all its finery, as he always did. His beaded horse blanket and matching pad saddle were well worn, the leather soft and pliable, faded to a light beige. He ran his hand over the beadwork, hooking his fingers in the looped fringe. His mother had made this set for him years ago. The four corners of the stuffed saddle were decorated with quillwork in bright yellow, red, white, and black, rather than the floral beadwork Marienne and Charlotte excelled at.

Some of the English people said the Métis were boastful for such displays, and perhaps that was true, but not showing the hard work that went into the beadwork and embroidery on their clothes and items would be a sin. Clément liked how his saddle stood out among the rest. People in St. Paul always commented on it. He would use it until it fell apart. His wife or his mother would salvage what they could and sew the beadwork onto moccasins or mittens. Or perhaps they'd take it apart and reuse the beads in a new design. Beadwork always lived on.

∞

"Yes, he came to see me, too," said Pierre.

They sat on stumps near the river, where Pierre's woodpile was. He'd been chopping when Clément rode up. They each took slugs of water from a canteen. Pierre wiped his forehead with his sleeve.

"Well, are they worrying over nothing or what?" asked Clément.

"Hard to say. But I think I'm going to go with Florian and other men he's rounded up to see what's happening out there. Just to see."

"You're not going to St. Paul?"

Pierre curled his lip. "I'll go next time. I think this could be important."

Clément pondered this. He was not surprised that Pierre was so eager to go see what the surveyors were up to. His whole life, Pierre had been easy to sway, keen to skip his regular routine for something new. He looked ahead to what was over the next rise, not what was in front of him. Something better was always waiting. He wasn't a dreamer exactly, so much as a restless soul.

They'd grown up in a small shack in St. Vital, the house more of a depot than a permanent home. They'd moved around, following the herds and the medicines, staying in different camps each season. So it was easy to understand why Pierre liked to move. When Pierre had built his log house a few lots over after they'd finished Clément's house, he'd been surprised. Marienne thought Pierre would find a wife next, but he never did. It had been over ten years now, and Pierre still had a dirt floor and the bare minimum of furniture.

"Be sure to tell me if something is going on," said Clément. "I want to know."

Pierre put his arm around Clément. "You know I will, brother. You know how it is—this is a chance for a small adventure that will probably turn to nothing. But I smell something in the air, and it calls me."

Clément laughed. "Something is calling you all right! Something that smells like merde!"

∞

That night, Clément squeezed close to Marienne in their bed. It creaked as he moved, the mattress ticking warm and scratchy. His mother was snoring lightly in her own small bedroom next to theirs.

He could hear Charlotte and Suzette whisper-bickering in the bed they shared upstairs. The children all shared the upstairs, which was one big room with a curtain separating the boys' side from the girls'. He remembered hanging the curtain, with Charlotte and Julien each eyeing the space, making sure one side didn't have even one extra inch than the other. He had made a show of taking them seriously, measuring the space with his footsteps and knocking his head on the low parts of the peaked ceiling. That night he and Marienne laughed about it. "I was the same way with Pierre," he'd said.

"Pierre says he's going to see what the surveyors are up to," said Clément.

"Are you saying you're going, too?" She shifted away from him a bit. "Move over, it's too hot."

He moved so he was closer to the edge of the bed, giving her space. "No, I'm not going," he said. "I'm going with Julien to St. Paul like we planned."

Marienne turned her head to look at him. The moon was nearly full and the room was surprisingly bright. "Pierre will tell us what's going on anyway. He likes having a story to tell, so this trip will suit him fine."

Clément grunted.

"How many are going with Pierre?" Marienne asked.

"Florian, one of the Boucher boys, a couple of men from St. Vital I don't know, and maybe a couple more yet—Pierre said Florian is still rounding people up. Pierre said he'd check some traps along the way. See what the crows are saying."

Marienne snorted. "Those crows, always talking."

They lay in silence for several minutes.

"We should maybe add some beadwork items to our trade goods," said Clément. "Pad saddles, maybe. People always talk about mine."

Marienne was quiet for a bit before she answered. "Pad saddles aren't quick; they take time to do right. But we can have some by winter. Charlotte is already strong in her beadwork, so anything she does won't take long. Suzette is getting there, even though her skills aren't as strong. The blankets and pad saddles, she's not ready to work on those yet. Maybe in a year or so. But we can get something going."

Clément kissed her cheek. "I don't want to be there when you tell ma bibiche that she's going to have to work harder with the beading and embroidery."

"That's because you spoil that girl and she knows it."

"And you're too strict with her."

"She needs to toughen up and realize that the sun does not shine for her alone. Charlotte dreams too much. Sometimes she acts like she's the lady of the manoir. She needs to get on with her chores and be useful. And I'm the one who always has to remind her."

"Yes, yes, you are right, as always." He squeezed close to her again, and she softened against him. "Just remember, Charlotte will only be pushed so far. If anyone needs extra honey, it's her."

"Pfft." Marienne let herself be squeezed. "Too many stings to get that honey, but I take your point."

They cuddled and kissed, and soon it didn't matter how warm the evening was; they were too wrapped up in each other to care.

CHAPTER 4

Julien

May–June 1869

Julien and his father rumbled in their Red River cart with the rest of the freighters heading south along the Pembina Trail to Minnesota and St. Paul. There were at least thirty other carts on this trip, all loaded heavy with different goods to trade. The Rougeaus had a modest supply of furs, as did Henri and his father, Claude. They'd been on the road for twenty days, and this night was their last before they reached town.

All the carts stopped in the same place for the night. The Rougeaus and the Lamberts made camp together, as they had throughout the trip, their carts side by side. In past years, the carts were parked in a big circle with the horses and the camp in the centre, protection from attacks by the Sioux. There hadn't been an attack for several years, so the freighters had relaxed.

Julien and Henri leaned back on their packs and enjoyed the sunset, their bellies full from their evening meal.

"We could be traders, too," Henri said.

"We could do better than this," Julien agreed, gesturing at the assembled carts. "We could sell more things, better things; really build a network."

"Yes! And we'd start with our own seed money. That way we wouldn't need credit like everyone else does."

Julien nodded. "I've already been saving. Credit is what keeps everyone tied down. You can't grow a business when you're always in debt. There's no way to get ahead."

"It's a trap. The trick is to see the trap before you get stuck in it."

"One day," Julien smiled, "we'll have our own store, and we can hire others to cart for us."

"Eventually we'll have a whole chain of stores!"

"An empire!"

"Listen to these two captains of industry," Claude said to Clément. "They'll rule this whole land yet." The older men chuckled. "Let's get through this trip first before you two crown yourselves, eh?"

∞

Julien looked into the flat blue eyes of the owner of the trading post, Collins. He was pleased with their furs, but he pursed his lips like there was a problem.

"You know," he said, pointing at the floral beadwork that decorated Julien's vest, "we're getting a lot of steamships through here. Lots of people from places like New York City and Boston, people who want to see what the 'Wild West' is like. There's an appetite for real Indian goods. Especially beadwork. They all love beadwork." He smiled. "You think you can get stuff like that?"

"Well, you're in luck!" Clément said in his heavily accented English. "I happen to have the best beaders in Red River living in my house. Next time I come here, I'll have a cart full of beadwork for you. Tell your customers."

Julien opened his mouth to add to the sales pitch, but his father cut him off. "My son here knows what I'm saying. His sister, Charlotte, is the best in the region. Get ready, we're going to make a lot of money." He slapped the counter for emphasis.

Julien leaned forward so Collins could see the beadwork better. "Look at the stitching," he said. "Not even a hair's width between those beads."

"Well, you're going to need some help," said Collins, all smiles. "Those beads need to go on something, maybe vests or coats. Have you seen the latest thing? It's a sewing machine. Been popular out east for a while, and now they're catching on here. Cuts your time in half."

"Oh? Then let's see it."

His father winked at Julien as Collins went into the storeroom. He clapped him on the back. "See how easy it is? Everything always works out, you just have to trust that it will."

Julien chuckled. "Papaa, you amaze me. But can we have enough items ready for the next trip?" He imagined Charlotte's face when she learned she'd have to do the lion's share of the beadwork. She was good at it and could work quickly, but she didn't like to be told what to do.

"We'll come up with something—no need to worry."

As soon as Collins brought the sewing machine out for them to see, Julien knew they'd be buying it. It was shiny and black, with gold paint decorating the machine and the table it sat on. He'd never seen anything like it.

"I keep this display model on wheels since there's so much interest in it. See the treadle here," Collins pointed at the bottom, "the lady uses her foot to power the machine. All the stitches are evenly spaced with none of the effort."

Julien felt the smooth, cool surface of the metal under his palm. "It almost looks like furniture, it's so elegant."

"It looks expensive," his father said, sucking his teeth.

"It will pay for itself in no time," Collins said. "I'm sure we can make an arrangement. Credit is always an option. Maybe that unique saddle of yours as a down payment?"

Julien looked at his father, expecting him to refuse.

"You don't want that old thing," Clément said. "I'll come back with a nice new saddle for you, with a blanket to match."

Julien watched his father negotiate with Collins. Sometimes he saw him as a bit of a relic, reluctant to try something new, but at times like these, when he was self-assured, Julien was proud. His father could smell a deal and profit. Julien believed him when he said everything would work out.

At camp that night, the four of them talked excitedly about their trades.

"You better not let Octavie see that sewing machine, Clément, she'll be after one for herself," Claude said.

"I might need to hide from Marienne, once she learns how much it cost!"

They all laughed.

Julien felt fired up after the day's events. He had too much energy to sit still, so he paced around their camp, looking for twigs on the ground to add to the fire.

His father lit his pipe and gestured to Julien with it. "You're pacing in a figure eight like a buffalo hunt capitaine, trying not to get your horse dizzy."

"I wish I could corral some buffalo now," Julien said. "I could hop on my horse and ride with no hands while I load my rifle, like a true hunter."

His father turned serious. "Not many men can ride while they tamp down the gunpowder, spit a ball-bullet down the barrel, and avoid fallen animals, gopher holes, other riders. A person could learn, but for the best, it comes naturally."

"Julien could do it," Henri said. "He and his horse move as one."

Julien inclined his head toward Henri, acknowledging the compliment.

"You can't be too proud, though, because that's when you make mistakes," Claude said. "Remember, Clément, what happened to my cousin Charles?"

"Not this story again," Henri groaned.

"I've never heard it," Julien said and sat down to listen.

Claude lit his own pipe and inhaled the smoke deeply. "My cousin was one of the best riders, always was capitaine. One time, he misjudged how much powder he'd stuffed down the barrel of his gun and blew off half his face when he spit his bullet in."

"Ah ben!" Julien gasped.

Claude continued. "The injury was fierce, and Father Benoît said it was time for last rites. Charles survived for three days, moaning in his tent. His wails kept half the camp awake. His wife tried to comfort him, but nothing could quiet him. It was a relief when he died, for him, but for us, too. We buried him near some trees because the priest said there was no way we could carry Charles' body back home to the churchyard for burial."

"Not in that heat," said Clément. "We were weeks away from home."

"Some of the elders tried to convince the priest it would be better to leave Charles on a platform high up in one of the trees, in the old way. The priest said the suggestion was horrifying. He didn't understand anything. I was fifteen when Charles died, and I think about him every time I load my rifle."

"Did this happen a lot?" Julien looked at Claude. "I've seen men with scars on their face and always wondered what happened to them."

"Enough times." Claude shook his head. "Too many times."

"But still," Henri said, "there's nothing like a hunt, and how it all comes together in the moment, with a présidente and capitaines. Like everyone was already in place and waiting."

Julien nodded. "The last hunt we went on, I was too young to ride like that. I wish I could have been part of it."

"Well, your Aunt Flossie and Uncle Joseph go out still," Clément said. "You can join them next time."

Julien hadn't seen his father's sister and her family in years. They lived west of St. Norbert, in White Horse Plain. Julien had cousins there he hadn't even met. "Maybe I should go visit them," he said.

"Sure, sure," his father said. "But not until the next trading trip is done. After how well you helped today with old Collins, I'm not letting you loose."

"We heard you boys talking all night about your big plans for your business empire," Claude said. "Maybe it should be the four of us instead of only you two."

Julien caught Henri's eye. Were their dreams about the future all just talk? Julien didn't want to be under his father's thumb.

"Let's survive bringing the sewing machine home first," Julien said with a laugh.

CHAPTER 5

Charlotte

July 1869

Charlotte stabbed her finger with her sewing needle. She was practising her embroidery, adding pink flowers to the edge of a handkerchief.

"Ah ben!" she hissed and sucked the blood that bubbled from her fingertip.

Suzette snickered.

Charlotte glared at her as she examined her finger. Her left thumb and index finger were calloused and rough. She could see all the points where the needle had poked her skin and healed over, a testament to her many years of sewing. Imperfections. She'd started sewing as soon as she was old enough to thread a needle. Her mother had been eager to put her to work. Charlotte wondered how many times her fingers had been poked. Too many times to count, probably. Her mother never showed any sympathy, said she should use a thimble if she wanted to keep her fingers pristine, but Charlotte could never get the feel of it right. The thimble was in the way, and her thumb was unprotected anyway, so why bother? Instead, she just learned to live with having rough fingers. It wasn't as though the rest of her hands looked any better. Her skin was often dry and cracked because of all the washing, gardening, hauling, chopping.

Drudgery.

She set the needle down and looked out the window, where an orange square of evening light from the setting sun filled the glass. Every day was the same: a circle, a loop of thread that pulled tighter and tighter, binding her to this life. In the mornings, she helped prepare their breakfast, then cleaned it all up after. Then it was the washing, or drawing water from the well, or tending the garden, gathering eggs, milking the cow, feeding the pig, sweeping the floor. Then more meals, more cleaning up after the meals, then finally some sewing by lamplight. No time left to wander the meadow, soak her feet in the soggy mud by the riverbed, lie in the grass and watch the clouds change shape in the sky. Only work, always more work. Even the work that she liked, such as embroidery and beading, had the joy stripped from it because all the other endless chores pressed so heavily on her.

She looked over at her grandmother, Mare, sewing in the same circle of lamplight as her and Suzette. Mare was Saulteaux and had been born in the northern forests, somewhere near York Factory. Mare's family had died when she was young and she had been taken in by some people from the fort at York Factory. She married a voyageur and ended up in Red River when she was sixteen, the same age Charlotte was now. Everyone called her Mare, because when Julien was learning to talk, he could never quite say "memayr," and so "Mare" had stuck. Mare had lived with them for Charlotte's whole life; her grandfather had died before she was born. When Charlotte was four or five, Mare told her the story of what had happened to him. "He dropped dead that winter when he was hanging bells and ribbons on the dog carioles. We were getting ready to go to a dance, and Pepayr was setting us up to arrive in style. Instead, when I went outside to leave, I found him in the snow, his eyes frozen open and lifeless, ribbons gripped in his hand, waving in the wind."

Mare had told this story matter-of-factly and that made it terrifying. For weeks afterward, she'd dreamed of those unseeing eyes and waving ribbons. Even now, the sound of tinkling bells and whipping ribbons on winter nights brought the dreams back.

Mare was absorbed in her work, her face close to the pad saddle she was working on. Her straight black hair was parted in the middle and pulled tight in the back; only a few gray hairs streaked the front, evenly spaced from the part. She kept her thumbnails long, to sweep the beads into place as she sewed, and to pull out stitches with the sharp corner of her nail when she needed to. The rest she kept trimmed short. Charlotte watched her wrinkled brown hands move in a smooth rhythm. Stitch, bead, stitch, bead, stitch, bead. Her chest rose and fell in time with her movements. Calm, steady. Sometimes Charlotte thought she heard a quiet drumbeat when she watched her grandmother work.

Suzette got up from her chair to show her rosettes to Mare, her face hopeful, expectant. How eager Suzette was to get even the smallest crumb of praise. Suzette was still learning, but her progress was slow. She was an adequate beader, even if her rows were jagged, each bead slightly off, not perfectly aligned and spaced like Charlotte's. Her embroidery was worse, the weight of her stitches either too heavy or too light. Charlotte had shown Suzette how to do it over and over and Suzette never got better.

Suzette held her hoop of fabric in front of Mare, her eyes downcast, waiting for Mare to inspect her work only when she was ready. Sometimes she looked up right away, and sometimes Suzette stood with her arm held out for several minutes.

Today, she didn't make Suzette wait. She snatched the hoop and looked at it closely. Then she handed it back without looking at Suzette.

"The thread needs to sing to you," Mare said. "This has no music in it."

Suzette hung her head and went back to her chair.

Charlotte asked to see Suzette's hoop. "Do you need me to draw the stitch marks for you to make it easier?" she asked.

"I can do it." Suzette snatched the hoop back.

"You just need to practise, that's all. It isn't hard."

"Maybe for you!"

"Enough, you two," Mare said. "You both have different strengths. Look how good Suzette's braided mats are. The weave is so tight you could turn them into bowls and carry water with them."

Suzette beamed and Charlotte gave her a half smile. The last year or so, nearly everything Suzette did irritated her. Suzette had grown nearly as tall as Charlotte, even though she was only twelve. Her limbs seemed too long for her body, and she'd become easily distracted and testy. Charlotte refused to put up with it.

She put the embroidery away and picked up her beadwork. She was working on a new project, something she was excited about, a decorative shelf valence made of velvet. She'd gotten the idea from the wall pockets she usually made. The wall pockets were pouches of various size and shape made from deer hide or any scrap fabric, and elaborately embroidered. Charlotte had made ones for her mother, Mare, and Suzette last year. They hung on the wall by their usual chairs in the sitting room and held their sewing supplies. The pouches were pretty to look at while also being useful. Charlotte wanted to make something that was decorative only. Something she could enjoy looking at for its own sake, that was simply beautiful. Décor, it was called. She liked the sound of it. Not everything had to be useful, to have a purpose.

Her Aunt Denise had given her a scrap of black velvet that she'd hemmed into a scalloped edge, then visualized her bead pattern: triple vines entwined together with red, pink, and white flowers interspersed among the leaves. The colours stood out against the black velvet. She was only part-way done on the beading, but already she could tell it would be her best work yet. She thought about this project as she scrubbed clothes in the wash bin and chopped vegetables for dinner. She usually rushed through these rote tasks so they would be over sooner. Lately she'd stretched them out, letting her mind come up with new design ideas as she worked. Inspiration came from whatever was in front of her. Carrot slices became orange flower centres or setting suns. At night, she'd lie in bed and look at the patch of sky she could see through the small window. Soon the idea of a star pattern with different phases of the moon took hold. She wanted to bring the night sky inside so she could look at it always. It calmed her thoughts. She hadn't told anyone about her star pattern idea yet; she could already hear her mother saying it was foolish. Mare would say nothing as usual, only stare at her long and hard until Charlotte reached the right conclusion and scrapped the idea. She decided to keep it to herself. Once this shelf valence was done, she'd see how it went. Maybe it would turn into something, maybe it wouldn't. And besides, having a secret idea was exciting in its own way. It was something she had just for herself.

The room was quiet except for the sound of rustling fabric as Suzette ripped out her stitches.

Sometimes Mare could be a bit too harsh. Charlotte watched Suzette's small but violent stabbing at her failed rosettes. She could see Suzette hardening inside. Mare's criticisms were usually right, but she could be blunt to the point of cruelty at times. Charlotte wondered if that was on purpose. Mare had layers to her. She could laugh at anything and seemed to enjoy watching the boys pull pranks on each other. But she would also fall into quiet periods, when her thoughts seemed to be far away, as if she was in another realm or perhaps lost in the past. Sometimes a story about Mare's childhood would come out mixed with instructions on how to do something, like how she told Charlotte about how much she missed the northern rivers when teaching her to properly dry fish. She tried to ask Mare for more stories directly, she was hungry for them, but Mare was good at evasion. Those stories always came in sideways and Charlotte collected them like treasures. Mare was a puzzle to be solved.

Mare cut some thread with her ulu knife. It had a curved, semi-circle-shaped blade with a wooden handle. It looked like a knife that would be better for scraping hides, but Mare used it for everything. She carried it in a leather pouch that she kept in her pocket at all times. She'd had it since she was a young girl; it had belonged to her mother. Mare said it was a sacred object, a woman's tool that was handed down from mother to daughter. If the knife were lost or broken, it was a bad omen. It needed to be cared for with reverence and protected always. Charlotte could not understand why Mare preferred to use the knife when sewing scissors seemed so much simpler to use. They offered better control. "Scissors make you lazy," she said. Yet she never chided the girls for using them.

When Charlotte was around ten years old, she tried using the ulu knife to cut thread. But she missed the thread and sliced her thumb open instead. She cried and ran to her mother for help as angry, red blood rushed from the wound. Mare had come to see what the commotion was and given her a knowing look. "You tried using the ulu knife, eh?" Charlotte had nodded and tried to suck the tears back up into her eyes. She didn't want to look like a baby in front of Mare. "The knife knew it was being used by the wrong hands and bit back. You can only use it when you're ready."

Charlotte rubbed the scar. Since that day, she'd avoided the knife as though it were alive. Something that plotted. Mare always made sure it was the sharpest knife in the house.

∞

Charlotte's feet crunched in the gravel. She and Julien and her parents were on Main Street in the village of Winnipeg near Fort Garry. After Papaa and Julien returned from St. Paul, they both talked nonstop about the beadwork they'd need to trade, so they decided on a trip to the Winnipeg shops to see what was on offer there. Charlotte hoped they could get more black velvet. It was a little more expensive, but the shelf valance she made had turned out well, and her father decided she should make more to trade in St. Paul.

The day was overcast and humid, with oppressive, thick air.

Charlotte pulled the collar of her dress away from her neck to try to get some breeze on her skin. She could feel sweat dampening the underarms of her sleeves. She hated weather like this, when the air was heavy and everything felt damp and sticky. All she wanted to do was jump in the river to cool off, even if the water was brown with mud. But of course, she would never do that. She imagined her mother's horrified face and that gave her a kind of relief.

The fort dominated the landscape. Its tall wooden walls formed a huge square with stone towers at each corner. As she passed by the arched stone gateway, Charlotte could see a cannon, pointing out. She supposed it was a warning but, with the grass grown up through the wheels of its support cart, it looked more like an artifact than any kind of threat.

The governor's stone house was visible in the centre of the courtyard. It was painted gleaming white and was two storeys tall with windows framed by green shutters on both levels. It was gigantic compared to Charlotte's house and she wondered what it was like inside. She imagined the lace tablecloths and curtains, the bone china dishes, the crystal glassware, the plush furniture. She wanted to wear boots that laced up and clicked on the floorboards instead of her silent moccasins, no matter how finely beaded they were. She wanted to wear a silk dress and earrings that dangled from her ears. Lace cuffs would brush her wrists and she would use cream on her hands to keep them soft. That was the life she wanted.

Winnipeg was a growing village, more like a town. Main Street was a dirt road with some scattered buildings: a few shops, a hotel, a print shop, a Presbyterian church and adjoining school. In the distance, more buildings were being constructed. The church's white steeple reached for the sky above the other buildings, almost as tall as the fort's towers. Across the river stood St. Boniface Cathedral and the Roman Catholic mission. Her family attended Midnight Mass there on Christmas Eve, since it was the only church with an organ, and the promise of music brought people in, even non-Catholics. They went to St. Norbert Church the rest of the year. The school there was where she'd learned from the nuns to embroider in the French style. Charlotte wished they'd learned to read and write. "The church only wants to create farmers," Mare had said. "So that's what they teach."

A rope pulley spanned the river, propelling a floating wooden platform that moved goods and people between the Fort Garry side and St. Boniface. It wasn't very sturdy, and Charlotte remembered seeing it tip over once when she was a little girl. All the cargo spilled into the river, and the ferryman had jumped in to save what he could. His angry swearing carried clearly to shore. She'd never heard such blistering language. The scene was funny, but she knew better than to laugh, although some men who were waiting on the other side did laugh before diving in to help. Today the waters were calm and the ferry glided easily, its cargo well balanced.

Many people milled about Main Street. Maybe it was the grey skies and humidity, but there seemed to be a sense of agitation in the air. People were brisk, talking to each other in clipped voices. Charlotte hung back from the rest of her family, letting her father and Julien lead the pack, followed by their mother. She watched her mother's head bob in front of her, not a hair out of place, even in this disgusting heat. They turned into a haberdasher's where they could get beads and sewing supplies.

The inside of the shop was small and cramped, and Charlotte knew she wouldn't have a say in what her parents bought anyway, so she stayed outside. She leaned against the wall, trying to give her feet a bit of a rest as she watched the people walk by. Around her a melange of languages came from all directions: French, English, Michif, Cree, Gaelic, and more, sometimes all in the same sentence. She knew French and Michif, of course, but also English, and a bit of Cree and Anishinaabemowin, which was Mare's first language. There was a lot of overlap between many of the languages if you listened carefully. Picking out the patterns and connections was like seeing the patterns between the natural world and the designs she could see in her mind. She saw connections in a lot of things.

She heard shouting from across the street. A boy a little older than Fredie held up a newspaper and waved it as he shouted in English. "Rupert's Land must be sold to Canada! Only in *The Nor'Wester*!"

A small group of men gathered around the boy and bought copies. Charlotte could hear the excitement in their loud voices.

"Finally!"

"Annexation is what we need!"

"We can get more farmers here from Canada. We need more industry and less indolence!"

"But will we have a say in how they govern?"

More people joined, and a man with greasy blond hair and dusty trousers bumped into Charlotte as he passed, almost knocking her over.

"Be careful!" she said in English, annoyed.

"Be careful yourself, you dirty half-breed! Do something useful with yourself instead of lazing around."

His ruddy face had heavy frown lines. He looked like he was about to spit on her but seemed to change his mind and rushed across the street to snatch a newspaper from the boy.

Charlotte couldn't believe what had just happened. She looked around to see if she could find sympathy from a passerby, but people just continued on without looking at her. She'd seen men behave roughly before, but never in the middle of the day on the street like this.

"Are you all right, miss?"

Charlotte turned and faced a young man close to her own age. He had light brown hair brushed neatly away from his face and curled behind his ears. He was clean-shaven, his skin pink and creamy. He smelled of soap.

"Thank you, I'm fine," she replied.

She looked him directly in the eye, refusing to look downward modestly, which was what her mother and Mare would expect her to do. Mare rarely looked people directly in the eye, especially a strange man. She'd admonish Charlotte if she was there. Charlotte didn't want to be old-fashioned like that.

The young man nodded at her and continued across the street where he joined the crowd around the newspaper boy. Charlotte watched him.

His clothes were different from those of the men around him, more finely made. He wore tan-coloured trousers that hung from his hips precisely as they should, neither too baggy nor too tight. Underneath his matching vest and jacket, he wore a white shirt with buttons down the front. A shirt like that was unusual in Red River. Most of the men wore pullovers with a wide opening at the neck. They were loose-fitting and made of coarse homespun fabric that softened over time. Charlotte could see how a shirt that buttoned at the front would have less wasted fabric and be more versatile. Even with the dust from the road and the sticky air, his clothing was unblemished. It had to be made from linen, she thought. She wanted to feel the fabric on her fingers. She discreetly patted the undersleeves of her dress. They were damp but not stained too wetly.

This man's clothes were tailored to fit his body. His outfit had rhyme but he didn't stick out; he looked like he belonged. He had an easy smile and seemed to be an affable sort as he chatted with some of the other men. She hadn't seen him before, she was sure. She would have remembered someone like him. He had to be new to the settlement. He was stylish, but he didn't sound as though he was from Quebec or England; his accent was all wrong. Maybe he was American—people moved fluidly across the Medicine Line and she'd heard of some Americans coming to the settlement, stirring up talk about Red River throwing in with the United States. It wasn't a bad idea, and it didn't really make much difference to her. It all seemed the same, one government or another. It was all so remote—a queen or a president or a prime minister, what did it matter? They were far away and had no idea what her life was like. They had no meaning for her.

He stayed with the men for a few minutes, bought a newspaper and walked north on Main Street, away from Charlotte. She considered following him, but just then her family came out of the store.

"What's going on there, ma babiche?" her father nodded to the crowd of men.

"The newspaper is out. It says something about Rupert's Land being sold to Canada. That's here, right? But who's Rupert?"

"Some long-dead Englishman who thinks he owns everything, even from the grave. I'm going to see what's happening." He crossed the street and bought a newspaper.

Her mother handed Charlotte a package wrapped in brown paper and tied with string. "What's he going to do with that newspaper? He can't read English. He can barely read French."

Charlotte shrugged. "Maybe Fredie can read it, or Father Courchene."

"That newspaper will be good to start a fire and that's it," her mother said, annoyed.

Her father came back with the newspaper tucked under his arm. "They're getting good and riled up over there," he said.

"Is it this surveyor business?" her mother asked.

"It's connected. We'll find out if what this says matches what those men were blathering about. Come on, we should get home."

Charlotte trailed behind her family again so she could look back over her shoulder to see what the stylish young man was doing, but he was gone. She hoped she would see him again.

She thought about Florian Dubeau. He'd visited their house a few times since her father and Julien returned from St. Paul. Charlotte had only half-paid attention to the conversations he had with her parents; she was focused on her sewing. But she noted Florian was focused on action. He mentioned a committee that he was part of, and he'd asked Papaa to join, but he'd declined. Fredie lurked during those visits, sitting quietly with his eyes wide. He practically sat at Florian's feet like a dog.

All their talk of the surveyors—and what would happen if more settlers came—hadn't bothered her. She thought new settlers might be a good thing for the community. Already there were new people from Quebec coming, moving to the next lot. They were cousins of Father Courchene, but still, new blood was good. If more people from Ontario came, maybe that would be good, too. Maybe they would make Winnipeg bigger and better, with more shops and other businesses. Maybe it could become a real city one day. That could only be a good thing.

They passed Red River Hall, which had a large window. Charlotte caught her reflection in it as she passed. She paused to look at herself. They had one small mirror at home that hung by the door. Charlotte could hardly see her whole face in it. In the window, with the fuller view, she turned her face slowly from one side to the next. At one angle, when she wasn't looking straight at herself, she saw Mare's features in her face: the high cheekbones and broad forehead, full lips. It was as though her face was overlaid on top of Mare's, and one day, when she was older, Mare's features would rise to the surface. It was unsettling, seeing her future buried in her face. It was doubly strange, because Charlotte felt different from most of her family. The boys and Suzette had dark hair and tan skin, like their father's, but her own hair was light brown and her skin paler. Her mother had had lighter hair when she was younger, so that's where it must have come from. She wondered if perhaps she resembled an ancestor who'd come from France many years before. Maybe there were still family members there—she could have a double somewhere living in the shadow of some château. Maybe she could visit France someday and see what it was really like. It had to be better than here.

Just south of the fort, a pair of tipis stood by the riverbank, with smoke rising from a fire between them. A small group of children chased each other in circles, laughing. A woman who looked a lot like Mare sat by the fire, softly beating a drum and singing. Something burned in the fire that smelled sweetly fragrant. It was a pleasant smell, warm and inviting. Charlotte wondered what the song was about. Mare might know, but she had stayed home. She didn't like being around the fort and rarely ventured near it. The village of St. Norbert was metropolis enough for her.

There were times when Mare would drum and sing. When Charlotte was small, she'd help Mare collect sage and sweetgrass and other medicines. She still collected willow bark from the trees that grew on the riverbank near their home. She realized sage was the smell in the fire. She filled her lungs and felt calm wash over her.

"Charlotte, don't dawdle," her mother called.

Charlotte hurried to catch up, still thinking about the stranger as she made her way back to where their canoe waited for them on the riverbank near the fort.

∞

Uncle Pierre was waiting for them when they got home. He sat at the table drinking tea with Mare and laughing.

"Hé-ho!" he called in greeting.

Her father sank into the chair next to him and slapped the newspaper on the table. Julien took another chair next to Pierre and patted his back in greeting.

"Finally came to see us, eh?" Julien said.

Charlotte joined them at the table. She was nearly marriage-age; it was time for her to be treated like one of the adults instead of left in the realm of children. She eased into a chair next to her father like it was the most natural thing in the world. He put his arm around her and pulled her close.

"Look at ma belle bibche! You should see what she's been making! A new venture that's turning out well for us, eh?"

Charlotte smiled. Her mother sat at the opposite end of the table and motioned for Suzette to bring tea for everyone. Suzette shot Charlotte a sharp look but did as she was told.

Charlotte leaned away from her father's embrace and sat taller in her chair. Yes, let Suzette serve everyone. It was her turn now, and Charlotte had earned her place.

Charlotte explained about the shelf valence project and opened the parcel that held their new supply of velvet and beads, carefully untying the string and folding up the paper wrapping. They'd reuse both. She was pleased to see the velvet she'd hoped for. Uncle Pierre enthusiastically crowed his approval. After their tea was finished and another round poured, he turned serious.

"We saw some excitement at Petite Pointe des Chênes," he said and paused for effect.

Her father nodded, urging him to continue.

"We found the road crew's camp," Uncle Pierre said. "We watched them for a day, then we rode up and joined them one evening by the fire. They seemed surprised that we would show up and join them like that, as if it's so strange to share a fire with passersby." He chuckled and shook his head. "They didn't want to say too much. But one of them said more surveyors were coming soon to Red River on behalf of Canada to see what the land situation was like and report back to Ottawa."

"And what are they going to report?" her mother asked.

"It sounds like they're most interested in the river lots—"

"Oh!" her mother looked worried.

"—but also the hay lands. And the reports were right, they meas-ure things oddly, not in the usual way at all."

"How so?" asked Julien.

"They didn't measure straight out from the river, the way the lots are already set up. Most of what they measured was nowhere near the river. Strange rectangles in a grid pattern with no river access at all."

"Well, there it is, they're not measuring lots for settlers, then." Her father folded his arms across his chest.

Julien scoffed. "I wouldn't be so sure. They're up to something. Besides, you know how some of those Selkirk lots are. Some of them are set up strangely too."

"Yes, they're up to something," said Uncle Pierre, "but that's not the interesting thing about our visit."

Charlotte leaned forward. The surveyor talk was boring, but now Uncle Pierre would deliver the real news.

"We were staying with Florian's cousins, the Fletts, right near the village. It was evening, but not getting too dark yet. We were having fun, playing cards, when we heard yelling from outside."

"Well, that's not so unusual," her father said.

"Let him finish!" her mother batted his arm.

"Fine, fine."

"We went outside," continued Uncle Pierre, "and some of the road men were yelling and shoving each other. So, of course, we went to see what was happening. They were yelling in English, but we could understand most of it. They seemed to be angry at their boss, mad about not being paid enough, or something like that."

"That figures," said Julien.

"One of the men was larger than everyone else, and he was the angriest by far. Shoulders like an ox and a thick neck with popping veins when he yelled. His hair was short and spiky and stood out from his head—maybe he had lice and that's why it was so short— you know how some of those English aren't very clean."

Everyone around the table laughed, except Charlotte.

"We didn't interfere with the fight," Uncle Pierre said. "It was loud but didn't seem too bad. Eventually they moved away to their camp on the outskirts of the village, and we thought it was over."

"Then what happened?" asked Fredie. Charlotte hadn't noticed him at the table, he must have snuck up like he was playing fox again.

"We went back to our cards and then everyone turned in," said Uncle Pierre, "actually kind of early, but we were all tired. But not long after we turned down the lamps, there was pounding on the door. I was up first because I was on the floor closest to the door. Then it banged open, and it was the big man from the fight, drunk as a skunk! Not only drunk but naked, too!"

"What? No!" her mother gasped.

"Not a thread on him! And smelly like old potatoes!" Uncle Pierre clapped his hand on his leg. "Well, everyone was up and the lamps were lit and once we saw what we were dealing with, I had to laugh, I couldn't help myself. I've seen many things in my time, but never an uninvited drunk English naked in my home!"

Mare gaped.

"What was he after?" Julien asked.

"We couldn't understand his drunk yelling," Uncle Pierre said, "especially with that strong accent, like he was talking with rocks in his mouth. Who knows what he was thinking, but once he focused on us, his face changed, and blood filled his eyes. Rage like I've never seen. His eyes locked on Louise Flett and he flew at her, his hands around her neck in an instant."

"How awful!" her mother said.

"Shameful!" said Mare.

"We all jumped on him," Uncle Pierre said, "but Louise kicked him in his soft spot between his legs and he went down. He cried on the floor for a while, then we tossed him outside. She wanted to horsewhip him! He ran off, howling at the moon. His clothes were nowhere to be found."

"Unbelievable!" her father shook his head.

Some chuckles rippled around the table, but everyone was stunned by the story. Soon they fell quiet, sipping their tea.

Her mother looked ill. "This isn't right. These people come here and act like savages. What right do they have to behave like that?"

"You know how it is," said Uncle Pierre. "Some of them go mad on the voyage over here, or they were mad to begin with. Only the desperate leave their homeland to start over in a brand-new place."

"Or opportunists," said Julien.

"But to act so wild, treating people like that! How is Louise? Was she hurt?" her mother asked.

"It was an ugly thing, to be sure," Uncle Pierre said. "I think she was more shocked than anything, but his grip on her was solid. She had red marks on her neck the next morning. She went on as though nothing happened, but said she'd carry a rifle the next time she went to the village, at least until that road crew was gone."

Her father nodded and picked up the newspaper he'd bought in town. "Is this who the Canadians want to come and settle here?" He jabbed the paper with his finger. "They keep saying they don't want Red River to become a new Quebec, but what are they offering instead? Violence and drunkenness? It's not right."

"Is that what the paper is saying, about new settlers?" Uncle Pierre took it from his brother and looked at it closely.

"The men in town said it's about Rupert's Land being sold to Canada," her father said. "And that they want English settlers from Ontario to come. At least, that's what they said, but who can say. We need to find someone who can read what it says."

"So it's true then," Uncle Pierre said. "Florian was right, everything is about to change." The table fell silent.

"How long before that road crew reaches here?" Charlotte asked.

"Probably by the fall. Before winter, for sure." Uncle Pierre put the newspaper back down and smoothed it flat with his hand.

That night, Charlotte lay awake. Suzette was fast asleep, her breathing slow and steady. Every now and then, Suzette's legs would twitch. Uncle Pierre's story was stuck in Charlotte's mind. It was disturbing, even if he had tried to make it seem funny. He could make anything seem funny. She could see the humour in his tale, but she also couldn't forget the looks of disgust and fright on her mother's and Mare's faces. They had looked worried, and Charlotte was worried, too.

CHAPTER 6

Julien

July 1869

Julien rode away from his house, fast. Most families were working outside, and Julien should be, too, but he left before anyone could notice, heading to Henri's place.

When Uncle Pierre visited, Julien had walked him outside and Pierre had told him about the committee that had been struck to deal with the surveyor business and the possible sale of Rupert's Land to Canada. "Your Papaa doesn't want to be part of it, but I do," he'd said. "We're setting up patrols to watch for any suspicious activity. I think you should come hear what it's all about. We're meeting at St. Norbert Church."

Julien knew Henri would be interested too, so he ignored his chores and rode straight to the Lambert house.

Henri's eight older brothers and sisters were grown and out of the house, so it was just him and his next-oldest sister, Claudette, living with their parents. Their house was smaller than his own, only one storey, and more of a modest cabin than a proper house. The mortar between the logs had been patched many times and moss grew between them. Julien had asked him once how twelve people had lived there at one time. Henri had shrugged, "Same as how a whole family can sleep in a tent when out on the land—close together!" Julien laughed but knew he wouldn't like such a crowded situation. Sharing a bed with Fredie was bad enough. He couldn't imagine having to share it with two more siblings, even in the cold of winter.

Henri stood with his father near their well. They were stringing new rope through the pulley, the old, frayed rope coiled at their feet. Julien dismounted and let his horse graze the nearby grass. He opened his arms wide in greeting and smiled. He was blessed with straight white teeth, and he liked to show them off, even to people he saw all the time. He was proud of his appearance, and why shouldn't he be? Gifts were meant to be displayed, not hidden away.

Henri clapped Julien's back in greeting while Claude nodded at him, picked up the old rope, and walked to the barn.

"Are you finished your chores, or what?" asked Julien.

Henri blew air through his teeth. "Eh, enough for now. Let's go to the racing strip, see who's around. Nice day like this, someone must be up for something."

"I have another idea. There's a meeting at the church Uncle Pierre told me about. Let's go."

On the way there, they met Henri's cousin, Jean, with his friend, Alain. Jean had acne scars on his cheeks that a wispy beard was trying to cover.

"Are you going to the church too?" Jean asked.

"Yes," Julien said. "Looks like there will be a lot of people there."

"I heard there will be some from St. Vital and St. Boniface, too," Alain added. "Everyone's talking about the patrol. Florian will be capitaine."

"So, like the buffalo hunt then," Henri said.

Jean nodded, smiling big. "It's like the camp, all our carts together, spokes out, protecting everyone in the middle. We're the spokes."

At the church, Father Courchene stood outside, ushering men in as they arrived. Inside the dim interior, Julien was greeted with the loud chatter of around forty or fifty men, some young like him, a few older ones, and more yet in their twenties and thirties. He recognized some from St. Norbert, like his Lavallee cousins William and Georges, and a couple of Bouchers from St. Boniface. A few men stood to the side. He saw his Uncle Pierre leaning against the

47

wall. He nodded at Julien and waved him over. Julien and his companions slid into a pew near him.

"I'm glad you came." Uncle Pierre said.

"I'll take this over chores any day," Julien replied. The chatter died down when Father Courchene went to the front and called Florian Dubeau to speak.

"See, I told you he was the capitaine," whispered Jean.

The main priest, Father Ritchot, stood in the back, watching. Julien leaned forward, eager to hear what Florian had to say.

Florian stood silent and scanned the crowd before he smacked his hand on the wooden pulpit with a loud crack. "We've all heard about the surveyors." It was a statement, not a question.

A few scattered nods.

"The Hudson's Bay Company has sold us out to Canada," said Florian, "without asking us or even telling us. We all heard the talk, stories of Canada sniffing out west, but the story changed a little every time. The Canadian Party has been asking for this for months—*The Nor'Wester* has been full of big opinions and not much fact. But then Canadian newspapers started saying the same thing and said Ottawa was sending surveyors, to take stock of Red River."

He nodded in the direction of Uncle Pierre. "We sat with the road crew and surveyors around their fire," Florian continued. "We tried to be friendly. But they did not want us there. Just like they don't want us here now."

"How can you be sure?" asked a voice from the pews.

"You've heard the talk in town, what they're saying in the saloons in Winnipeg. They call us indolent, lazy, say we don't belong. But who needed our help during the floods and droughts? Who depends on our work and sweat when they need it? Who built the HBC? Who built Red River and keeps it alive? Without us, there is no Red River."

Florian stepped from behind the pulpit and spread his arms wide. "This is our homeland, our nation. We belong to it. But the HBC thinks it belongs to them. They can't give it away without asking us what we want, without any kind of negotiation."

"What does Governor McTavish have to say about this?" one of the Bouchers asked.

"Pfft, he's been sick in bed for months, he's no help," said the other Boucher brother.

"The Canadians will probably send a new governor," said Florian. "Someone English."

Julien looked around and saw faces that had grown angry. He felt his own anger rise.

"Maybe we should negotiate a treaty, like Peguis and the other chiefs did with Selkirk," said another voice.

"And look how that turned out!" someone replied.

"Why would we want to join with Canada? Look how they talk about us—they hate us and see us as nothing," an older man with a long grey beard said from the front pew.

Many people spoke at once. The voices grew loud.

Father Ritchot came to the front and stood next to Florian. The voices hushed as the priest took his usual place behind the pulpit.

"Perhaps something like a treaty would be a good thing," he said. "Perhaps something else. First, we need to see what the Canadians really want. There's room for more river lots."

People murmured, and a few nodded in agreement.

"That's not what we saw at Petite Pointe des Chênes," said Uncle Pierre. All faces turned to him. "We spied on the road crew and surveyors first and heard them talk. They spoke of carving up big acreages, bragging that their people would be the new owners when Canada takes possession. Their stakes and chains cut through existing lots. They don't see us as rightful owners. They can't be trusted. We need to stop them."

Voices erupted again. Some whooped and stamped their feet on the wooden floor. Father Ritchot narrowed his eyes at Uncle Pierre. "We must be patient," he urged.

Julien felt hot.

Florian held his hand up, and the men quietened. "The first thing we need to do is start patrolling our parishes, so we know what's happening. We can expand the patrol farther when we need to. We can talk about finding someone to speak to the Canadians later. For now, we need to survey the surveyors."

Julien looked at Henri, who sat on his left, then Jean, who sat on his right. In their eyes he saw the same excitement he felt. Florian's words sparked something in him. He had a focus now. Whatever came next, he would be part of it.

Uncle Pierre rode home with him. "Clément needs to know what's happened here. Some of us were talking with Florian and Father Ritchot before you all showed up, and the committee is choosing representatives to talk to Canada."

"Are you going to be one of them?"

He shrugged. "Depends on how it turns out. Right now, the patrol is what interests me."

Julien was glad to be so close to the action. Maybe he could play a part in things, too. He just had to keep his eyes open.

∞

"What!" his mother said when Julien and Uncle Pierre told everyone about the patrol.

"So you're just going to up and leave us? It's going to be haying time soon," his father said.

"Things are getting serious, Clément," Pierre said. "This is more important than some hay."

"Of course you would say that! I expected you to go chasing these imaginings, but now you're dragging Julien into it. He's turning into you!"

"Like that's so terrible," Uncle Pierre looked like he was going to spit.

"And what are those horses of yours going to eat if there's no hay?" Mare asked, giving them pointed looks.

"Ah ben!" Uncle Pierre scoffed.

Julien didn't like how this was going. "Mare, Papaa, this is important work too. Let's see how it turns out. Maybe we won't need to patrol for long, who knows? I might be back before the haying even starts."

"I understand you think this is important, and maybe it is," his mother said. "But your family is important too. So you need to come home and help out when you can. The patrol doesn't need all of you. Right, Pierre?"

Pierre opened his mouth to speak but thought better of it and nodded instead.

"It's settled then," said Mare. "Now someone pour me some tea. My cup's been empty for too long."

CHAPTER 7

Marienne

September-October 1869

Everything was falling apart.

First Julien joined the patrol, which was fine at first, but now it was leading to strife between him and Clément, which meant Clément was now grumpy with everyone else. Mostly with her.

He refused to give much weight to what was happening. It was all a lot of talk, he insisted. "Young men with nothing better to do trying to prove their worth. They need some real work," he'd said.

"Like carting?" Marienne said. "Disappearing for weeks while life goes on without you? How is Julien being away with the patrol any different? The surveyor business isn't all just talk."

He glowered at her and stomped out, and that was the end of that.

She didn't understand why Clément was so upset. She told him that he should also join the patrol, to see for himself how it was. "That's for Pierre," he'd said. She gave up asking about it. Clément and Pierre had always been close, but sometimes they clashed like water and hot grease. Marienne's two older brothers had been the same, and her strategy then was to stay out of it. Things always calmed down. She could see Clément didn't like Julien growing closer to Pierre; he wanted to be the one Julien looked up to. Marienne thought it was best for Julien to figure out what he wanted for himself, but she didn't dare tell her husband that.

She wished they could go back to how things were when they had come home with the sewing machine. Clément had beamed when he unloaded it from the cart and called them all over to see. With a flourish, he removed the drop cloth that covered it and grinned. Charlotte was the first to react.

"Papaa! A sewing machine! I can't believe you got one for us!" She hugged him tight.

"How can we afford it?" Marienne had asked.

Clément waved his hand. "With all the success ma bibiche will have with her works, it will pay for itself in no time."

He'd bought it on credit, then. Clément was fond of credit.

Suzette and Charlotte exclaimed over the machine and fiddled with its moving parts. Mare hung back and scowled at it. Clément gamely tried to show her the machine's features, but she refused to touch it.

"Maman," he'd said, "think how much easier it will be, how much time you'll save."

"It just means we'll have to produce more in less time."

"Ah ben! It's a good thing. Why can't you let it be that?"

Mare said nothing. But she did lean forward to watch the girls explore the machine.

Marienne could see how the sewing machine was a tool for making money, but it was mostly a gift for Charlotte, who was Clément's favourite, even though he denied it. It was easy to see why; Charlotte was charming from the beginning. On the hunt, Marienne carried her on her back in the cradleboard, so she was at the same height as the adults around her. She smiled and made faces at everyone who passed. Her eyes were big and always searching. She became known as the laughing baby and people made a point of walking and camping alongside them. Marienne was sure it was these interactions that led to Charlotte speaking so early. And speak she did. Soon she was the baby who babbled nonstop, and people enjoyed her more. Now that she was grown, Charlotte seemed to have inherited the best from all of her ancestors: height, curiosity, fearlessness, all carried with a quiet confidence.

Beauty was a blessing, but it was also dangerous. Charlotte garnered different attention as she grew older, not all of it good. Clément liked to joke about auctioning her hand in marriage, but Marienne said it was bad luck to joke like that—it would give people ideas. He told her she was worrying over nothing, but he did stop.

Henri had been making moon eyes at Charlotte ever since they were small. He wouldn't make a bad husband, but would Charlotte want him? She hadn't shown any interest in anyone yet as far as Marienne could tell. Maybe that was for the best. When the time came, she would encourage Charlotte to think carefully about who she chose. Her mother had told her the same thing. But it was Mare who had given her the best advice.

When Marienne first married into the Rougeau family, she was surprised at how small it was. Most families had at least six children, sometimes as many as a dozen. She herself had eight siblings, now scattered all around Red River. Clément had only Pierre and a sister, Florence, who everyone called Flossie, who lived in White Horse Plain. Marienne assumed that some of Mare's children had died young, or perhaps she'd had a few miscarriages. Such things were common. She herself had a younger sister who died at only three months. But no, Mare told her that she'd deliberately spaced her children out and chose to have only three. It was what Saulteaux people did, and she urged Marienne to do the same. Marienne was shocked at the idea. Wasn't it a sin to make decisions like that, and worse, act on them? Mare scoffed at that. She dutifully attended church and went through the motions of practising their religion, but she was always cold to it, with an edge of contempt. "I accepted their medicine of pouring water on my head, but that didn't mean all people offering such medicine have good things behind it," she'd said. Marienne asked what she meant by that, but Mare didn't elaborate.

Sin or no, she'd said, Marienne's life would be easier and her children more likely to live if she did as she suggested. Marienne herself would also be more likely to survive. "Each birth takes something from you," she'd said. "You only have so much to give before you have nothing left."

Now, Marienne could see the wisdom of that. Suzette's birth had definitely taken something from her; she'd been afraid the whole time she'd been pregnant with Fredie because of it. How many times had she attended births where either the baby or mother died? Or both? The heartbreak that followed, plus hard times for everyone left behind. It seemed irresponsible to put her other children at risk like that, no matter what the priests said. So she quietly drank the tea Mare made for her and helped her collect the white flowers it was made from when they went on their medicine-collecting trips. When her own mother asked why she only ended up with four children, she said it must have been God's will. When Charlotte and Suzette's time came, she planned to give them the same advice.

Marienne's father and grandfather had both been voyageurs, and their family's livelihood depended on movement. When her father gave up the voyageur life, they kept their base in St. Laurent, near Lac Manitobah, but continued moving, going from seasonal camp to seasonal camp, and spending weeks on the buffalo hunt. She didn't question it. It was how it was.

That's where she'd met Clément. Her family joined with other carts from Red River and White Horse Plain as they headed west for the buffalo. She and Clément had seen each other many times over the years as they grew up on the hunt, and when Clément was in his prime, a little older than Julien was now, he'd been one of the youngest capitaines. All Marienne's friends and cousins noticed him. He was hard to miss. Marienne was interested, too, but she didn't fawn over him as the other girls did. Instead, she made sure she stood out in her own way. Her brothers had taught her to ride like they did. She was good, and once, when wolves had approached their camp, lured by the butchering and rendering of meat, hadn't hesitated to leap on a horse, load her rifle, and shoot at the beasts. She hit one clean between the eyes before others joined her to protect the camp. She'd been hailed as a heroine and got to keep the wolf's fur. She still had it, rolled up and wrapped with her clothes. She never made anything out of it but liked to unroll it and feel the smooth fur in quiet moments alone.

Her actions caught Clément's attention, and he rode home beside her all the way until her family turned away to St. Laurent and his continued to Red River. A month after they got home, Clément rode up and asked her father if he could marry her. "It's up to Marienne," her father replied. Marienne had held up the satchel she hadn't bothered to unpack and said, "I'm ready."

She'd been happy with their life, but by the time Suzette was born, she was tired of moving. Each birth had been hard, but Suzette's was the hardest. When HBC was handing out lots for settlement in St. Norbert, she'd insisted that they take one and build a good home.

Clément didn't seem to understand why she wanted to settle. He saw a home as a depot, a place to store your things, rest, and resupply before the next journey. When Marienne tried to explain how hard it was for her, with two small children and now a toddler to care for, he shook his head. "Other families have twice as many kids, and they manage just fine," he'd said.

"Well go marry them, then! That's not how it is for me. I'm tired now. I want a settled life."

Her husband sulked for a few days, but he didn't press her. He could be rigid in his own thinking, but he didn't often force it on others. Instead, he put his energy into building the finest house in St. Norbert. If they were going to settle down, they were going to do it in style.

When the first foundation stone was set, she felt at peace. Home was now on the river lot, not on the open prairie.

She knew Clément could adapt his thinking, which was why his reaction to Julien was so surprising. It should be easy for him to see how, for Julien, nothing could compare to the excitement in front of him. Marienne worried Clément's dismissal and outright disdain might cause a permanent rift between father and son. Maybe it was a good thing Clément had left in a huff that morning. He could stew about it on his own. It was her job to keep the family together.

At church and around town, she asked others what they heard. A leader who was educated in Montreal had emerged; his name was Louis Riel. Marienne knew of the Riel family, but it was her sister, Denise Lavallee, who was acquainted with them. "The story changes every day," she'd confided. "The young Louis has formed a council to turn back that new governor, McDougall, who made some sort of proclamation saying the transfer of Rupert's Land is set and done. The English side want to let him come and hope for the best. Well, that's set the hostilities on fire! Riel says it's up to us to govern ourselves. Honestly, I agree with him. This won't stand."

Marienne didn't know what to think. Their lives had been calm for quite a while, which, in her experience, meant something bad was bound to happen.

CHAPTER 8

Julien

October 1869

Julien had been patrolling in St. Norbert in shifts for months. The church was their headquarters, Florian was the patrol's *presidente*, and Uncle Pierre was their group's *capitaine*.

At first, Julien had returned home when he wasn't patrolling, but he didn't like his attention split in half like that, so now he and Henri camped at the church. They found no surveyors in St. Norbert, and the other patrols in St. Vital and St. Boniface hadn't found any either. However, they had found stakes in the ground, which they promptly removed. Julien felt the patrol's presence was important. People smiled and waved at them when they passed by. They were keeping everyone safe.

Julien decided to visit home, since it had been a few weeks since he'd been there. He found everyone in the meadow, cutting hay. Even Fredie was helping, although the haystacks were taller than he was.

"Julien!" Fredie called out as he ran to meet him.

Julien remained on his horse, wanting everyone to get the full effect of him in his new patrol uniform. He wore a blue *capote* cinched at the waist with a red sash, dark homespun trousers, and knee-high moccasins. The effect was better when all members of the patrol were together in formation, but still. His family had to be impressed.

"Well, look at you," said his father. "A real *soldat*."

Charlotte stood up from her work, pressed a hand to her lower back and shielded her eyes from the sun. She looked at Julien for a long beat, then scowled. "Are you here to take a break from your prancing to help the rest of us?"

"We don't *prance*," he said, his manly façade broken already.

Charlotte smirked.

"Enough!" shouted Marienne. "Ah ben, you two. Julien is doing important work. We're all proud of him."

She smiled at her son, but Julien didn't feel warmth behind it, more like indulgence. Like when he was a boy, and she'd feigned amazement when he first learned to set a snare. Sometimes she looked at Fredie the same way.

"Of course we're proud of him, and all the other boys, too," said Clément. "But we could use your help here if you're finished your patrols for the day."

This was not how Julien expected things to go. They were supposed to stop what they were doing and remark on what a dashing figure he cut.

"Things are happening, you know. Just yesterday we were by the fort and some of the Company men were talking about annexation to Canada and how good it will be. But what about us? It was all done without any say from us, it's all lawless. Someone has to protect us!"

His father had been leaning on his hay rake, but now he tossed it to the ground. "Yes, that's important, but Julien, you have responsibilities to us. Your friends can do without you for a few days."

When his father talked to him like that, he felt like a child again. Why couldn't he see him as a man, someone important? Frustrated, he turned his horse around and rode to the house. He'd go back to the church when he could. Florian would have to understand.

For three days, Julien cut hay and resented every moment he wasn't patrolling. He imagined what he was missing while he was mucking hay. He should be mucking invaders. Already his hands were raw from the scythe. He walked toward the meadow, to join the rest of his family, a rake over his shoulder.

Henri rode up, fast, his horse in a lather. "We need to go, come on!"

Julien dropped the rake where he stood and raced to get his capote and sash. He didn't even bother to ask what the rush was all about.

"Hey!" his father called. "Where are you going?"

Julien turned around. "We've been called up, we have to go!"

"Called up for what?" his mother said, walking toward him. "You have work here."

"Sorry, madame," Henri said, trying to smooth things over. "But it is true, we've been called to the Nault farm. The surveyors have come."

She covered her mouth with her hand and looked from her husband to Julien. "Go! But send word when you can."

In a flash, they were galloping toward the Nault farm. This was it. Finally! No one could say they were just a bunch of prairie chickens all puffed up for show. Julien was excited and maybe a little afraid of what they were going to find.

Halfway there, they caught up with Florian and the rest of the brigade. When they arrived at the Nault farm, they found the yard with its wooden house quiet, except for the penned-up dogs who yelped and paced, eager to escape.

"Over there!" Henri pointed toward the hay meadow, where they could see a group of men and their horses. They rode over and found the men huddled around a pair of surveyors who sputtered in English. Julien's group stayed mounted. The surveyors grew quiet and stepped backward, away from them.

One man spoke for the patrol group. He was tall with dark curly hair that waved out from his face and a thick moustache with long pointed ends. Julien briefly wondered how the man had trained his moustache, and if he could grow one like that, too.

The man stood evenly on both feet, with one foot slightly in front of the other—a fighting stance. Julien was riveted. He wore black trousers, a white shirt, and a multicoloured sash under a black frock coat, different from the brigade in their light blue capotes and red sashes. He looked to be only a few years older than Julien, in his mid-twenties, but still he held the attention of everyone there.

"You have no right to lay these chains here," the man said to the surveyors in English. His French accent was not too pronounced, but it was still there.

"Look, we're just doing our jobs," said one surveyor. He was pale. He looked from one end of the gathered men to the other.

"But you are disregarding the fact that these lands are already settled, as you can see." The man gestured to the surroundings.

"The government simply wants to know what's here," said the other surveyor.

"Understand we have no quarrel with you specifically," the man said in a calm, soft voice. "But we can't have this. This action goes against the law of nations in the name of an alien authority."

The surveyors looked at each other. They seemed surprised to encounter this sophisticated and charismatic Métis man. Julien was also a little surprised to hear him speak this complicated legal talk so smoothly. In English, yet.

"We must ask you to leave and trouble us no further."

"Yes, well, but the Canadian government—"

"Again, they have no business here. No one consulted us when the transfer of Rupert's Land took place. Never mind our Indian brothers and sisters. We've been here for generations and Canada needs to negotiate with us, nation to nation. Now, it would be best if you would pack up your things and return home."

The two men stared at each other.

One surveyor still held an end of the chain in his hand. "Let us just finish this one measurement, and we'll be on our way."

The Métis man stepped on the chain, pulling it taut in the surveyor's hand.

"Perhaps I was not clear. You need to leave, now."

The surveyor held the chain firm. The man stayed where he was. The two stared each other down as Florian dismounted his horse and stood on the chain, pulling it tighter. The surveyor still held it fast. One by one, Julien and the rest climbed down from their horses and stood on the chain until it was yanked from the surveyor's hands. It clinked as it fell. The surveyor turned to his partner, who looked at the crowd of men around them and shook his head. "Let's go," he said. They got on their horses and rode away fast, leaving the chain behind.

The brigade erupted in cheers. Florian lifted the chain above his head in triumph.

"Who is that?" Julien asked Henri, gesturing at the man in black.

"That's Louis Riel," Henri answered. "He came back recently from Montreal. He went to school there."

"That's him?"

Henri nodded. "He came back at exactly the right time."

"I'm glad he's on our side. I wouldn't want to argue against him."

He watched Riel smile at the men rallied around him. With a man like that as their spokesperson, things should turn out well for sure.

∞

After celebrating with the brigade at the church, Julien rode home to tell his father about all the excitement. He felt light as he galloped home, as if wind was sending him along.

He found his father in the barn.

"Papaa! We pushed the surveyors back! They ran away like scared rabbits! You should have seen it!" Julien was breathless.

His father nodded but didn't look up. He said nothing.

"You should have heard the man who's leading us, Riel. He speaks like no one I've heard before."

At this, his father looked up. "Who?"

"Louis, son of the Riels in St. Vital."

"I remember his father, he was part of the Sayer case, when the Company tried to sue Métis traders, maybe twenty years ago. Now the son is a leader too? What happened?"

Julien told him about stepping on the chain. His words came fast.

"I know this seems exciting," his father said. "But I don't want you becoming so involved. We need you here."

"I'm already involved," Julien said. "Uncle Pierre said a new governor is on his way here, and we're going to stop him. They're talking about building a barrière on the Pembina Trail, near La Rivière Sale."

"Keeping the governor out? I thought you boys were having fun riding in your matching coats, feeling important. But this is something else! Who's making these decisions? This Riel?"

"Not just him! There's a whole committee. Father Ritchot is part of it too. We know what we're doing, Papaa. We're taking a stand."

"Bah, a stand! What happens when they kick your legs out from under you? I think you should step away from this now. I'm building a winter hunting cabin in the bush near Lac du Bois, like we've always talked about. I could use your help. Working with your hands could help clear your head. We should start before the snow comes."

"How can you ask me to leave now, when things are just getting started? Maybe in the spring I could come. But who knows how things will be then. A lot could happen. Maybe I'll be an officer or something."

His father scoffed. "You think you're a man," he said, "but you still have a lot to learn. Look at this patchy beard you're growing. All of this with the surveyors and Riel, it isn't for you. You need to grow up more first."

The artery in Julien's neck pulsed. "This is me growing up! You have no idea what you're talking about. I thought you'd be proud.

This is something big. Bigger than some cabin in the bush. I don't need to be here—I don't need any of this from you."

Julien left the barn in a huff, stamping his rage into the ground with each step. He opened the house door with a bang and ignored the surprised looks of everyone inside. He took the stairs two at a time and gathered his few belongings into a pillowcase, slung it over his shoulder, jumped on Julienne and left without looking back.

CHAPTER 9

Marienne

October 1869

Marienne decided she should see what Julien was up to at St. Norbert Church if Clément wasn't going to bother.

She'd expected Julien to cool off after his blow-up with Clément and come home after a few days, but he never did. Fredie had seen him ride by on patrol once and had followed them down the road, running to keep up, but Julien hadn't stopped. He probably thought ignoring his family made him seem mature, but real maturity meant taking responsibility for the family. It was time to remind him of that.

She walked to the church. The day was grey with a strong cold breeze, so she tightened her cloak around her neck. She thought she saw his horse, Julienne, among those tied up outside but wasn't sure. Maybe he was on patrol. If he was, she'd just wait until he returned, no matter how long that took. She pulled open the heavy wooden door and stepped inside, pausing for her eyes to adjust to the dim light inside the church.

She was greeted by a pair of muddy boots dangling from the end of a pew, sticking out into the centre aisle. The young man who wore them lay stretched out and dozing on the pew. Not many people wore boots in St. Norbert, since they were expensive and couldn't be repaired as easily as moccasins. She wondered who he was. Marienne refused to dodge the feet and nudged them out of the way as she walked up the aisle.

"Hey!" the man said as he sat up. He looked ready to lash out, but when he saw it was Marienne, he sat straighter and apologized. "Pardonnez-moi, madame."

"You should know better than to lie like that in church." She wanted to bop his ears.

She saw Father Ritchot talking softly with a small group of men near a window and stepped toward them. The abbé noticed her first.

"Madame Rougeau, you must be looking for Julien. He should be back soon. Please, sit and wait."

Marienne had worked herself up to a low boil, ready to question Julien and scold him, but Father Ritchot's mild manner knocked that out of her.

"Merci, Father."

As she sat in the front pew and waited, she tried to listen to what the abbé and the men were saying, but they'd quietened their voices and angled themselves away from her. So they were trying to keep her in the dark. Why? She was part of this community too; she should know what was going on. That's what bothered her about the surveyors and the patrols—nothing was shared with the people at large. Everything was a rumour, and no one knew what was what. It seemed haphazard. Were they whispering because she was a woman? Because she was Julien's mother? She had opinions. Her voice had value. Women were not usually cut out like this. This was a turn she didn't like. That low boil was back.

Just then Julien sat down next to her. She'd been so lost in her thoughts she hadn't noticed him come in.

"Mamaa," he said and grinned at her.

Despite herself, she softened at his smile. She worried about his charm—it could backfire on him one day. She could see the man he'd become, but she also saw the little boy who used to like playing in the mud. The time between those two stages was short, too short. It was hard to accept him as an adult, but here he was. How did that happen?

"You haven't come back to see us," Marienne said, "so I had to see for myself what keeps you away."

"What's wrong?"

"My son has abandoned us."

"Ah ben, Mamaa! You've got Charlotte and Suzette and Fredie to help. You can spare me for a while."

"You couldn't stop in at least? You patrol right past us! Are you pretending we don't exist or what?"

"Of course not. But I can't have Fredie following us like a dog. It's embarrassing."

"So now your family is embarrassing."

"No! You twist everything I say! I'll come by tomorrow, all right? I'm leaving the day after, anyway. I'm going to la barrière."

"What's that?"

"We're blocking the Pembina Trail, to keep soldiers from coming to Red River."

"Soldiers! What soldiers? No one said anything about soldiers. All I hear about is surveyors. Why are you keeping secrets from me?"

Julien scoffed. "I'm not keeping secrets, no one is keeping secrets. Again with the twisting!"

"Well, the abbé and those boys were whispering and they got even quieter once I sat here. That sounds secretive to me."

"They're just being respectful to the men who are resting. Mamaa, calm down."

Being told to calm down had the opposite effect on Marienne. Her face got red and she took a deep breath, eager to lay into her irritating son.

"Madame, how thoughtless of me, you sitting here all this time with no refreshment. Perhaps you'd like some tea?"

Marienne turned around to see the priest smiling at her.

She sighed. Good manners took over and she nodded silently. She wasn't about to yell at Julien in front of the father and a crowded church. These men probably all deserved a good talking-to, but losing her temper now would make her look bad, not them. So she recalculated. "Julien, we'll talk more about this when you come home tomorrow."

Still, she wasn't going to let that low boil go to waste. "Father Ritchot," she said sweetly, "what's all this about soldiers and la barrière?"

Julien looked at the floor, away from the priest's gaze.

Father Ritchot didn't miss a beat. "A precaution, more than anything," he said, his voice soft. "We've heard rumblings from some of the Canadian Party men in town. With everything going on with the change-over to the new governor, and the talk of him bringing a full retinue with him, it's important to be cautious."

Marienne gasped.

"But not to worry," he said. "No one thinks a full complement is coming. Probably a few old men with rifles, full of their own superiority. Nothing to worry about."

Marienne looked the priest in the eye for a long beat. Eventually, he blinked and looked away. She knew there was more to the story than he was telling. But he was good at seeming calm and reasonable, so it was hard to argue with him in the moment.

"If you say so, Father. But I hold you responsible for these boys."

"Of course," he said, bowing. "You have my word."

He walked away and she gave Julien a hard look.

"He's slippery, that one."

"You sound like Mare."

She sniffed. "Even so, I want you to be careful, and don't just accept what he says. Pay attention and listen to the voice you have inside."

"You worry too much. Everything will be fine! I'll see you tomorrow."

She left without a word. The priest never did bring her any tea.

When she got home, the sun hung low in the sky. Instead of going inside, she went to the riverbank and sat on an old stump. She liked to watch the water and think. The wind had calmed to a light breeze and the sunlight danced on the water's surface reminding her of her childhood, of Lac Manitobah. They had spent summers near a shallow beach with white powdery sand. The fishing was good in that spot and her father and brothers caught plenty. She helped her mother smoke and dry the catch. But there was a lot of free time for her in those days, and she spent most of it splashing in the water, feeling the muddy bottom squish between her toes. She collected shells and pebbles along the shore and kept them in a pouch. They were her treasures, and she held on to them until she was grown up. She wondered where they were now. She wished she could hold them in her hands again, feel the cool, smooth rock between her fingers. It was such a comforting thing.

Once, there was so much fluff in the air from the cottonwood trees, she pretended it was snowing. It collected in her hair and eyelashes. It whirled in the air, coated the sand and grass, and eventually collected in drifts. She gathered as much as she could to try and make a snowball, but it was too soft and crushed into nothing in her fists. The fluff kept falling and eventually it swirled up and up, high in the sky, then settled in long strings on the lake's surface, floating away to the horizon. She wondered about the seeds in that fluff—how far they would travel, the seedlings that would sprout once they found purchase. *If* they found purchase. Perhaps there were thin trees climbing to the sky somewhere on the other side of the lake, trees that sprang from the seeds that had clung to her years ago. The idea was satisfying. She felt as if she'd had some small part in those lives continuing on.

The feeling of dread that had been growing in the back of her mind since her visit to the church hadn't eased. Instead, it was firmly snagged on her like a sharp burr. What was the priest not telling her? She needed to know what the English people were saying. Maybe she should visit the Bouchers in St. Boniface, see what they had to say. They did most of the entertaining for their community, since they had the largest house. They always had news first. If Julien wasn't more forthcoming when he came home, off to St. Boniface she'd go.

She rose from the stump with a groan. Her left hip had been aching lately. It was hard to stand up quickly, and the chill in the autumn air only made it worse. Soon she'd be like her own grandmother had been, stooped over and needing to be carried into church. Marienne refused to let that happen. She vowed she'd never be a burden like that to anyone. If she had to, she'd limp into the bush, alone, and lie down in the pine needles to die.

∞

The next day, Julien was all smiles when he rode up. Fredie hugged him and clung to him the whole visit. Suzette was eager to hear anything he said, like he was a traveller from far away. Marienne was warmed, watching them. Suzette was in that in-between age where half the time she wanted to be grown up like Charlotte and Julien, and sometimes she was still a child. She wanted Suzette to stay like Fredie for a little while longer but knew that was hopeless.

Clément hadn't said anything to Julien; he just huffed and went to work outside.

Later, just the two of them sipped tea at the table. Marienne asked Julien what was really going on. She took a gentle approach this time, thinking he'd be more likely to answer honestly if she did.

"The thing is, a new governor is coming," He pressed his thumb into a groove in the table's grain and didn't meet her eyes. "Riel and some of the council think he should be stopped before coming here. They've heard he's bringing an army, and we want to stop them from coming. A group is riding to Pembina to stop them there, but we're also blocking the trail here, to keep things secure. If they see how strong we are, they will be forced to turn back. Maybe we can change the future of this place. For the better."

He looked up at her.

She sat quiet for a while before speaking. "What you're saying, it's no small thing," she said. "When you were just patrolling nearby and pulling up those surveyor stakes in the night, that was one thing. But where is this Riel and his advisors getting their information from? Is it reliable? Maybe no soldiers are coming. Maybe these stories are a trick to keep you distracted from other things."

"They've thought of that. Mamaa, you should hear these men, especially Riel. He talks like the English do, like he knows their ways and systems. With all this change here, now, we have a chance to do something to make things better. For everyone."

"So you've said. I want to believe you. Just promise me you'll keep your eyes and ears open, like I told you. In times like this, things don't always go the way you think they will. Just remember to think for yourself, too. And if you hear something that we should know about, come and tell us, no matter what anyone says. Your family comes first."

"I will. You can be proud that I'm serving the Métis National Committee with honour." He hugged her, then left.

The next day, the family went to church in St. Boniface. Since the brigade had taken over St. Norbert's church, many people had migrated to St. Boniface for services. She spotted Denise's family so they sat together. She and Denise whispered to each other nearly the whole service. Neither heard much of the sermon.

"So what have you heard?"

Denise replied while still looking forward at the priest. "A lot of conflicting things that amount to a whole lot of nothing. You know how boys get."

"But what about the governor bringing soldiers, and us blocking the south road?"

"Change is coming for certain, but it doesn't have to be all bad. There might be some skirmishes, but nothing to be worried about.

And besides, the brigade could be mobilized into something bigger quite quickly, if they needed to. Our men will rise up ready. Just like always."

Marienne started to feel better. Even as a child, Denise could explain things simply, and then they didn't seem so bad. Marienne relied on this.

When they left the church, they found a crowd had formed at the foot of the steps. A young man, handsome with thick wavy dark hair, was speaking to the group around him. He stood out in his stiff collar, vest, and black frock coat. He raised his fist as he spoke in French. He cut a striking figure.

"That's him, Louis Riel," said Denise, pointing.

"We have to start somewhere!" Riel shouted. "Let's start with a government!"

A flurry of chatter rose from the crowd. A few people cheered.

"What is he saying?" Marienne asked a man next to her.

"He's saying it's time for a new government here, a proper one that represents all the people of the settlement, not just the interests of Canada."

"He's right," said Denise. The people around them nodded and murmured agreement.

"Canada had no right to conduct surveys without the express permission of the people of the settlement," Riel said. "The Canadians are going to keep coming until they are as plentiful as the grasshoppers were last year, when they ate every blade of grass and left us starving." He paused for effect. "We'll fight if we have to. We're ready. We can't be crowded out by invaders in our own country. Our National Committee will prevent this governor, McDougall, or any other governor, from entering Red River, unless Canada negotiates with us first. No union can happen without it."

He looked across the crowd. "We are Métis. We are a nation. It's time we show them who and what we are. And if one Métis falls, a handkerchief should be dipped in his blood, and that will be our flag."

The crowd whooped and cheered. Marienne wanted to cheer also, but felt frozen. She stared at the handsome man who looked every bit the politician and knew the fate of her family would be tied up with his. She hoped it would be a good one.

CHAPTER 10

Julien

November 1869

Julien's breath formed little clouds in the night air.

It was the first of November and he'd been at la barrière for a week. With most of the patrol south at Pembina, la barrière had been mostly quiet. He was paired with a young man from St. Boniface—Martin—and they got along well enough, but he was disappointed that he hadn't been paired up with a more seasoned soldat, someone he could learn from. After being around the brigade men and getting a taste of that life, he wanted more. Martin seemed more blasé about things. He acted as though all the patrolling and maintaining of la barrière was just one more thing to do. Julien couldn't understand it. Martin even said he was bored at times. The biggest excitement they'd seen so far was when some drunk American traders rode up and tried to argue their way past the gate. They had been more boisterous than belligerent, and after talking in circles for a while, they turned back and disappeared into the night. So maybe Martin had a point. McDougall's men hadn't come. His mother had worried for nothing.

The pair were sitting by the fire, keeping warm. Martin handed Julien some dried bread. "They better send some more supplies soon, or I'm going home," he said.

Julien was shocked. "You can't leave your post!"

Martin shrugged. "I can if we don't have any food left. There's nothing to patrol here anyway. All the action is at the fort. That's where we should be."

Julien considered this. All this time he'd thought he was at the forefront of the action and serving an important purpose. He hadn't thought at all about what was happening at the fort. "You think we could get posted to the fort?"

Martin nodded. "When we get back, I'm going to talk to Florian about it. I can read, so maybe I can help Riel. Can you read?"

Julien shook his head. "I know numbers, though. How did you learn?"

"I got lessons from the priest. He said I had potential."

"My little brother Fredie is getting lessons from the priest. My father thinks it's a waste of time but my mother says it's good for him to learn. Now I wish I'd learned, too."

"You still can. It's an important thing to know. I think it's going to become even more important, if things go the way I think they will."

"What do you mean?"

"Red River and the whole Northwest will change no matter what we do. It's up to us how it turns out. If we want to rule ourselves, then we need people who can do more than just farm and hunt. I'm going to be one of those people."

Julien sat up straight. He looked at Martin with new eyes. Martin might not be a seasoned soldier, but there was more to him than Julien could have guessed.

"Should we wait for our relief," Julien asked, "or do you want to just go back?"

Martin laughed. "Now look who wants to leave his post!"

Julien laughed too. Martin poked the fire, stirring up a cloud of sparks that lit the night like fireflies.

"Stick with me, Julien. We'll get you sorted so you're in on all the action, eh!"

Two days later, their replacements arrived and Julien and Martin rode back to St. Norbert as if they were being chased by McDougall's soldiers. When they got to the church, they found it humming with activity. Men were readying their horses, and others were packing up their belongings.

Julien found Henri inside. "What's going on?"

Henri seemed irritated. "Well, look who's returned from his big adventure. We're moving from here to the fort. That's our new base now. You should get ready too."

Julien was already packed and his horse was ready, so he looked for Martin and found him with Florian and Uncle Pierre, who waved Julien over. "Ride with us, we're going now!"

Julien looked for Henri, but he was still inside. He considered waiting, but the sense of urgency was too strong. Henri would catch up.

When they reached the fort, they found it shrouded in fog; only the corner towers were visible. The sky had gone grey overnight, and the clouds hung low. As Julien passed under the limestone blocks of the arched gateway, he expected to be entering a new world.

He'd never been inside Fort Garry before. The Company store was outside the fort, and when he'd gone with his father to trade or get provisions, that's where they'd gone. Julien had always wanted to see inside the walls, but his father had refused to let him go in. He said he always felt trapped in the fort, like a penned-up cow, and always came home in a foul mood afterward. Now that he was there himself, Julien was surprised how ordinary everything looked. Wooden buildings, some stone ones, dirt paths, yellowed grasses bending in the breeze. The soil they trod on was the same as the soil outside. He expected the air to be different, or something, but nothing was.

They tied their horses with the others and made their way to one of the wooden buildings, where everyone was heading. Julien recognized a lot of the men from the St. Norbert patrol, but there were even more he didn't recognize. He heard snatches of conversation in French, English, and Michif. Their voices were excited, their steps quick.

"How did we end up in the fort like this?" Julien asked Martin.

"They say Riel and his men simply walked in. No one met them or resisted. Nothing! So it's ours now," Martin laughed.

"What about the Company governor, McTavish?"

"He's still here, in his house. They say he's ill, but I think he just wants to stay out of it."

Inside, the room was lit with several lamps, giving it a warm glow. Some men sat around a long table, all talking at the same time. Others crowded around them, filling every nook in the room.

"Someone shut the door!" Just then, Henri entered and closed the door behind him. Julien caught his eye, and Henri scowled at him. Julien guessed he wasn't happy about being left behind. He shrugged; Henri would get over it.

A voice called for quiet, and the men settled down. Riel stood and addressed the room. "This fort has stood as a symbol of our oppression, but it's also been a symbol of stability. Does anyone remember the cannons ever being fired? How many of you have never been inside these buildings before? It's where all official business takes place. This place rules us, but it hasn't been for us. Now it is."

"I think this is a mistake," a man with a bushy moustache said in English. "We're only causing trouble here. We should have waited until the new governor came so we could see what he would have done. Now we'll never know."

"If we waited, it would have been too late!" another man piped up. Several others argued, all talking over each other, getting louder.

Florian whistled over the din and everyone turned to look at him. "The Company sold us to Canada like cattle. Now is not the time to sit quiet like docile cows. What's done is done, and now we have to decide what we do next."

He suggested guards be set up around the fort and Uncle Pierre volunteered to get a roster set up. Julien perked up at this, eager to join the effort.

The man with the moustache spoke up again. "Some of the local men aren't happy about what we've done here. They're all at the Emmerling Hotel, getting angrier and angrier the more they talk and the more they drink."

"All the more reason for guards." Uncle Pierre called out to his St. Norbert patrol and Julien joined them in the corner.

"Our National Committee of the Red River Métis got us here," Riel said, "but we need representation from all people of Red River, English and French alike." He nodded at the man with the moustache, who crossed his arms and gave a single nod back.

Julien followed Uncle Pierre's group outside and fell into step beside Henri, who ignored him. "What's wrong?" he asked.

"You disappeared! Left me alone with Jean, doing the boring work. Then when you get back you ignore us and follow your new friend there," Henri jutted his chin toward Martin, who walked ahead of them.

"Bah! What are you talking about? I was sent to la barrière, as you well know. It's not my fault you got assigned somewhere else."

"You volunteered for that post! You didn't even ask if I wanted to go, you just left."

Julien frowned. Henri was acting like a child. He didn't want to argue, not when things were getting interesting. He put his arm around Henri's shoulders. "You're right. But let's not worry about that now. Look where we are! Look who we're with! Let's enjoy this time."

Henri sighed, but one corner of his mouth turned up in a half smile. They quickened their pace to catch up with the group.

∞

Julien and Henri paced outside the fort's walls, near Main Street. It was night. The fog had dissipated, but the clouds remained, blocking out the moon and starlight. Light from nearby windows cast the only illumination. This assignment was already more interesting than la barrière had been. Many people moved in and out of the fort all day, and Main Street had been busy with activity, too.

"There sure were a lot of people out here today," Henri said. "I can't remember ever seeing so many people just walking back and forth, with no obvious destination."

"It's curiosity." Julien turned to face Henri. "Who can blame them? I'd probably do the same."

A small group of men came up to them from the direction of Main Street. They spoke slurred English and smelled of liquor. A man with yellow hair, a barrel chest, and almost no neck seemed to be their leader.

"You half-breeds think you're something, don't you?" He laughed in their faces. His cheeks were ruddy and unshaven. His eyes were deep-set, like finger holes poked in dough.

Julien tensed. His rifle was slung over his shoulder, and he grasped it in his hand, ready. Henri moved a step closer.

The man shoved Julien in the shoulder.

"Can't you talk?" the man said. "What are you, Swampies? Maybe we need to play some tom-toms to get you to understand."

He stepped close enough that Julien could see the crumbs caught in the man's beard and smell the sour odour on his clothes. His companions also stepped closer, surrounding them. Their breath formed little clouds in the cold air. Henri gave Julien a sideways glance, but Julien kept his eyes locked ahead on the thick-necked man.

"Why don't you men go home?" Julien said. "I don't think you want any trouble." His English was good, but his accent was strong.

The man laughed. Flecks of spittle flew and hit both Julien and Henri in their faces. "Listen to it speak!" said the man. "You hear that? It can talk after all."

His companions laughed.

Julien got hot with anger and wanted to crack his rifle across the man's smug face. But he and Henri were outnumbered, and they were far enough away from the fort gate that help might not reach them in time. Things could turn deadly in an instant.

"If you're not happy about something, I'm not the one who can help you," Julien said, keeping his voice calm, his tone reasonable. "We're not the ones making decisions here. We're just keeping watch and enjoying the night air."

The man seemed disappointed that Julien was not taking his bait. In that moment, Julien saw the men not as a threat, but as a source of curious amusement. They could cause harm, yes, but they were a bunch of drunk buffoons, full of their own imagined importance. His racing heartbeat slowed and he took a deep breath. He held the man's gaze.

"What's going on here?"

Julien turned around and saw Uncle Pierre with a group of men, all in matching capotes, forming a wall behind them.

"These men were just making their way home," Julien said.

The no-neck man seemed to deflate a bit. He took a step back. "Just having a friendly chat, nothing more."

"You best be on your way, then," Pierre said, his voice firm. He held the man's gaze for several beats.

"Come on, Thomas, let's go," one of the man's companions said, tugging on the thick-necked man's sleeve. Thomas scoffed and looked like he wanted to say something more, but then turned around and led the group back the way they'd come, muttering to each other.

"Let's go," Pierre said.

He led them to the headquarters building in the fort. It was quieter, with a few men still sitting at the table, talking in low voices. Martin sat with them, writing things down as they spoke. Someone brought Julien and Henri cups of steaming tea that they sipped eagerly, perched on a couple of wooden crates by the wall.

"That was close," Henri said. His hand shook a bit as he held his tin cup. "I thought they were going to beat us—or worse."

The tea had warmed Julien, keeping his calm state intact. He waved Henri's concerns away. "They were just a bunch of drunks. You saw how they swayed; they could barely stand straight. I doubt that no-neck man could have hit me if he tried."

"I'm not so sure. They weren't that drunk."

They sipped the rest of their tea in silence.

The next morning, Martin found Julien and brought him back to the headquarters building.

"Come on," Martin said, "he wants to talk with you."

"What? Who?"

"Riel."

Julien couldn't believe it. He smoothed his hair and made sure his sash was tied neatly around his waist. He felt like he was being summoned to an audience with a priest, or even a bishop.

The room was quiet, the way it had been the night before. Uncle Pierre and Riel sat at one end of the table, an empty chair next to him. Riel nodded for Julien to sit, and Martin sat beside him. Though Riel was in the same clothes as the day before, and had likely been awake most of the night, he looked fresh, alert. He gave Julien a warm smile.

"I hear you handled yourself very well last night," Riel said.

Julien felt his face flush. "It wasn't anything special."

"He calmed those drunks down and sent them on their way with no bloodshed," said Pierre. "That's no small thing."

Riel spoke in a smooth French, not the more common Michif, though Julien had heard him speak Michif to Florian the day before. He sounded like Father Ritchot.

"Pierre and Martin tell me you're keen to serve here," Riel said.

"Yes, sir."

"Young men like you are the future of this place. Your help is important."

Julien tried to keep his face still. He looked at Riel closely. Up close, Julien could see his youth, but his carriage and demeanour were of someone at least a decade older. His education was evident in both what he said and how he said it.

"I want to do all I can," Julien said. "It feels like we're at the start of something here, and I want to be part of it."

Riel smiled. "I'm happy to hear it. Pierre wants to post you inside the fort, with us. We're setting up a council here, but, as you've seen, not everyone wants us to succeed. We need to protect everyone here. I want you to be part of that protection force. Pierre will lead it."

"It's an honour, sir, maarsi."

Martin clapped him on the back. "I told you we'd get you sorted."

CHAPTER 11

Clément

December 1869

Clément shovelled snow away from the door of his house, where it had drifted. It was the first big snow of the season and was heavy enough to stick now that the temperature had dropped. He'd have to get the dog carioles prepped.

"Hé-ho, Clément," Claude Lambert called.

Clément put the shovel down. "Claude! What news?"

"Henri came home yesterday and said twenty-four delegates from all parishes of Red River had been elected. English and French, evenly split. Looks like we have a new government!"

"What? How come Julien didn't come to tell us? He's supposed to let us know when something big happens."

"He's probably too busy. Henri says he's with Pierre and the special guard inside the fort. Protecting Riel himself."

Clément thought he would fall over. "I can't believe it! Julien?"

"It's true. But there have been some big happenings outside the fort, too. Henri said Schultz and the other Canadian Party men aren't happy about this government. Well, Schultz kept about sixty men at his compound, but Florian had three hundred men surround them. They surrendered quietly, which Florian and Riel found suspicious."

"I'm sure they were right," Clément said.

"They were. When Florian and Riel walked through the place, it was cold inside, with no fires lit. So they checked the stoves and pipes and found gunpowder stashed everywhere. If anyone had lit a fire, the whole place would have gone."

"Tabernac!" Clément gasped.

"Schultz and his men were arrested, and his paper, *The Nor'Wester*, was shut down. Schultz is mixed up with some others, like this Charles Mair who said he was reporting for the *Montreal Gazette* but was stirring up trouble instead. And there's another one, calls himself Major Boulton, who's also part of it."

"But they've been arrested, so the trouble is over, right?"

Claude shrugged. "It seems so, but who knows? Henri sounded worried when he told us about it."

They stood in silence for a moment, absorbing the news.

"There's going to be an announcement tomorrow at the fort," Claude said. "A big celebration with a brass band and everything. You should come with us."

"We'll all be there," he said.

∞

Clément, Marienne, Charlotte, Suzette, and Fredie stood in the crowded courtyard of the fort. The snow had turned brown from the mud and melted to slush from all the footsteps.

"Look at all the people!" Fredie said, clearly thrilled.

Suzette hopped up and down, trying to get a better look over the crowd. "I see Julien!" she said. "He's standing with the men holding the rifles!"

"Where?" Charlotte said, craning to get a better look.

"I see him too," Marienne said. "He's at the end. Even in their uniforms, he stands out."

"I want to see!" Fredie said, tugging on his father's sleeve.

Clément hoisted him up on his shoulders. "You're getting too heavy for this."

The president of the council was introduced as John Bruce, a carpenter from St. Boniface who Clément knew only in passing. He was surprised it was not Riel.

"I thought Riel was the leader," Marienne said.

"There must be a reason, maybe Riel doesn't want the spotlight."

Marienne scoffed. "You heard him on the cathedral steps. He likes the spotlight well enough."

"It must be something else, then. Listen, Bruce is saying something."

John Bruce spoke to the crowd. "Today, we govern ourselves, and honour this with a new flag."

Florian stepped to the flagpole in the centre of the courtyard, pulled down the British flag and folded it neatly. He handed it to John Bruce who passed him a new flag to replace it. Florian unfurled it with a snap and raised it up. The new flag had a shamrock and a fleur-de-lis side by side. As it waved in the wind, first the shamrock was visible, then the fleur-de-lis, twirling in a dance.

The president spoke, projecting his voice to the crowd. "We resist against the Company that sold us, and against Canada, which pretends to have a right to coerce us and impose upon us a despotic form of government, contrary to our rights and interests as British subjects. There can be no takeover without consent."

The cannon was packed with gunpowder and lit, its crack echoing across the fort and beyond. Clément stood in stunned silence as each successive bang split the sky. The twenty-four shots took longer than he expected and left his ears ringing. Then the rifles fired one after the other in a feu de joie. He watched as Julien raised his rifle and shot. Clément was surprised to feel emotion swell up inside him. His eyes watered and he looked away so Marienne wouldn't see.

The boys' brass band from St. Boniface played a lively tune, and people clapped along and tapped their feet. Fredie cheered and waved at Julien, who didn't respond. Clément lifted him off his shoulders and set him down. After the band played, the president invited everyone to march up Main Street to the Emmerling Hotel for cakes and beverages. As Clément and his family followed the crowd out of the fort and down the street, Suzette and Charlotte pointed and exclaimed at the assembled soldiers.

"How handsome they are!" Charlotte said.

"They are impressive! And the band! Did you see them?"

"Julien was my favourite part!" Fredie said. Marienne ruffled his hair and pulled him close.

Clément looked back to catch sight of Julien, but he and the others had left the dais. He hoped they'd join the crowd at the Emmerling Hotel. Once they had eaten their cake, he made everyone wait a little longer, hoping Julien would arrive. But he never did.

CHAPTER 12

Charlotte

Christmas 1869

Charlotte worked on a new pair of dancing slippers for the Christmas season. Getting hard shoes with heels that clicked was out of her reach; they were impractical, rare in the settlement, and the imported ones were too expensive. So she improvised with soft white leather that she fashioned into snug slippers embroidered with delicate pink flowers and pale green vines around the edges. The effect was subtle yet striking. She used buffalo hair inside for warmth and to cushion her feet against the stitches. She was proud of them. With all the work she'd done with the shelf valances and other beadwork goods she'd made for sale in St. Paul, she'd become more adept with her stitching. Her hands moved quickly, she hardly needed to think about it anymore. Sometimes she dreamed of stitching as she slept, and her hands would be cramped in the morning.

Their house was busy preparing for the festivities. Her father had brought some rum back from his last trip to St. Paul, as well as tobacco, especially for the season. It was December 24, and they were getting ready for Midnight Mass, the start of celebration season. She and Suzette were making bannock, while her mother and Mare prepared a ham for le réveillon after church, when they would have dinner and exchange gifts.

Julien had come home to celebrate, but all he talked about was the fort and Riel. "This new government changes everything," he said. "We're going to be called Assiniboia and become a province of Canada, all with no bloodshed or any real fighting. Our future is bright. Anything can happen."

Charlotte had to admit she was proud of her brother, and she couldn't help but get swept up in his excitement. He'd looked sharp on the dais, and she liked the ceremony of it all. Her father hadn't said much since the flag-raising, but he seemed happy to have Julien home. There were good times ahead, she could feel it.

In the evenings leading up to the holidays, she'd mended her calico dresses to make sure they were in good repair, especially the hems, which tended to fray. She added ribbon to cover the worn edges and reinforce the hems. She was happy with the result.

When it was time to go to mass, she put on her nicest dress with an embroidered shawl and her winter moccasins. She wore her hair in a long braid that hung in a thick rope down her back. She could have wound the braid into a low knot the way her mother and Mare did, but that style was usually for married women. She was still in that in-between state where she was an almost-adult. She had turned seventeen in November, and her father had already been making noises about finding a husband for her. She ignored him whenever he started, but she caught his sidelong glances and half-smiles. She knew he wouldn't force her into a marriage she didn't want. Still, she was wary when the subject came up.

Her father shook snow off his buffalo robe and stamped his feet as he came inside.

"Let's go!" he cried. "Rapide! The carioles are ready!"

His shout caused a flurry of activity as she and the others donned their coats and moccasins. Marienne blew out the lamps and banked the coals in the fireplace before latching the door behind her. Most people preferred to go to the cathedral in St. Boniface for the Christmas service; it was grander and could hold more people. Sometimes Anglicans and Presbyterians came, too, to be part of the big event, and because the cathedral had the only church organ in Red River. Music could always draw people in. Charlotte wondered who she'd see there.

Two carioles with dog teams of four waited for them, each with a lantern to light the way. The dogs were decked out with ribbons and bells on their harnesses. Sensing the excitement of their passengers, they jumped and yipped, making their bells jangle. Charlotte climbed into one cariole with Suzette and Fredie, with Julien standing on the runners behind them to mush the team. They sat in the cariole single file, with Fredie in front and Suzette in the middle. Mare and Marienne sat in the other with Clément mushing. The night was clear, full of brilliant stars, and a nearly full waning moon that made the snow sparkle.

Julien led them off with a shout and they swooped down the sloping trail to the frozen river. Fredie raised his hands in the air and cried out as they raced down to the ice. They were packed tight together, covered in blankets and hemmed in by its tall sides. It was a warm and cozy way to travel.

They followed existing tracks in the snow and then pulled up beside the other cariole. "Go! Go!" Julien shouted to make the dogs run faster. He just couldn't help racing, even on their way to church. Fredie and Suzette waved as they passed, shrieking with delight. Charlotte enjoyed the cold wind on her face as the snow crunched under the runners. She exhaled little clouds of fog into the crisp night air.

Shadowy trees lined the riverbank and outlines of a few houses could be seen. Some had faint glows in their windows, others were dark. The odd bonfire flickered in the distance, glowing beacons in the night.

When they passed through The Forks, the intersection of the Red and Assiniboine rivers, they were joined by more carioles and sleighs. Soon the cathedral came into view, set back from the river, ablaze with light. "Look at it! It reaches the sky!" Fredie said.

The peal of the church bells echoed down the riverbank, calling people to service. Charlotte and her family pulled up near the cathedral and climbed out of the carioles. The bank was steep at this part of the river. A rope fastened to a tree hung down the slope to help people climb up the trail. Charlotte grasped the rope behind Fredie and Suzette. Fredie slipped and slid backwards into Suzette and they both fell flat, laughing.

"Fredie!" shouted Suzette, as she righted herself. She let go of the rope to grab a mittful of snow and threw it at him. The snow was dry and didn't stick together in a ball, so half of it flew back in her face. This would usually turn into a royal scrap between them, but instead they just laughed and continued on their way. Charlotte looked over her shoulder to see her father and Julien on either side of Mare, helping her up the bank, with Marienne behind.

At the top they saw crowds filing into the church. Two large bonfires flanked either side with blanketed horses and dog teams resting around them. Julien and Clément ran back down the bank and brought the carioles to join the others by the fires, standing on one runner and pushing up the hill with the other leg. Charlotte and the rest of her family waited for them to catch up so they could enter together. They waved at people they knew as they passed on their way inside.

The church glowed in candlelight; it was nearly as bright as day inside. Pine boughs adorned the ends of the wooden pews, giving a clean, welcoming scent. Soft murmurs bounced off the vaulted ceiling. Nearly all the seats were full, but Aunt Denise waved them over; she'd saved seats for them next to Uncle Robert and her cousins Marie, Juliet, Georges, William, and little François, who sat on Aunt Denise's lap. The sisters sat next to each other and chatted excitedly.

"There are more people here than last Christmas!" Marienne said. "I don't even know everyone!"

"Yes, it's like people just want to be in the same place. To be seen, maybe. I see some Kildonan people over there," Aunt Denise said, gesturing ahead.

"Where are the Bertrands? Have you seen them?"

"They haven't come back from the hunt. I think they're wintering on the plains again."

Marienne nodded. "The McKays are too. I heard some of the Touronds are trapping."

Aunt Denise leaned forward to look past Marienne to Charlotte, who sat next to her mother.

"And look at mademoiselle all dressed up!" she said.

Charlotte was afraid her aunt would reach over and pinch her cheek, but she was too far away. She smiled.

"Joyeux Noël, Auntie," she said.

She left her mother and aunt to their gossip and scanned the crowd. She saw more cousins and neighbours, but many people she didn't know. It was energizing to be in such a large crowd. The candles and stove heated the church, but all the people crammed in the pews kept it warm, too. She loosened the shawl from around her shoulders and shifted in her seat. When she looked up, the people in the rows in front of her had shifted and she could glimpse the profile of the handsome man she'd seen on Main Street in the summer. She was sure it was him. He was chatting to the person next to him, who she could not see. She held her breath. Then the woman behind him shifted again and blocked Charlotte's view. She wore a fur hat that sat nearly a head taller than everyone else. Charlotte moved from side to side trying to see around the giant hat, but she couldn't catch sight of him again.

A hush fell over the crowd as the Bishop Taché came out and began the service. Everyone faced forward. Organ music filled the room. Charlotte fidgeted in frustration.

Her mother tapped her leg.

"Sit still. You don't need to see the bishop, you just need to listen to him."

Charlotte continued to try to peer around the crowd but was more subtle about it. The service whizzed by. She heard none of it. When it was time to take communion, she caught a glimpse of the man standing to let others in the pew pass to join the line for the sacrament. She saw him more clearly and was sure it was him. She focused on the back of his head and the smooth lines of his felt frock coat. The back of it had a martingale with two shiny brass buttons that glinted in the soft candlelight. She was mesmerized.

It was her turn to stand in line. She hoped she could catch his eye when she passed. She was sure that if he could see her, he would return her interest. It had to be so.

When she took the wafer and wine, it barely registered. The wafer turned to pasty gum in her mouth; the splash of wine was not enough to wash it down. She sucked on it like a lozenge, feeling it disintegrate.

Suzette was in front of her, so she focused on the back of her head. When they approached the row where the man sat, she dared to look in his direction. She locked eyes with him and felt lit from within. His blue eyes were the colour of thick winter ice. His hair was swept back as before, and he was clean-shaven. He smiled at her, showing his straight white teeth.

Boldly, she held his gaze. He stopped speaking to the person next to him and focused on her, his gaze following as she inched past. Her legs shook as she took her seat. He'd noticed her! What this meant exactly, she didn't know. But that didn't matter.

∞

It was New Year's Day, and ever since Midnight Mass, Charlotte had not stopped thinking about the handsome man. She'd savoured their brief interaction and, in her imagination, it grew bigger than it actually was. "Quit your daydreaming and knead the dough!" her mother snapped at her. Charlotte was embarrassed and pounded the dough hard.

They were cooking food to pack for the New Year's Day parties.

She didn't mind this work; it was for something she looked forward to, so she helped without complaint. She couldn't wait to wear her new slippers and dance into the wee hours, starting at the Boucher house in St. Boniface, then on to other houses to continue the party for the next three days. There would be bonfires, food, drink, naps on the floor, then back to dancing. You never knew who you would see or what would happen.

They packed food, rum, tobacco, and some extra clothes into the sleigh; Julien followed in a dog cariole. The festive feeling Charlotte carried grew and held fast.

It was mid-afternoon when they arrived at the Boucher house, and children were already chasing each other around the bonfire. Two of the Boucher sons were busy splitting firewood and adding it to the pile, which had grown taller than they were.

"Ho! I think you have enough there," her father said.

Inside was a bustle of activity, even though only a few families had arrived. The dining table had been pushed into a corner and was laden with food. A large enamelware water pail sat on a washbasin table where a pitcher and ewer would normally sit, with a tin ladle hanging off the side. Another pail of melting snow sat on the floor beside it. It was the job of the smaller kids, like Fredie, to fill the extra buckets with snow to keep a steady supply of cool water at hand.

Charlotte was restless waiting for more people to arrive, so she went outside. The sky was overcast. Sunshine at this time of year meant deep cold and sun dogs in the sky. Clouds kept the warmth in like a blanket, so she wore only her shawl around her shoulders instead of her heavy coat.

Henri and Julien had joined some of the other young men to race dog carioles. Some of the younger kids had snowshoe races. Laughter and whoops echoed across the fields. She moved toward the cariole races and found her friends Sarah and Hyacinthe Berard watching and gossiping.

"Look at Henri, how his hair blows behind him as he races," said Hyacinthe.

"You say that every time he races," said Sarah.

Sarah and Hyacinthe were cousins. Sarah lived in St. Norbert and Hyacinthe lived in St. Vital. Sarah liked to know everyone's business, hoard it, and then parcel it out to her chosen audience. Knowledge was a commodity and Sarah knew how to use it. Charlotte had been burned by Sarah's talk before, so she was cautious, but Sarah was also a lot of fun to be around, so sometimes the price was worth it. Besides, ignoring Sarah would be worse, because then her focus would be unrelenting. It was better to stay on the periphery and in her good graces.

Suzette had been watching the snowshoe races but came over to join them instead. "Those races are boring," she said.

"You came to the right place," said Sarah. "Things are just getting started."

"Look how wide his shoulders have gotten," said Hyacinthe. "And did you see him in his blue capote when he was on patrol?" She fanned her hand in front of her face as if she were warm.

"Henri et Hyacinthe, ooh la la!" said Sarah, nudging Hyacinthe with her elbow. The girls laughed as Hyacinthe blushed and looked away. Charlotte suspected Hyacinthe would regret mentioning Henri—now Sarah would never let it go.

Julien sped by, loudly mushing the dogs to go faster. Henri's lips were pressed together in a tight line. He didn't usually look so grim when racing. Maybe he was trying to look serious for his female audience. The bells from their carioles jangled, the sound crisp in the air.

The girls cheered the boys on as they passed.

"Go, Julien!" Sarah shouted.

Charlotte looked at Sarah with surprise, then realized Sarah was watching him closely. She remembered Sarah dropping Julien's name in conversation a lot over the last year. She always asked Charlotte about him, her tone casual, polite. Now Charlotte understood why. She smiled. This was information she could use.

"Julien said he'd be staying at the fort for good," she said to the group, but looking at Sarah.

"Oh?" Sarah turned to her.

"Yes, he said with this new government, he's going to be part of it. He's even learning to read and write."

Sarah narrowed her eyes. "Really?"

Suzette nodded. "Oh, yes. He talks about it all the time. He practises with Fredie."

To them, the fort was an exotic place where the governor held fancy dinners and dances. But, of course, no one they knew had ever been to one.

"Are they saying Riel will be the new governor?" Hyacinthe asked.

"He has to be," said Sarah. "You've all heard him speak. That time he spoke on the steps of the cathedral after Sunday mass was like something out of a story. He *seems* like a governor."

The girls nodded and murmured agreement.

"Haven't you heard?" said Charlotte. "Riel has already replaced John Bruce as présidente of the council. It happened a few days ago. Uncle Pierre came and told Julien all about it. An election and a permanent government will be next."

Sarah and Hyacinthe gasped. "Présidente!" they said.

"It's true," Suzette said. "Oh, Julien was upset to have missed it! He stomped around the house all day."

Now they circled around Charlotte, eager for more. Julien's cariole had looped back, with Henri finishing a full length ahead of Julien. Fredie and some of the younger kids cheered and gathered around him. Julien looked up toward the girls and frowned to see them huddled around his sister. Charlotte caught his eye and turned away from him. He always had an audience. It would do him good to not have everyone fawning over him for once.

"Maybe Henri and Julien will be capitaines!" said Hyacinthe.

"Probably not both of them," said Sarah.

"Maybe even part of the government somehow," said Charlotte.

A new pair of boys were getting ready to race.

"Life in the fort would be a nice change from the freighting life," said Sarah, looking Julien up and down.

"A government man's wife might even have servants," said Hyacinthe.

"As if you would be a government wife!" Sarah shot back. "You'd be the servant, more like."

Hyacinthe scowled. "We'll see about that."

More people had arrived. The bonfire raged and a small group stood around it, talking and laughing. More men had joined the races, but the sun was going down, so soon most would move inside.

"It'll be dark soon," said Charlotte.

"That means the dancing will start!" Suzette clapped her hands in excitement.

"I love how it gets dark so early this time of year, it makes the night last longer," Sarah said.

"New Year's Day is the best time of year," said Suzette. "There are no rules!"

Charlotte and the girls went inside, leaving the boys to race in the dusk. There was no set mealtime, since there was nowhere for anyone to sit and eat. All the furniture had been moved aside or out of the house entirely. Any chairs or stools were arranged against the walls, and they were reserved for the elders, like Mare. Some men sat on overturned crates. Everyone else stood or sat on the wooden floor out of the way. The girls grabbed some food from the table and stood near a window that looked onto the bonfire. In the fading light, Charlotte could see the lane that led into the property. She tore off pieces of bannock and nibbled, licking her buttery fingers.

In the orange light, she watched an ornate sleigh arrive, pulled by a team of four horses. Most sleighs were uncovered, but this one was enclosed, more like a stagecoach. She couldn't see who was inside, but it could not be anyone from the Métis parishes. No one had a sleigh like that. It seemed much too cumbersome to move efficiently. Plus, feeling the wind in your face was part of the joy of riding in a sleigh to begin with. Why add more weight and take away the fun? It was odd.

The fiddles started up. Her father and two others sawed their bows across the strings, the sound calling everyone's attention—the real fun was about to begin. Charlotte slipped away to the corner where she'd stashed her belongings and changed out of her winter moccasins into her dancing slippers. The white leather glowed in the lamplight. It was the effect she'd hoped for. She kept her shawl on, but knew she'd shed it before long.

When she rejoined the group, Sarah gasped and pointed at her feet.

"Did you get English shoes?" She tugged at Charlotte's skirt to lift it above her feet.

Charlotte put one foot forward and dipped in a mock curtsey, showing off her slippers.

"No heel!" said Hyacinthe. "But you would never guess at first."

"Did your memayr make these?" Sarah asked. "It looks like her work."

"No, I made them," Charlotte said. She was annoyed but tried to keep it out of her voice. Sarah always knew how to irk her, but Charlotte didn't want to get snared by her this night. She gave a bright smile instead.

"Who is that?" Suzette pointed.

As one, the girls turned toward the door.

Four new people had arrived. A blast of cool air followed them inside. The handsome man from Main Street, a young woman, and an older couple who must be their parents. They wore tailored felt coats and fur hats. The woman and her daughter wore black-heeled boots with tight laces. The two men wore black leather knee-high boots. They stood close together and looked around the room, as if they were unsure if they should stay. Daniel Boucher emerged from the crowd and embraced the older man, welcoming them inside.

Charlotte vibrated with excitement. She had hoped he would show up at one of the parties, but she'd been afraid to dwell on it too much, in case wishing for it made the possibility vanish. But here he was, at the first and best party! She didn't know what to do, but she had to do something. This opportunity was a gift that she would not let pass her by.

"Those are new faces," said Sarah.

"Those are the Wakefields," said Hyacinthe. "They moved here in the spring, from Toronto. They live in the big house in Point Douglas, you know the one. My father talks about them a lot."

Sarah narrowed her eyes at Hyacinthe. "You've never mentioned them before. Have you met them?" Her tone was icy.

"Well, no, but I've seen them around. Look at them. They stand out."

"I saw the son on Main Street in the summer," said Charlotte. "I wondered who he was." She tried to keep her tone light, but worried her voice was too high and strained.

"Father says they're opening up a bank," said Hyacinthe.

"A bank and a big house in Point Douglas," said Sarah. "Why is this the first I'm hearing of this? Hyacinthe, since when do you keep secrets?"

Hyacinthe sputtered. "It was no secret! Just boring business. I never thought twice about it."

Charlotte didn't like the tension in this conversation.

"What does it matter?" she said. "Now we all know of these new people. Let's enjoy ourselves. I think this is going to be a good night. Look, the dancing is starting."

The fiddles raced like the carioles outside. People danced the reel of four, arms linked with skirts swinging.

Charlotte and the girls joined in, weaving into the throng like threads in the sashes men wore around their waists. Soon she was laughing and sweating, her heart pounding. She felt relaxed, happy to take up space in the room, where she belonged. As she turned about the room, she kept her eye on the Wakefields. She tried to catch the eye of the young man, but his back was turned to her. He worked the room, moving from one deep conversation to the next. If his family was opening a bank, it made sense for him to be forming ties with the community. If he was here with the Métis, maybe that meant his bank would serve everyone in Red River, not just the English side. She wondered if he would make his way to her father. She had to make sure she was nearby for that conversation.

The jigs had started. Tired, Charlotte moved to the side for a drink of water. It was refreshing on her throat. She dipped her fingers into the cup and wiped her brow. The water mixed with the sweat that dripped down the side of her face.

"You're not dancing the jig?"

Charlotte turned and locked eyes with the young Wakefield. Up close his blue eyes were almost transparent. A hint of gold stubble shadowed his jaw. He smiled.

"Just needed a bit of refreshment," she said. "I'm Charlotte."

She held out her hand. She surprised herself by being so forward. It was as if someone else had taken control of her. She had no idea what she would say next.

"Callum Wakefield," he said and kissed her hand. His lips were soft, feather light. He let go of her hand but the spot he kissed still tingled. "What's your family name?" he asked.

"Rougeau," she said. "My father is Clément—he's there, playing fiddle."

"Ah, so Julien must be your brother then," he said.

"You know Julien?"

"We met at the fort. My family has business there, and I've seen Julien many times. He's charming."

"As you can see."

She nodded her head toward the centre of the dance floor, where Julien was jigging so quickly his feet were a blur. The fringes of his sash bobbed in time with the music. His long hair was tied in the back, but pieces came loose and swung around his face. People had cleared space around him, forming a circle. They all clapped and whooped. Sarah was right in front, calling his name. She caught Charlotte's eye and gave her a look of surprise when she saw who was standing next to her. Sarah would no doubt soon be along to see what was happening.

"Look at him go," said Callum.

Just then, Henri unwrapped the sash from his waist and threw it down on the floor in front of Julien. The crowd cheered. It was the signal for a challenge to out-jig each other. Everyone loved a good dance-off.

"Here we go," said Charlotte.

Julien bowed deeply to Henri in mock gallantry. The music swelled and Henri began to jig. Julien stood back, clapping in time with the music. They took turns dancing, each getting more frenzied, until they both collapsed on the floor, laughing.

"That looks like fun," said Callum.

"Henri and Julien compete at everything," said Charlotte. "I don't think they'd know what to do with themselves if they couldn't race or outdo each other somehow."

"Maybe he needs someone new to compete with."

"You can try."

Charlotte was surprised how at ease she felt with Callum after only a few minutes' conversation. His face was open and he kept his full attention on her as she spoke. She was used to being barely heard in her crowded house, where there was always noise, usually several people talking at once. Here, in this loud house full of people, they were in a little pocket, just the two of them. Callum offered to refill her water cup and came back with another for himself. They sipped and smiled at each other.

"Callum, who is your new friend?" said the young woman who had arrived with him. She'd appeared at his side seemingly out of nowhere.

"Alyce, meet Mademoiselle Charlotte Rougeau," said Callum. "Charlotte, my sister Alyce."

"A pleasure to make your acquaintance," said Alyce.

Charlotte smoothed the front of her dress. Alyce wore a rose-coloured silk dress with puffed sleeves and lace around the collar. She smelled of rose water and Charlotte wondered if Alyce always matched her scent to her dress. Her light brown hair was piled on top of her head in big curls. Silver earrings dangled and grazed her neck. She felt shabby next to this exotic creature. Were these the types of women Callum was used to? What he expected? She'd felt relaxed with him, but now she felt awkward and unsure of herself. He probably saw her as an amusement, not someone to take seriously.

"What darling shoes!" said Alyce, pointing at Charlotte's feet. "I've never seen anything like them."

Charlotte pulled her feet under her dress. "Maarsi," she said, the Michif a tiny act of defiance. She straightened her shoulders then added in English, "I made them."

"They are certainly unique."

Alyce looped her arm through Callum's. "I think Mother wants to go home. She seems tired."

"But it's still early," said Callum.

"You know how she gets," Alyce waved her hand.

"I should check on her," Callum said and crossed the room, leaving Charlotte and Alyce alone.

"You must know some exciting people, Charlotte. It's been frightfully dull in Point Douglas. Hardly any company, and all anyone wants to talk about is land and money. Please, save me from this." Alyce grinned, flashing a matching set of Callum's white teeth.

"Nearly everyone here is a cousin of some sort."

"How charming!"

"You should meet Sarah—she knows everyone and everything."

"Perfect! Lead on."

Sarah was regaling Hyacinthe and the others with a story that had them rapt. Sarah's arms waved around in the telling. Everyone turned toward Charlotte and Alyce when they joined them.

". . . and then he said—" Sarah was cut off mid-sentence.

"Sarah, this is Alyce Wakefield, from Point Douglas," said Charlotte.

At first, Sarah seemed annoyed at the interruption, but she recovered when she noticed who stood in front of her. She offered a bright smile. Charlotte introduced Alyce to the rest of the group. Sarah's English was not as strong as Charlotte's, so she took the lead.

"Alyce was saying how dull it's been in Point Douglas," she said. Turning back to Alyce, she added, "This must be a nice change."

"This is the right place for you," said Sarah. "Much more for you here."

"How wonderful these little houses are," said Alyce. "So warm, yet sparse. It's a wonder all these people can fit inside, never mind dance like dervishes!"

Sarah seemed confused but continued. "Yes, the fête is a nice one."

Alyce gave Charlotte a disappointed look, which matched one from Sarah. This was not the sparkling conversation Alyce surely expected. Charlotte would have to think of something to ease the awkwardness.

"Why don't we dance?" Charlotte hooked arms with Sarah and Alyce and led them to the dance area.

"I don't know these dances!" said Alyce.

"Sarah's a great teacher," said Charlotte.

She nudged the two so they were side by side and urged Sarah to show Alyce how it was done. Sarah seemed happy to be somewhat in control again, since showing Alyce the steps in the midst of the loud music sidestepped the need for talking. Soon Alyce was hopping and laughing, not seeming to mind that her steps were inelegant and jerky, like the small children who hung out on the fringes of the dancers, copying the adults. Alyce's heeled boots made the jigging difficult; she kept stumbling and needed to hike her skirt to keep from tripping on the hem. Charlotte could see how her dancing slippers were actually superior—for jigging, at least.

It was hot in the house, so Charlotte left the girls to their dancing and went outside to cool off. She waved at Norbert-from-St. Norbert, who was petting some of the dogs.

"Needed a break from the noise, eh?" he said.

"It's too hot in there." Charlotte always felt comfortable around Norbert. He had a gentle nature. Some people said he was simpleminded, because he preferred the company of animals over people. But she knew he just didn't like noisy crowds. That didn't seem simple-minded to her. He was known as a good worker and woodcutter, and Julien said he was keeping all the fires going at the fort.

"I see you got Alyce to try her hand at jigging," said Callum, appearing at Charlotte's side.

"She's a natural," said Charlotte, being generous.

"I'm glad you introduced her to your friends. I think she's been lonely since we moved here."

Charlotte was touched by the care he showed for his sister.

"It's good for us to have new people around, too," said Charlotte. "I think Sarah would really take to Alyce if her English was better."

"Your English is excellent. And you speak French too?"

"Yes, but at home we speak Michif more. Sometimes a mix of

French and Michif, it all kind of flows together sometimes. I know some Anishinabemowin from my grandmother—she's Saulteaux—and most people can speak at least a few words of Cree."

"I've noticed most speak a mix here but had no idea the people of Red River were so accomplished. I only speak English myself and feel at a disadvantage."

"You should try to learn some French at least. Especially if you're intending to open a bank here that serves everyone."

Callum appraised her. "I can see that will be important. So you've already heard about my family's plans." It wasn't a question.

She nodded. "News travels fast here."

"Well, perhaps you can help me with my French. Alyce too. We'll gladly compensate you."

Charlotte was intrigued by the prospect. Would her father let her do it? Would it matter that she couldn't read much? How would she even teach someone French? She only learned herself by doing, by being immersed. Most kids learned new skills by watching the adults and then trying things on their own. Figuring things out made people self-sufficient. She was proud of that but wasn't sure how to teach someone else to do that. But she was willing to try.

"That's something my father will have to decide."

Her shawl slipped and one end fell to the snow. Callum reached down and brought it back up around her shoulder, brushing her arm as he did so. Charlotte found the gesture comforting and thrilling. She smiled.

"Everything all right, mademoiselle?" said Norbert.

He must have been watching their exchange. Charlotte hadn't noticed.

"Yes, maarsi," she said and lowered her gaze. Her face went hot, like she'd been caught doing something wrong. She looked around, worried she'd be the next gossip story. "I should get back inside and help with the food."

She turned and hurried inside, her heart pounding. She found her father taking a break with Julien and Henri, who were both red in the face, with dripping hair. They were laughing.

"Papaa," Charlotte said, "I've been asked to help some English people learn French."

The three stopped laughing and stared at her.

"What English people?" said Julien.

"The Wakefields."

"The new Point Douglas ones? Who wants to learn French, the daughter?" said Henri, suspicious.

"The whole family, I think. To help with their business."

Her father took a puff from his pipe and exhaled a cloud of sweet smoke at her. "And why should we help these English with their business? And why you?"

Charlotte didn't want this chance to slip away. "Well," she said, "I think the daughter, Alyce, needs a friend. They said they'd pay me."

The mention of payment seemed to pique her father's interest. "Well, they'll need to talk to me," he said. "You have to watch with new people. They can be slippery."

"We've seen the son, that Callum, at the fort," said Julien. "Their family is opening a bank. Maybe them learning French is a good sign."

"Maybe," said Henri, frowning. "But I don't like it."

"Well, I'll need to talk to him before even thinking about this," her father said. "Being a friend to this new girl might be a good thing. But we'll have to see."

The festivities continued long into the night. Charlotte returned to dancing and chatting with her friends and Suzette. She looked around for Callum, but lost sight of him many times. Alyce had danced with them for a while, then returned to her mother's side. Charlotte noted that Mrs. Wakefield seemed to be enjoying herself and didn't appear to be tired at all. She wondered if Alyce had interrupted her earlier conversation with Callum with the excuse of their mother's fatigue in order to send him away.

She was considering taking a rest in a corner, perhaps even a short nap. A few people had done so already, even as the music and dancing continued. Some of the older men had set up card games off to the side. They sat on three-legged stools or overturned crates, yelling out when someone slapped down a winning hand. The room had a heavy air of pipe smoke, sweat, and rum. It was pleasant. Fredie sat with some of the younger cousins in a circle on the floor, out of the way, against the wall. They seemed to be telling stories, as though they were sitting around a fire at camp.

There was a commotion at the door. The house was dim and smoky, and she couldn't see through the crowds of people, but she could hear angry shouting. People looked toward the sound.

"Look at these half-breeds, drunk like Swampies!" a blond man shouted. He was stout with a thick neck, like an ox.

Some of the men who had been playing cards stood up, the stools and crates they sat on toppling over. More men, including Mr. Boucher, gathered around the intruders.

"All proud of yourselves after stealing the fort, eh?" said the ox's companion.

"Trying to act civilized! It's like seeing a pig in breeches or a dog in a dress," said the third member of the group.

Charlotte moved closer to get a better look and found herself next to Sarah.

"Who is that?" she asked.

"I've seen them before," Sarah said. "My father says they're part of that group that supports annexation, the Canadian Party. They're always causing trouble. They want the whole Northwest to be annexed and they want to fill it up with Protestants from Ontario. They are always publishing nasty things in the newspaper."

"Why would they show up here?"

"To cause trouble, why else? I heard there were fewer parties this year, so of course they show up here. Calling us drunks! They should look at themselves. They say we're savages, but they're the ones who act like it. Shame on them."

The ox reared his fist and punched Mr. Boucher. This was a mistake, because Boucher stood nearly a foot taller than the ox and he knocked him down with hardly any effort.

Everyone shouted at once.

The other two men tried to throw punches and landed a few, but they were soon overtaken. In an instant the three men were on the floor, obscured by a mass of swinging arms and kicking legs. Someone knocked over a lantern, which started a small fire on the floor. Mare and a few nearby women quickly beat it out with their shawls.

Callum made his way through the crowd to the mêlée.

"Friends, friends, stop this now! These poor fools are only here to cause trouble. Let's not reward their stupidity." He pushed his way between the fighting men.

"They deserve everything they got!" shouted someone. More shouted in agreement.

"Yes, but let them go lick their wounds. They can sleep it off in the snow."

"Might do them some good," said one of the fighters.

"All right," said the man who'd been punched by the ox. He kicked the ox in the shoulder, hard, before picking him up by the collar and tossing him outside. The other two were also tossed outside. They landed on the ox. The Métis men clapped each other on the back and laughed.

"Enough of that nonsense," Clément cried out. "Back to the jigging! We'll make sure that fire is out by dancing on its embers, eh?"

He picked up his fiddle and screeched his bow across the strings. He played "Chanson de la Genouillère," a song about the Métis victory of Frog Plain in 1816, which was always a crowd pleaser. Claude Lambert sang the opening lines:

> *Would you care to hear sung*
> *A song of truth?*
> *Last June 19th,*
> *The band of Bois-brûlés arrived —*
> *A band of brave warriors*

The crowd joined in for the rest of the song and danced like nothing had happened.

Charlotte was impressed with how deftly Callum had stepped in and helped calm things down. She looked for him. She spotted him making his way through the crowd in her father's direction. Was he going to talk to him about the French lessons? Should she join them? She weighed the options. Callum had charmed her and put her at ease right away. Perhaps it was best to let him do the same to her father. Let him judge for himself. If she joined them, her father would more likely be skeptical and defensive. She sat in the corner and watched.

Callum offered his hand to her father and gave him a warm smile. Her father had had a few rums by then and was affable. Their chat appeared friendly. Callum spoke at length, gesturing with his hands as her father nodded along, appearing to agree. Or to not disagree, at least. Charlotte held her breath.

He reached out his hand and Callum shook it eagerly. They looked like they'd just struck an agreement. Charlotte smiled. It had to be good news. Julien joined them and he and Callum shook hands. Soon they were all laughing and clapping each other's backs. Charlotte relaxed, and before long, she'd fallen asleep against the wall, using her bunched-up coat as a pillow.

When she woke, it was morning. Half the people had gone, others were sleeping on the floor like her, and others sipped tea and picked at the leftover food. Fredie and the other young kids were gone. She could hear voices outside; the small kids were probably already back to their snowshoe races or other games. She didn't see the Wakefields anywhere. She stood up to look out the window, and their sleigh was gone. Her mother and Mare were in the kitchen area, working. Her mother stirred a large pot of porridge that steamed on the stove. Charlotte joined them.

"You seem to have made some new friends last night," said her mother. She handed Charlotte a bowl of porridge.

Charlotte's stomach sank. She was hungry when she first smelled the cooking porridge, but now not so much. Her mother's expression and tone seemed calm, but Charlotte knew a storm could erupt at any moment. She had to be careful. "Yes, the Wakefields. They're new in town. Only been here a few months, I think."

"And now you'll be giving them French lessons."

Charlotte gaped. "What? Did Papaa say so? Really?"

Marienne laughed. "Yes, he said so. He's a charming one, that young Wakefield. Had your Papaa eating out of his hand in no time. Julien, too, of course."

Relief flooded through Charlotte. She picked up a small wooden spoon and eagerly dove into her porridge. "What did he say?"

"He said you could go to their house and give them lessons, but you need to be accompanied by either Julien or Suzette. Julien seemed happy to oblige, but said he'd be busy a lot of the time, so it will mostly be Suzette. Make sure you include her in things." Mare pointed a finger at Charlotte. "I mean it."

"Oh yes, of course I will!"

Charlotte felt as if she could float like a cloud. She would get to go to their house! A large, fancy house, with servants! It would be like seeing the inside of the governor's house. Oh, she could just see Sarah's face. She turned to look for her but didn't find her. Just as well—better to have time to savour the moment for herself first.

CHAPTER 13

Marienne

January 1870

"I said no," said Marienne, "and that's it."

She was tired of Clément going on and on about Fredie going on the next carting trip. They were talking in circles at this point, and she refused to continue.

"By the time we're ready to go on the next trip, he'll be older, ready."

"So why are you asking me now, then?"

"We're just talking!"

"Well, I'm tired of talking about this."

"Bah!" Clément threw on his buffalo coat and stomped outside, slamming the door behind him. Soon, she heard him splitting wood, each crack resounding through the air.

She'd been cross with him ever since he told her how he'd gone and given permission for Charlotte to spend time with the Wakefields, without even talking about it with her first. Now he wanted to take Fredie away. He said he wanted to replace Julien's help on the trips, but Fredie couldn't offer much. She suspected he really wanted to get Fredie away from Father Courchene and his reading lessons, which she thought was ridiculous. Why had everything turned upside down? Things weren't making sense.

Charlotte and Suzette whispered to each other nonstop ever since the New Year parties. The French lessons hadn't started yet, but Marienne could hear them at night, when everyone was in bed and supposed to be asleep, trying to be quiet but failing. Marienne couldn't make out much, but she could guess what they were saying.

Just like the wind whistled through any gap between the boards, so too did any whispers. It was hard to keep secrets in their house.

After the third night of chatter, Marienne had split up the girls so that Suzette shared a bed with Fredie, now that Julien was gone, and her elder daughter got a bed to herself. Charlotte now walked around like a queen, and Suzette sulked. Fredie seemed to take it in stride. He could easily find the good in any situation.

The girls continued their not-so-secret chats when they could, and when they sat sewing with Mare and Marienne, the whispering turned into animated conversation. They talked about what they imagined the Wakefield house would be like and what kind of exotic treasures they would see.

"I'm sure they'd have fine china and all kinds of crystal!" Suzette said, barely able to keep focused.

"They'll have all that and much more," Charlotte replied, knowingly.

Mare shook her head at both of them. "You girls need to keep your eyes on your work and your heads down. Nothing good will come of all this daydreaming." She glared at the girls and slashed a length of thread with her freshly sharpened ulu knife. The blade was grinning metal. When Mare punctuated her statements with the ulu, everyone got in line. Even Marienne felt chastened.

Their sewing projects were now an industry. Suzette had taken to the sewing machine quickly. Charlotte liked the machine, too, but Suzette was faster with it. At last, she was better than Charlotte at something. It brought equilibrium to things. Suzette smiled when she pulled the thread through the housing and then through the needle. Her foot moved on the treadle in a smooth, even rhythm. Marienne found herself hand-stitching in time with the sound. Mare did too. At first, Mare seemed to be disturbed by its presence and didn't want to learn how to use it. But she watched the others use it and made approving noises whenever Suzette got going.

Marienne expected the machine to fail every time, but eventually admired how quickly it could produce perfectly spaced stitches. But if anyone, especially Clément, noted her admiration, she'd frown and say the machine would prove to be a novelty and nothing more.

When Charlotte worked in the kitchen, which seemed to be less and less, Marienne would catch her finding ways to look at herself in the mirror that hung near the door, above the washstand with a pitcher and ewer. "Don't be so proud, it leads to vanity," she scolded. But Charlotte ignored her.

Marienne didn't know how to feel about Charlotte now that she was grown. She loved her fiercely, of course, but sometimes the girl seemed like she was from somewhere else, somewhere foreign. From one angle, Charlotte looked like Clément or Mare, but from another, she looked like her own mother. She looked like everyone and no one at the same time.

As a toddler, she'd been especially inquisitive, hungry to learn about everything, almost angry at the world for all the knowledge she didn't have yet. But for all her energy, she could also sit still and focus when she needed to. Mare would sit Julien and Charlotte down when they were small and tell them stories. The kids had to sit still and listen, no matter what. One time, a fly landed on Charlotte's nose and she didn't even try to swat it away. She kept her eyes locked on Mare and scrunched her face, but otherwise didn't budge. Mare said Charlotte's ability to maintain focus must be why she was so good at beadwork and embroidery. Such skill took discipline.

Marienne looked up from her own sewing and studied Charlotte. She sat in a little square of sunlight, her brows drawn together, a half-finished valence held close to her face. Marienne felt a gulf growing between them. Her elder daughter was moving away from her. This association with the Wakefields was sure to change her life, maybe all of their lives.

Clément didn't agree. "Again you're worried over nothing," he'd said. "You're worse than an old woman lately, trying to keep everyone at your skirts. Look how good things are going. Why do you need to find something wrong with it? Why can't you just enjoy it for what it is?"

A gulf was opening between them, too. She wasn't sure if she could hold everyone together, or if she even should. Julien was already gone, now Charlotte was going. With Suzette acting as chaperone, Marienne worried about her, too. Her children would all become strangers to her. Even Fredie was spending more time with the priest, which she supported but now felt anxious about.

Clément said she liked to find the worst in things, but was that actually true? She merely pointed out risks or consequences, and wasn't that a good thing? He was far too quick to skip over those risks. And she was right more often than he was. These opposing viewpoints had always been one of their strengths as a couple. They could reason through problems and arrive at good solutions. Now nothing seemed to fit right. Maybe he was right, though. Things *were* going well. She shook her head and got up to pour herself some tea.

Fredie was at the table, a pencil held so tightly in his hand that his knuckles were white.

"Loosen up a bit, it will go easier," she said, ruffling his hair.

Fredie relaxed his hand and looked relieved. "Father Courchene says I have to get better with my penmanship before he'll teach me to read English."

"So that's why you're here at the table every day. Why don't you take a break and play outside for a while?"

"I can't. Julien said it's important to learn English, so I have to keep going."

Marienne rested her hand on his shoulder and looked at his blocky, jagged writing. She could recognize letters and a few words.

That's how it was for her generation, especially for women and girls. Marienne wished she could have learned. Maybe Fredie could teach her.

"It is important, but not so important that you can't rest sometimes," she said. "How about some tea?"

Fredie sipped from the steaming cup and looked out the window. A lone cow ambled in the distance, nosing in the snow for buried grass.

"Do you ever wonder what cows are thinking about?" he asked.

Marienne turned to look at Fredie. "Why do you say that?"

Fredie shrugged. "Some cows are allowed to roam free all winter. They can go where they want and eat what they want. They don't need to worry about anything. Sometimes I wish I was a cow."

Marienne sat next to him and held his hand, massaging his sore knuckles. "Aen rinaar, what do you have to worry so much about?"

Fredie looked down, not meeting her eyes. "I just want to help, like Julien. He says he's learning to read, too, and I wanted to learn before him."

Marienne smiled. "It's not a race, even though Julien thinks everything is one. You can learn at your own pace. Don't worry what Julien or the priest says, it'll come."

Fredie put on his coat and ran outside to play in the snow. Marienne poured more tea and sank into her chair. She felt as if she had no substance, an empty sack. She watched the cow outside. Its jaw moved from side to side as it chewed. It looked serene out there, with the sun making the snow sparkle. Maybe Fredie was on to something, maybe it would be nice to be a cow.

∞

Marienne trudged through the snow. The path to the village of St. Norbert was packed down, but narrow, and when she misstepped, one foot sank knee-deep. She had her winter mukluks on, tied tight to her legs so no snow got in. She was glad; she hated the feeling of wet feet. She moved at a steady pace, and felt warm, despite the deep cold. She breathed it in, invigorated by the cold air. She loved the winter. She loved travelling by cariole, loved the sound of the runners gliding on the snow. The world was quieter in winter; the snow dampened sound and made things seem closer than usual. She removed her mittens and tucked them under her arm. Her hands were sweaty. She kept walking, but felt one mitten fall away, so she bent to retrieve it. It was beaded with four red-petaled flowers arranged in a diamond shape. The flowers stood out against the undisturbed snow, like drops of blood. She shook her head. Why did she think that? All she did was drop a mitten. Mare would say the vision was an omen. She kept going forward.

A sharp cry pierced the quilted quiet. Marienne snapped her head toward the sound and trudged off the trail to get closer to it, following some fresh tracks in the snow. It led to some bushes off the path. The cries grew louder and sounded more frantic. Marienne hurried.

When she cleared the bushes, she saw Sarah Berard fending off a man much taller and heavier than she was. He gripped her close to him with one arm and grasped at her flailing arms. Sarah looked more angry than frightened, but fear was what Marienne felt as she came upon the scene.

"What's going on here?"

Sarah and her attacker looked to her but continued struggling.

"Move on, old woman, or there will be trouble for you, too."

Marienne's fear burned away into rage. Looking at the man's doughy face and soft paunch barely covered by a too-thin coat, she could tell he wasn't a local. His head was uncovered and his bright pink ears poked through his unwashed brown hair. He smelled like a midden pile. She didn't think—she launched herself at him. She hit him on his back and the arm that gripped Sarah. The girl broke free, and both she and Marienne pushed the man to the ground. He shouted angry filth at them, but grew quiet when Sarah sat on his chest and shoved fistfuls of snow in his mouth. He coughed and sputtered. Sarah then stood over him and kicked him in his side. He groaned. Sarah kicked him again.

"I wish I had English boots!" she said as she kicked.

The man curled up on his side, away from Sarah's kicks. Marienne put her hand on her arm, in a calming gesture.

"All right, my girl, you can stop now," said Marienne, her voice soft.

Sarah gave one last grunt of disgust, kicked, and stood back.

"Let's get you home," Marienne said.

She put an arm around Sarah, who shrugged it off, but gently. She offered Marienne an apologetic half-smile, and they hurried away. They looked back to make sure the man wasn't following them. He remained in the snow, moaning.

"What happened?" Marienne asked.

"I was just walking home, and he grabbed me and pulled me off the path. I didn't see him coming. Why would he do something like that? Oh, I feel so stupid for not seeing him and letting him get a hold of me like that!"

"You did nothing wrong; he's the one who should feel stupid! Grabbing a young woman like that! In the middle of the day yet! Do you know who he was? I don't think I've seen him before."

Sarah shook her head. "He's no one I know."

"Well, let's get you home safe, and then you tell your father and brothers and anyone else what happened here. Maybe we need the brigade to patrol here again, instead of being all piled up at the fort."

Sarah agreed. "Oh, I'll tell everyone, all right. And then some."

They passed a dead tree that stood alone in a clearing. It rose above all the nearby living trees. It had been dead for many years, probably before St. Norbert even existed. It would have been green when the buffalo grazed under it and rubbed their sides against its sturdy trunk to get relief from itchy mosquito bites. Now its bark had long ago crumbled away, the exposed wood weathered to smooth silver. It looked like a bony hand grasping the sky. What was it pulling down? For a moment, Marienne thought she saw it move, beckoning her. She felt an urge to go to it, to feel the smooth wood against her face. Would it come alive and trap her in its grasp? Would she be swallowed inside somehow and end up in another place? Maybe with the invisible little people of legend, the ones who never showed themselves but still took care of people's crops when they were away. She kept her eye on the tree as they passed. She felt better keeping it in sight. A fat crow landed on its topmost branch and looked at her. It cawed once, then flew away.

CHAPTER 14

Charlotte

February 1870

"It's called aspic. You should try it, you'll like it."

Charlotte looked at Alyce, who grinned at her. She looked back at the shivering grey jelly full of suspended bits of meat and vegetables.

Suzette sniffed the mould and made a face.

"Think of it like solid soup," Alyce said.

Charlotte scoffed. "Solid soup would be frozen and *solid*. This is not that. Besides, I don't want to be the one to ruin its shape. Your mother would be upset."

Alyce frowned. "That's probably true. Another time then."

"Now say it en français."

"Une autre fois."

"Très bien!"

Charlotte had been coming to the Wakefield house for several weeks, trying to teach French to Alyce with a sprinkling of Michif. Alyce showed little interest but was a quick study when she bothered to apply herself.

Charlotte hadn't seen Callum much on these visits. Suzette went with her to act as chaperone, because even though she was now seventeen, a young woman like her could not be alone with any young man, especially one like Callum. It was unseemly. Suzette was considered a perfect chaperone; even Fredie would have been acceptable.

Callum had picked them up in his sleigh carriage on their first visit in late January. Her father had arranged weekly visits with the conditions that Charlotte would be paid fifty pence per month, Suzette would accompany her, and the Wakefields would provide transportation. When the carriage arrived, Charlotte and Suzette had jumped in anticipation. "Look at that! All for us!" Suzette had exclaimed.

The Wakefields had a hired man, Johnson, who drove the carriage, so Callum rode inside with them. "It feels like it's going to tip over," Suzette said, gripping the seat's armrest to steady herself.

"You'll get used to it," Callum said, laughing. "It's more stable in summer when the wheels are on instead of the runners. It's not as smooth on snow."

"We're just not used to a covered carriage like this. We always travel in the open air," Charlotte said.

After that, Johnson came alone, and in an open sleigh instead of the carriage. Charlotte was disappointed, but she enjoyed the language lessons and discovered she liked teaching. When she sat at home in the evening doing her beadwork, she thought of new ways she could teach Alyce beyond the basics.

One evening it came to her: she could teach Alyce to bead while speaking only in French. Alyce was good at embroidery, and recently learned lacework, which Charlotte knew little about. Perhaps when Alyce was more proficient in French, she'd get her to teach her lacework in exchange.

The Wakefield house was more than she imagined. It was larger than any house she'd ever seen, with a wide staircase and three stories, with many glass windows that were not warped like the windows in her house. The views were undistorted. There were several fireplaces and wood stoves, and a summer kitchen that was nearly the size of her whole house. She couldn't imagine what such a small family would need with so much space. Alyce had an entire room all to herself, with a wardrobe and trunks full of dresses and shoes. Alyce noticed Charlotte eyeing her many pairs of shoes and urged her to try some on. The fit was close enough if she laced them tight. Alyce laughed at Charlotte's tentative steps in the heeled shoes.

"You wobble like a fawn!"

Charlotte felt that Alyce was laughing at her, rather than with her. She was polite with Charlotte and Suzette, but not always warm. As if she was holding herself back. This left Charlotte feeling inadequate, and she wondered what Alyce really thought of her.

It was easy to enjoy the comforts of the Wakefield home, because it had been built for comfort. It had plush chairs stuffed with horsehair rather than the un-cushioned chairs at home. Once, when alone in Alyce's room, Charlotte stretched out on her bed. What luxury! She imagined she was La Cendrieuse, one of her favourite stories. Perhaps, like the mistreated orphan girl, she too could be plucked from her life of drudgery and placed into one of comfort and ease. She didn't need any glass slippers; regular English shoes would suit her just fine.

Mrs. Wakefield smiled at them too much, and the warmth in her voice never seemed to reach her eyes. Charlotte knew her first name was Elodie but would never refer to her that way. Mr. Wakefield was similarly friendly, but his smile was warm.

Mrs. Wakefield did take Suzette under her wing, though, and liked to sit with the girl, needlepointing forget-me-nots on napkins and drinking tea. Mrs. Wakefield chattered on as Suzette sat quietly, listening. Mrs. Wakefield seemed happy to have a passive audience. Suzette kept her expression neutral—a perfect blank slate.

One day Charlotte and Suzette were alone with Alyce in the parlour when Callum walked in.

"And what's going on in here?" he asked, flashing a wide smile.

"Callum!" Alyce exclaimed. "You've hardly been home these last few weeks. Well, months practically. Come sit with us and tell us all about your adventures." Alyce patted the settee where she sat.

Charlotte sat straight in her chair, feeling out of place in such a fine room with her plain dress and boring, braided hair.

"How are the language lessons coming along?" Callum said. "Fluent yet?"

"I thought you were supposed to be my student, too," Charlotte said. She smiled at Suzette, who gave a knowing smirk back.

"Of course," said Callum. "We'll have to remedy that, won't we?"

He patted Alyce on the arm, then vanished almost as quickly as he'd appeared, with vague promises of joining for lessons, but no real commitments. Charlotte realized Callum's ease and charm also made him fickle. She wondered if she'd ever get the chance to spend time with him at all.

∞

"You need to do a double stitch to hold the beads in place on every second bead," Charlotte said, holding her work so Alyce could see. "Every second one, la deuxième."

"Deuxième," Alyce repeated, holding her piece close to her face.

Suzette sat with them, also beading. She looked over at Alyce's progress. "Beadwork is supposed to sing—it's a prayer to the ancestors. Yours doesn't."

"She's still learning! And she's doing very well for someone just starting out." Charlotte smiled at Alyce.

"That's not what Mare would say," said Suzette.

"Well, Mare isn't here, and her way isn't the only way." Suzette sniffed and returned to her work.

"What does that mean, 'a prayer to the ancestors'?" Alyce asked.

"Something our grandmother says," said Charlotte. "She rips out our stitches if she doesn't feel any music in them."

"That seems harsh," said Alyce.

"Well, it is frustrating when it happens, but that's how we get better," Charlotte said. "Once you see beadwork with melody, you understand. It's a way to show respect to the ancestors and the spirit helpers."

"Spirit helpers!" Alyce exclaimed. "That sounds positively pagan. Don't let my mother hear you talk like that. She's already suspicious of Catholics, never mind Indian witchcraft."

Charlotte frowned. "It's not witchcraft. I've heard you talk about fairies and sprites. That's the same thing."

"That's completely different. Everyone knows about fairies!"

"Not everyone," Suzette piped up. "They sound evil if you ask me."

Alyce dropped her fabric in her lap, spilling the beads from her needle. "Look what you made me do! Fairies? Evil? I can't imagine."

The companionable mood they'd had was gone, replaced with a growing tension. Charlotte rose to help scoop up the spilled beads. She glared at Suzette, who stayed in her seat.

"It's getting late," Alyce said. "You both should make your way home before it gets dark."

"What about the sleigh?" Suzette asked.

"It's not here," said Alyce.

"The carriage?" Charlotte asked.

"Johnson can't take you, he's too busy."

Suzette and Charlotte looked at each other. They'd been dismissed. Without speaking, they gathered their coats and left. When the house was out of view, Charlotte spun on Suzette.

"Why must you ruin everything? Now we'll never be asked back!"

"I hate it there, it smells weird. Besides, you'll be back there soon enough. Alyce needs entertainment, and you're all she's got. So don't worry, you'll be pinching your cheeks to make them rosy for Callum in no time."

Charlotte fumed and pulled her shawl over her head. She had to admit, the Wakefield house did smell odd. Their own house was infused with the smell of countless pots of tea and fires that had seeped into the very frame of the house. It was a comforting smell, familiar and right. The Wakefield house smelled pleasant, but empty. Clean. Not the refreshing clean that comes after a rain, but clean as in the absence of anything else. She couldn't figure it out—the house had more stoves than hers did, so if anything, it should be smokier. But it wasn't.

Suzette had pointed it out on their first visit. "Do you smell that?"

"Smell what?" Charlotte answered.

"Exactly," said Suzette.

They neared the fort and noticed Julien marching with a group of men who surrounded Riel, who walked tall with his coat open, showing the purple vest he wore underneath. Suzette called and waved, her arm raised high. Julien spoke to Riel and broke formation to go to them.

"What are you doing out here alone?" he asked.

"We had to leave the Wakefields' early," said Charlotte, "and no one could take us home, so we're walking. We're going to use the river."

"I don't want you walking all the way there alone," Julien said. "Things aren't safe. Wait here and I'll see if I can find a cariole or someone to escort you, at least."

He hurried away into the fort. Charlotte watched Riel walk past. He moved with purpose.

"Is he wearing a bishop's vest?" Suzette asked.

"It looks like one. Why would he wear that? He's handsome, but with that vest and coat he looks like he belongs in a big house like the Wakefields'."

"Maybe he does. Or he will soon enough."

Julien returned with Henri and a cariole led by two dogs. "Henri will take you home. You never would have made it home before dark on foot."

"We don't want the kookoush to get you, eh?" Henri laughed.

Suzette laughed with him, but Charlotte didn't. Mamaa had told her what had happened to Sarah and the stranger a few weeks ago. She looked at the river with new eyes. It was a busy thoroughfare, but the steep banks would make it hard to escape if someone were to chase them. What was once safe now seemed threatening. The light was fading fast.

"Allons-y," she said and climbed into the cariole.

When they arrived home, Marienne welcomed Henri inside. "Stay and eat, you must be hungry after bringing the girls home."

"Maarsi, I would love some home cooking." He sat at the centre of the table, across from Charlotte. Fredie, Mare, and Suzette filled the rest of the seats. Henri hunched over his bowl of steaming stew and hungrily scooped spoonsful into his mouth, hardly taking a breath in between.

"Have a second bowl," Marienne insisted, ready with the ladle.

He ate the second helping more slowly, smiling at Charlotte. She looked away.

"Are they not feeding you at the fort?" Marienne asked.

Henri seemed embarrassed. "Your cooking is wonderful. It reminds me of my mother's. I miss it."

"What is really going on there?" said Marienne. "Julien never sends word. Or visits."

Henri shrugged. "There is a lot of activity. Pierre is involved with a lot of the talks and he's gotten Julien to be part of Riel's personal guard."

"Personal guard!" cried Marienne.

Henri nodded. "Julien's learning to read a bit, too, when he has time. But with all the attention on Riel, there have been threats, serious ones, from those Canadian Party types, especially John Schultz and Charles Mair. They've been stirring up all kinds of trouble. And they're mixed up with this so-called Major Boulton, so there's danger everywhere. Now Riel has a guard at all times. He even wears a purple vest now. Some people don't like it."

"We saw him in it today," said Suzette. "I thought it was strange."

Mare gasped. "Does he think he's a bishop? I've never seen such a thing."

"People say purple is the colour of sacrifice, so I think it's more about that," said Henri. "But I'm not sure. I heard he wanted to be a priest, that's why he went to Montreal in the first place. I'm not sure why he didn't become one, though."

"Not everyone is cut out for the priesthood," said Marienne. "And I can see why people don't like him wearing a priest's vest. He needs to be careful with that."

Mare agreed. "He's inviting bad luck."

Charlotte tensed up. She hoped Mare wasn't going to start in on one of her speeches about luck. She said luck was a living thing, hungry, and it could be good to you or not. Mostly it was not, so it was best not to draw its attention. Once bad luck caught hold, there was no shaking it.

Tea was poured, and Henri relaxed in his chair. Eager to be away from his gaze, Charlotte cleared the table and washed the dishes without being asked. Her mother mimed surprise, but Charlotte kept her eyes on her work. Afterward, she said she was tired and went upstairs to lie down. She could still hear the conversation below clearly. Henri was loud.

"How long has Charlotte been going to the Wakefield place?" Henri asked.

"Since January," Marienne replied.

"And Papaa Rougeau is fine with this?"

"Yes, he's made all the arrangements."

"And you?"

Marienne was quiet for a few beats. "Charlotte seems happy to go there. It's good to give her something new to focus on."

"That Callum has been spending a lot of time at the fort, and in some of the saloons around town, talking to everyone. I know he's probably not home much when Charlotte is there. But you should tell her to be careful around him. We don't know what he and his family really want. Their intentions might not be all good."

Charlotte fumed. She'd known for years that Henri was fond of her. Her siblings teased her about it, and even her parents joked about arranging their marriage. Charlotte hated this teasing. She didn't know anyone who'd had an arranged marriage, not even her parents or Sarah's or Hyacinthe's. They had all married for love, with their families' blessing. But she knew she didn't have the same choices as her brothers, so there was always some risk it could happen. She didn't think her father would actually broker a marriage for her without asking her feelings first, but she couldn't be certain. She wished Henri would stop sniffing around her.

Henri stayed for another cup of tea, then said he would go home to visit his family. He sounded happy about the visit, and not too eager to return to the fort. He talked about how Julien was standing out like he usually did, and Henri was left in his shadow. Was a rift forming between Julien and Henri? Maybe that would be a good thing. She didn't wish him ill, she just wanted him to leave her alone.

∞

The next week Johnson pulled up like before and brought Charlotte and Suzette to the Wakefield house. Charlotte wasn't sure if he'd show up. "It looks like we've been forgiven," Suzette said. "Or maybe Alyce is bored."

When they went inside, Alyce acted as if nothing happened. Charlotte was relieved; she wasn't sure what to expect, and she didn't want tension to fester between them. She was careful to offer extra praise for Alyce's efforts and told Suzette to make herself scarce. She didn't want to upset Alyce again. Suzette went to sit with Mrs. Wakefield in the drawing room, to help her sort note cards. With the unpleasant episode behind them, Charlotte put all her energy into her lessons. "You've gotten quite skilled at beading," she said.

"I find the detailed work similar to lacework," Alyce replied. "It requires dexterity and patience."

Without Suzette disturbing them, Alyce spoke more openly.

"I miss our life in Toronto. There was so much to do and new things were happening all the time. The city is really growing! And Father took us to New York once. If you think Toronto is big, you should see New York! I got the loveliest silk there. They even have shops with gowns and dresses already made—you could buy it and wear it right then! Can you imagine? Father promised we'd go back there, but that will probably never happen now. We're too far away from everything." She set her needle down and stared out the window.

Charlotte didn't know what to say. To her, Winnipeg was also growing fast. Brick buildings were going up on Main Street and the adjoining streets. You couldn't even see the river anymore from some parts of Main Street, because of all the new buildings.

"Things are changing here, too," she said quietly.

"Not fast enough. There's so much snow! And more falls all the time. It seems like spring will never come."

Alyce often complained about the weather. After the lack of society and entertainment, it was her favourite subject.

Callum entered the room and sat next to his sister. "Summer will be here before you know it," he said, "and then you can complain about the heat and mosquitoes."

"Oh you!" Alyce laughed and playfully hit her brother on the arm.

He turned to Charlotte. "Mademoiselle, I understand you and your sister were left to return home on your own on your last visit." He gave Alyce a sharp look. "We won't let that happen again. I will personally escort you home from now on."

"Merci, that's very kind," said Charlotte.

When it was time to go, Callum helped them into their coats and into the sleigh. She sat next to him in front, with Suzette in the seat behind. They were pressed close together in the small seat. This close, Charlotte could see him in detail. His earlobes were detached, like hers, and his facial stubble glinted gold in the afternoon sunlight. She wondered why he didn't grow a beard like the other men did, especially for the winter. She liked his clean face, the novelty of it, even if it made him seem younger. But she knew he would be turning twenty in April. Alyce had mentioned it.

"How is the bank business going?" Charlotte asked.

Callum chuckled. "Not as easy as you might think. Father is doing all of the real work; I'm just there to learn."

"You're being modest. I hear you're talking to all kinds of people, getting future customers. You're sure to be successful."

Callum seemed thoughtful. "We need to be successful. Father's poured everything we have into this. I don't know what will happen if we fail."

"I'm sure everything will work out."

When they arrived at her home, Charlotte invited Callum inside to warm up with some tea. He agreed without hesitation. He helped her climb down from the sleigh, guiding her with his hand on her back. Callum helped Suzette down, too, but didn't place his hand on her back.

"I saw that," Suzette whispered to her, once they were inside the house.

Her parents and Mare were already drinking tea and sitting around the table. Her father stood to greet Callum and ushered him to a seat. Charlotte quickly poured tea for Callum and refilled the cups of the others.

"Charlotte, you're being so helpful. I wonder why," Suzette teased.

Charlotte ignored her.

Callum took a sip and seemed surprised by the taste. "Oh, that's strong—and sweet."

Charlotte fussed over him. "That's how we make it. Don't you like it?"

He coughed. "It's fine, just a surprise, is all."

Charlotte cast her eyes around the table, trying to gauge people's reactions. Mare's mouth was a thin line and she looked at Callum as if he were an insect. Her father smacked the table and laughed.

"We'll make a Métis out of you yet, my boy!" he said.

Callum smiled and laughed too. Relieved, Charlotte sat at the far end of the table, next to Mare. Her father dominated the conversation, asking Callum about his father's business, and when they could expect to be banking with them. The idea of using a bank was new; most people used strong boxes. Only business owners and the wealthy used the fort as a bank. No one kept much money around anyway, because for most people it flowed away as quickly as it arrived. And credit took care of the rest. Charlotte was surprised to hear her father talk this way. He normally didn't like to talk about money. He shared Mare's ideas about luck and preferred to act as though money simply arrived when it was needed. Her mother didn't agree, and the two argued about it often. Charlotte had never thought much about money. She never had any, but she had everything she needed, so what was there to worry about?

The conversation wound down and Callum rose to leave.

"So you'll be bringing ma bibiche home every time now, eh?" Clément said. "Taking good care of her? Maybe she'll be making some moccasins for you soon!"

Everyone around the table laughed, except for Charlotte, who felt her face burn. Callum looked confused. "What does that mean?" he asked.

"You give someone moccasins as a gift when you want to get married," Suzette answered. She grinned at Charlotte.

Charlotte wanted the floor to open up and swallow her. She could feel everyone looking at her and her cheeks getting hotter, and there was nothing she could do to stop it. It was humiliating.

"Well, I'll be sure to let you know my size," Callum smiled at her.

After he left, she ran upstairs, using the newel post to swing herself up the first few steps. In her haste, she forgot to duck at the top step to avoid the sloped ceiling and smacked her head.

"Merde!" She rubbed her head. "Merde, merde, merde!"

CHAPTER 15

Julien

February 1870

The mid-February blizzard raged all night and into the next day. By the time it was over, the snow had drifted as high as doorways in some spots, and knee-high in others.

"There's trouble coming!" Martin banged the door open, letting in cold air.

Julien leaped from his cot, instantly awake.

"What trouble?"

Martin tossed Julien's coat to him. "Boulton's men are back from Portage la Prairie. We thought they were hiding out, but they're back. They just attacked the Coutu home, looking to kill Riel. They terrorized the family and ransacked their home—made a real mess of it. Now they're on their way to attack us here at the fort. Get ready!"

Julien dressed in a flash. "I thought we were finished with those fools."

Martin shook his head. "I don't think we'll ever be finished with them."

A small path of packed snow led from their barracks to head-quarters. Some of the younger men swept and shovelled the heaps of snow, creating a maze of pathways throughout the fort. Others tamped the snow to make a walkable path. The wind had died down after howling all night, but it still bit. Inside the headquarters, Julien and Martin joined the rest of the group led by Florian and Pierre. Florian paced in his buffalo coat; his thick hair and puffy beard were frosted white. When the group was assembled and quiet, he spoke.

"This gang, led by Major Boulton, has been trying to raise an army in Portage la Prairie. We know they are funded by Orangemen in Ontario, perhaps even Ottawa itself. When these men escaped from the fort here in early January, we thought they would move on and go quietly, but we've heard that they are getting ready to attack us. Now we've gotten word that some of them are amassing in Kildonan, and they've got war on their mind."

"War!" someone from the crowd shouted. "After all the work we've done together?"

Florian held up his hand and continued. "We took this fort and set up a fair government without spilling a single drop of blood. Now we need to worry that they will bring bloodshed to us. Let's make sure that doesn't happen."

The ride to Kildonan was slow. It was hard for the horses to pass through the heavy snow. When they reached Point Douglas, Florian called them to a halt and urged them to turn back. "This isn't working. Let's head back and make a better plan. Besides, if we can't make it through, neither can the Portage gang."

Julien wanted to push forward. He held Martin back with him. "Let's go see what we can find out on our own," he said.

"In this mess? It'll take most of the day to get there, and we wouldn't be able to return quick enough for our information to be useful."

"Bah! You heard Florian—if we're stuck, they are too. But with only two of us, we can move faster and follow our own tracks back."

Martin looked at the sky, which was grey. "It could snow more, yet."

"So what if it does? A little more snow won't matter at this point. Think about when we get back—we'll be heroes! Join me if you want or not. I'm continuing on, me."

Martin looked south toward the fort, then north toward Kildonan. "Let's go then."

It was dark when they got to Kildonan. They rode past houses but saw no activity, other than people digging out of the snow. They paused under a stand of trees where some bare ground was visible. The horses nosed for some buried grass.

Martin rummaged in his fire bag. "I think we're stuck out here for the night. Do you have any food?"

"Why don't we go to one of the houses? That one over there has their lamps lit."

Martin shook his head. "You can't just walk into a house in Kildonan. It's not like home."

"But travellers are always welcome, especially someone in need. Everyone knows that."

"I'm telling you, they won't be friendly. Think about where we are and why we're here. Going to that house could be dangerous. We're here to gather information, and to do it quietly."

They hid in a copse of pine trees. Martin broke off some boughs and arranged them in a cone, like a tipi, as a shelter. Julien built a small fire inside. They blocked off the opening and soon they were warm.

"I found some pemmican in my bag," Martin handed Julien some. "That should do for now."

They ate and tried to sleep. In the morning, they were stiff and in bad moods.

Martin left the shelter first. "Look over there, someone's coming," he said, gesturing toward the road.

A man in a heavy coat tied with a sash walked toward them. His head was down, his face obscured by the hood of his coat. Even though he walked slowly through the snow, Julien recognized his gait.

"That looks like Norbert," he said.

"The woodcutter? From the fort? What's he doing here?"

Julien thought about the last time he saw Norbert. He'd been at the New Year's celebrations at the Boucher house, but now he couldn't recall seeing Norbert for a couple of weeks.

"He doesn't live out this way, does he?" Martin asked.

"No, he's from St. Norbert. Norbert-from-St. Norbert."

"He must have been working out here before the storm hit, and he's just going home now."

Julien was about to call out to Norbert when a group of men burst from the house he'd suggested visiting the night before. Martin held Julien back, and they stayed hidden in the trees, watching.

The men swarmed Norbert, knocked him to the ground and took turns kicking him. He groaned. More men came out of the house.

"We got him!" a big man who'd done the most kicking shouted to the new arrivals. "He's a dirty half-breed spy! We saw his fire last night! Look at this ugly pig."

The men made snorting noises, then grabbed Norbert and dragged him into the house. His head sagged to his chest and his feet barely moved.

"What just happened?" Julien asked.

Martin shook his head, his breathing heavy. "What was that about a spy? And a fire? Did they see our fire last night? How? Why didn't they attack us?" He looked at Julien. "Is this our fault?"

"We need to go in there and get him!"

"You saw how many men there were, and who knows how many others inside. We need to get back and tell Florian about this."

Julien punched a tree trunk. His thick mitten absorbed most of the blow, but it was satisfying nonetheless. He sighed. "You're right," he said, "but we have to be careful. I don't know how they didn't see our horses or our tracks."

"I don't want to stay here and find out."

They led their horses through the trees toward the riverbank, then down to the frozen river. They were able to follow a few cariole trails, making the journey back a little faster.

When they returned, they found Uncle Pierre and told him what they had seen. He was alarmed but remained calm. "We need to tell Florian and Riel. You two rest and eat."

Uncle Pierre came to find them after the meeting. "Julien! Riel is pleased with you and Martin. He's going to send a message to the Portage gang, and you're coming with us to deliver it."

Julien looked at Martin. "What did I tell you? I knew we'd be heroes!"

Just then Florian and Riel came in, with more men. Riel faced them and placed one hand on Julien's shoulder and the other on Martin's, almost in an embrace.

"You boys did well. You brought us some valuable information. To help ease the tensions and to avoid civil war, our government has decided to release the rest of the Canadian prisoners, and they've sworn to keep the peace. We're asking the Canadians to join us and complete the provisional government. We take responsibility for our past acts, and we ask them to do the same in the cause of peace."

"A wise decision, sir," Martin said.

"Florian and Pierre will deliver the message, and you both will go with them. We don't want to look like a threat; we go to them in peace."

The next morning, they rode north to Kildonan. They took the river again, and a day after the blizzard, its pathways were easier to traverse. More travellers could be seen ahead of them in the distance. When they neared Kildonan, they heard the crack of a gunshot. Florian gestured for them to stop. They heard shouting. A large man with light hair dragged a bound man down the riverbank to the ice. The man's legs were tied together with a sash—one that matched the sashes of the Métis men.

"They've got Norbert!" shouted Julien.

He didn't think, just kicked his horse forward, leaning into it the way he did when he raced. Only this time the race wasn't for fun. This time everything was at stake.

"Wait!" Florian called. "We have to deliver the message so they know we mean no harm!"

Julien focused only on Norbert. The large man had tied another sash around Norbert's neck and then tied it to a horse. He then got on the horse and kicked it to make it run. Norbert weakly reached for the sash around his neck. His strangled cries soon turned to hoarse gasps, and his hands fell away. The man circled the horse back, dragging Norbert through the lumpy snow. More men raced down the bank from Kildonan. Norbert looked dead, but Julien could see he was still breathing. A thin man ran toward Norbert with a hatchet raised high. He screamed and buried the blade in Norbert's head. A fountain of blood spewed forth, soaking the snow red.

The sight shocked Julien to a stop. He leapt off his horse and ran to Norbert, who didn't move.

"What have you done?" he yelled. "You've killed him!"

The hatchet-man scoffed. "We held this simple-minded half-breed spy overnight at Kildonan Church and he escaped this morning. He shot an innocent man, John Sutherland, who was only on his way home. Look!" He gestured up the bank where a figure lay in the snow, surrounded by several men.

"That was the shot we heard? Why were you holding him prisoner at all? This man is a woodcutter, that's all. Not a spy. He'd never hurt anyone! He must have been frightened to death." Julien raised his arm to strike the man, but someone held him back.

"Julien! Wait!" It was Pierre.

Florian, Pierre and Martin surrounded them. So did a number of the Portage gang. Florian and the large man who had tied Norbert to the horse faced each other. Neither spoke for several beats. Julien looked from one to the other, afraid of what could happen next.

Florian took a deep breath and spoke evenly. "Remove your hatchet from this poor soul at once."

The thin man looked to his friend, who gave a tiny nod. He stepped slowly up to Norbert and removed the blade with a tug. Fresh blood spilled from the wound. The thin man wiped the blade on his trousers and tucked the axe into his belt. Julien knelt by Norbert and untied the sash from around his neck and wrapped it around his head, trying to staunch the blood. Blood soaked through it almost instantly. Next he untied Norbert's legs.

"We came here to tell you the rest of the Canadians have been released," said Florian, "and they've promised not to raise arms against us. They've chosen peace, and we ask the same of you."

"What's this ox saying?" the large man said to the axe-man. "I can barely understand his accent. Must get it from his squaw mother."

The tendons in Florian's jaw pulsed. He slammed an envelope into the man's chest. "It's all written here for you, in English. If you can read, that is. Maybe you should take it to your leaders."

The man spat at Florian's feet. Florian ignored the gesture.

"We come with an extended hand but this," he pointed at Norbert, "this won't be borne. You'll answer for this. Now go."

Florian turned his back on the gang members and gestured to his men to gather around Norbert, forming a protective wall. The Portage gang watched them, then went back up the riverbank. Martin and Julien gathered branches to fashion a travois to carry Norbert back to the fort.

"He won't make it on a horse," Florian said.

"He looks like he won't make it at all," said Martin.

The journey back to the fort was slow and sombre. They stopped several times to tend to Norbert, who remained unconscious, but groaned periodically. When they got to the fort, the men patched him up as best they could, but the wound in his head was serious and likely fatal. After a day, it festered and developed a foul smell.

He fevered and shivered but never woke. Word came that before John Sutherland died, he didn't blame Norbert for shooting him. "He knew Norbert was frightened out of his mind," Uncle Pierre told him. "He insisted Norbert hold no blame; it was his dying wish."

Julien stayed with Norbert, speaking softly. "Remember judging all our races? The bonfires? The jigs? We'll do that again, eh?"

After five days, Norbert's breath rattled and he died.

"At least now he's at peace," Uncle Pierre said, putting his arm around Julien.

Julien tried to go back to his routines, but he could not shake the image of Norbert's head split open, revealing his brain matter. It was there every time he closed his eyes. He couldn't sleep. All he could think of was the buffalo hunt, and how they used the buffalo's brains to treat the hides. Wasting any part of the animal was the ultimate sign of disrespect, so brains served a purpose in death. He considered Norbert's brain, and how it looked the same as a buffalo's. The same, yet so different. Julien wanted to leave Norbert in a tree, for the scavengers, like the old way. Then his body would serve a purpose. But he knew the priests would never allow it.

He'd never seen a death so brutal and deliberately cruel. He knew he'd never see the world the same again. He reached into his coat pocket, removed the sash that had bound Norbert's legs and pressed it to his lips. He would give the sash to Norbert's mother. She could unravel it and reuse the yarn in either a new sash or something else. Maybe it could live on.

He slipped out of the room and packed his things. It was time to go home.

CHAPTER 16

Clément

February 1870

Clément was surprised when Julien came home. He looked differ-ent, older. His complexion was ashen and his voice was flat. There was no life in his eyes. He ate little and didn't speak much. The son he knew had disappeared.

"All this time at the fort has changed him. For the worse," he said to Marienne. "I was worried this would happen."

She started to argue, but then reluctantly agreed.

"Pierre told us what happened to Norbert," Marienne said. "Julien was there, saw it all, and stayed with him until he died. Mare said he told her he's been having nightmares. Fredie says he's restless all night. He needs to talk about it. It's not good to keep it inside."

A week later, Julien hadn't improved much, but he ate more and helped with the chores. He sat with Mare in the evenings. She whis-pered to him; as she talked, the desolation left his eyes and his face softened.

One evening, Mare pulled out her smudge bowl. She crumbled some dried sage from her medicine pouch and lit it. Aromatic smoke filled the room. Clément went to the kitchen, alerted by the smoke. The rest of the family followed and sat at the table to watch.

Clément stood off to the side. He hadn't smelled sage like that in a long time, but as soon as it hit him, memories came back in a flood. He was a child again, Fredie's age, and was with his mother in the bush. She was teaching him about medicines and how smudging cleared your thoughts and healed your energies. He liked watching the smoke curl as it rose, and he did feel calm when he breathed it in. His father didn't approve of smudging. When he saw them, he said they needed to stop and insisted they start going to church. The smudge bowl was put away but his mother continued to smudge with his sister Flossie sometimes, in private. Always outside, away from the house. Clément wanted to tell on them. He thought if his father found out and he hadn't told, he'd be in bigger trouble for not telling. But he stayed quiet, unable to act. The priests frowned on smudging, said it was pagan. Mare said it was not any different from the incense burned in church. Why was incense not considered pagan? His father never had an answer to that.

Now here it was in his house, and he didn't know what to think. His instinct told him it was wrong, that God would see it and be angry. The thought made him jumpy.

Fredie leaned far across the table, stretched almost in a straight line. His knees rested on the seat of his chair and his feet stuck out. "What is that, Mare?"

"This is medicine. It helps heal you."

"But how? Why?"

"Just watch and you'll see."

Mare cupped the smoke and passed it over her face, her front, and over her head. She nodded to Julien and he did the same. She spoke softly in Anishinaabemowin, which no one else in the family could fully understand. Mare held the bowl in front of Fredie, who copied what Mare and Julien had done, but with exaggerated movements. He smiled big at Mare, proud. The bowl went next to Charlotte, Suzette, Marienne, who all smudged. Quiet settled in the room. Then Mare gestured to Clément to come forward. He froze and refused to move.

"This isn't good for Julien. He should go to confession instead."

Mare gave him a hard look. "This will help him more than a priest can."

Anger rose in him like bile. "This will bring bad luck!"

"Bad luck! Bah! The priests will bring bad luck, more like."

"Look what's happened already! This needs to stop." Clément snatched the bowl from Mare. A few embers spilled onto the table, and Marienne patted them out with a tea towel before they could burn the wood.

"Papaa, what are you doing?" Julien reached for the bowl.

"This doesn't belong in our house. This ends now."

He opened the door with a bang and marched outside with no coat and only his house moccasins on. His feet sank in the deep snow, but he didn't feel the cold.

Chairs clattered as everyone got up to follow him outside. Clément didn't care that he was making a scene. He wanted his family to follow him and watch. He turned to look at them, their faces shocked. Fredie was crying. He dumped the still-burning sage in the snow and stomped on it for good measure.

"Clément, no!" Marienne yelled. When the embers died, everyone fell silent.

"If you wanted bad luck, I think you just called it," Mare said, her arms crossed.

Clément looked each of them in the eye. "Let that be the end of it now." He went back inside and left them in the cold, stunned.

For the next few days, his family barely spoke to him. His mother wouldn't speak to him at all. His anger at the smudging still simmered.

"I don't understand you," Marienne said. "Since when is confession so important to you? You didn't want Fredie to get lessons from Father Courchene. You act like we should be wary of him. Now you act like Mare's medicine is from the devil. Why?"

He hadn't replied because he didn't know what to say. Now that the moment was over, he wasn't sure why he reacted so strongly. He just knew he didn't want that medicine in his house. It was seeing Fredie so proud of himself that tipped him over. He wanted Fredie to be free of everything that had held him back. All his life he'd heard nasty comments about his heritage. Calling him half a person. He wanted his children's lives to be different, but if they held onto those Indian ways, they'd never get respect.

The tension in the house got so uncomfortable he decided to go to the fort and see for himself what the situation was like. He didn't know why his gut sensed danger, but there it was. He didn't like change, because change led to uncertainty, and now Red River was in the midst of huge change. Permanent change. He couldn't picture his future. The rhythm of the seasons and finding game could be unpredictable, but that kind of unpredictability didn't worry him. There was a reason behind it, something you could plan for. But this new change rocked his foundation. The old patterns didn't apply. He couldn't plan ahead. It was worrisome, and there was nothing he could do to stop it. He was powerless. That's what bothered him the most.

There was commotion on Main Street. He could hear shouting and saw people lined up along the road. Some leaned out of open windows and some stood on rooftops. He joined the ranks and asked the man next to him what was going on.

"Those Canadians are trying to start a war, it looks like," he said.

A group of about forty men, led by a man with a long moustache and wearing a shabby military-looking coat with shiny buttons marched along Main Street. The men shouted and raised their fists.

"Not many men to start a war with," Clément replied.

The man laughed. "True, true, but look, they do have support." He pointed to people waving and shouting from upper windows in the buildings on the street. "They could get their war yet."

The marching men drew closer, and Clément could make out more of what they were shouting. They were angry at the death of John Sutherland and were calling for Riel to be hanged. They carried rifles and one man carried an axe. He swung it as he marched, making a show of it. Clément was shocked at the display, knowing how the young Norbert died. Was this the man who'd done it? Was that the very axe? He was disgusted.

An alarm pealed from the fort, causing the Canadians to pause. Their shouts grew louder, as did those from the spectators. Clément couldn't understand much in the din, but could tell some were against the Canadians, and some were not. The tension increased when the cavalry burst from the fort's gate and surrounded the marchers. He saw Pierre and Florian among the ranks. There was a skirmish between the groups, but the Canadians were outnumbered. After volleys of insults, they were corralled, led into the fort, and arrested.

"So much for that. I hoped we'd get a show at least," said the man.

"Well, that's a relief," Clément said. "Better to have them locked up for now. The surveyors last summer started this whole thing. What did they expect to happen?"

"But look around us here, not everyone is happy about the outcome. And that Boulton, the one in front, with the jacket? Calls himself Major. But major of what, eh? He was trying to gather hundreds of men to avenge the death of John Sutherland, but old Mrs. Sutherland wouldn't have it. Convinced most of them to disband, said it was John's dying wish. So maybe there are not as many on their side as you might think."

"Let's hope so. All this and for what? We need to move on from this, get things back to normal. We're losing out on precious carting time."

The man gave Clément a strange look. "I don't think this is over yet. Canada won't take any of this quietly. My nephew is in Ontario and the talk there isn't good. I think there's much more to come. We need to be ready."

"Well, let's hope for the best, then."

Clément rode home in the dark, thinking hard. Seeing the tensions in the town and how quickly things could turn violent gave him a new perspective. Maybe Julien had been right. Things were serious, it wasn't just a bunch of boys playing soldier. But so much had changed so fast, it was hard to keep up. He hadn't expected a revolution, but that's what was happening. He'd wanted everything to blow over, so the spring could be the same as every other. He knew now that he was wrong. What that meant for him and his family, he couldn't say, and he was afraid to guess.

He spurred his horse on, eager to return home. He had never told Julien how proud he felt seeing him in December at the flag-raising, firing his gun salute. Maybe it was time to tell him now.

CHAPTER 17

Julien

March 1870

The screaming was unbearable.

Julien was back at the fort. When his father had told him about the arrests of the Canadians and what he'd seen, Julien knew he had to get back. But what really surprised him was the change in his father's attitude. He seemed softer, subdued.

"My boy, you belong there," his father had said. "I see now that you're part of something important, and it's time for you to follow that path. It's all right. I want you to go."

He'd hugged Julien and helped him pack his things. He'd brushed down Julienne and gave Julien his own saddle, the one with Mare's quillwork he was so proud of. Julien was humbled—and relieved.

When Julien returned to the fort, he was assigned to guard duty at the jail. The jail consisted of some locked rooms on the second floor of one of the buildings. Several men were housed together in one room, and the remainder were in another. They passed the time playing cards or sleeping. Considering the number of imprisoned men, things were mostly uneventful. Until they weren't.

At first, Julien was eager for the posting but, after a few days, he wished he were somewhere else. Norbert's attackers were in jail, and he was glad to keep watch over them, but it had gotten to be too much. The barrel-chested man who had tied Norbert to the horse was Thomas Scott, and he had been separated from the others in a small room where he wailed and shouted profanities at all hours, keeping everyone awake. Even by himself, he agitated the others. Julien guarded his room, because Scott talked at length about how he would escape. When Riel visited the jail, Scott's cries grew frantic and even more vicious, calling for ever more degrading horrors to befall him. The other inmates joined in, causing chaos. Riel ignored the comments, but they must have disturbed him. How could they not? Such language was beyond anything he'd ever heard before. Some words he didn't even know, but he could tell their meaning. Riel seemed untouched by the hate and carried himself with a quiet dignity that Julien admired.

Julien wished he could tap into that quiet dignity now. It was late, well past midnight, and Scott continued with his garbled nonsense. He'd grin at Julien with his yellow teeth and explain in detail how he would split Julien open and wear his intestines like a necklace. It was his favourite taunt, and Julien was tired of it.

"You need to come up with some new insults," Julien said. "This one is getting old."

Scott banged on the door in rage. Julien laughed, which incensed Scott more.

"Shut up!" a prisoner in the next room shouted, and the others joined the chorus. This egged Scott on. Julien shook his head. He sat on a stool opposite the cell door, crossed his arms, and tried to sleep.

He was startled awake when dawn broke, surprised to have slept at all. Scott had fallen silent. Julien was relieved and hoped maybe the man had died in the night. He rose to look inside the cell and saw why it was quiet. Scott was smearing something on the wall, trying to write with it, but the result was unreadable. Julien peered more closely, then recoiled.

"What are you—" he gasped. "Hey, stop that!"

He called for help. When the other guards arrived, they too recoiled. Scott had smeared the contents of his latrine bucket on the wall. The odour was overpowering. The men all backed away, gagging.

"Get Florian!" Julien coughed out.

When Florian got there, he swore loudly.

"Tabernac! Everyone out, go! Get some air."

He ushered Julien and the others outside and once there, they huddled together and breathed deeply. They all spoke excitedly, talking over each other.

"You see what we're dealing with?" said one of the guards, Alain.

"Something needs to be done. That Scott is the worst, but the others aren't any better," said Jean, another guard. "But they've done nothing like he has. How long before the others get the same idea? Or worse?"

"What should we do?" Julien asked.

"Cut a hole in the river and drop him in," Alain growled.

Julien shook his head. "It's not up to us. Florian and the others will know what to do."

"I'm not so sure anyone would know what to do with the likes of them," Jean said as he spat on the ground.

∞

Julien was relieved to be off guard duty. The government and other leaders were shut up in meetings. There was a lot of talk in the fort, with people blaming Scott, not Boulton, for the attack on Norbert. The hatchet man was also imprisoned, but he'd been quiet since his arrest. Julien wondered if he regretted what he'd done. More and more people said Scott should be executed, since he was the instigator. His unpleasantness and threats didn't help. Martin told him that some of the guards had pulled Scott from his cell and "knocked some sense into him" until one of the members of the government stopped them.

Julien couldn't forget the hatred in Scott's face when he tied Norbert to the horse, or his glee when he dragged him. He agreed with the calls for execution. Something had to be done.

"I think executing Scott would be a mistake," Henri said. He was sharing a meal with Julien and Uncle Pierre.

Pierre frowned. "Why? He deserves it."

"Does he?" Henri said. "What about the one who used the axe?"

"He deserves it too," said Pierre.

Julien nodded. "Yes, both of them."

Henri scoffed. "We can't kill all of them. Where does it end?"

"But they murdered Norbert," said Pierre.

"Bah! You weren't there, Henri, you didn't see their faces," Julien said. "They were celebrating what they did to him. And you know they would do the same to us if they had the chance."

Henri set his cup down with a bang. "Maybe so. But killing for revenge is wrong."

"So is murder," said Julien.

Pierre tried to smooth things over. "Listen, you're both right, and it's not up to us anyway. Don't let those thugs tear us apart on top of everything else. They're not worth it."

The two friends looked anywhere but at each other. Pierre tried to change the subject, but they finished their meal in silence, and Henri stormed off.

Julien avoided Henri after that. He felt hard inside, like he was part stone. He saw things so clearly—this was wrong, that was right. He didn't understand why Henri couldn't see it. Was it only a few months ago that he was peacocking at the New Year's dances? It felt like another lifetime—all their races and contests seemed childish now. How proud he was to have worn through his moccasins out-jigging Henri and almost every other man there. Like that was some big accomplishment. Six months ago, that was what he cared about. And his daydreams with Henri of building a trading and carting empire! He wanted to laugh. They had no idea about anything.

Julien spent more time with Martin when he was available. "So what is the government going to do about Thomas Scott and the rest of them?" he asked him.

"No one knows," Martin answered. "Or, they haven't said anything, at least."

"They can't just leave it alone. A price must be paid. I hope they know that."

"I'm sure they do. It's all anyone is talking about, wherever you go."

"I hope so." Julien sounded doubtful.

∞

News of Scott's execution flew through the fort. Pierre had come to find Julien to let him know.

"I thought nothing would happen!" Julien said, surprised.

"I told you to have faith that they would do the right thing."

"When is it happening?"

"Tomorrow, I think. From what I heard, Scott's ravings took a toll, enough so there was no ignoring it. And him being so proud of what he did to Norbert, well, that kind of talk is catching. The other prisoners were repeating his words, and it was getting bad. Especially against Riel. Those Canadians seem to be focusing all their rage on him. Riel said an example had to be made, so the court found him guilty and set the sentence—firing squad."

"Good. I want to be there to see it, but I'd rather be one of the shooters."

Pierre shook his head. "Julien, don't say that. You don't want to live with that on your soul."

"Right now I'm living with Norbert's death on my soul. It won't leave my mind. But if I see his killer get shot, that might help."

"I don't think it will. Please don't volunteer."

Julien nodded. "You're probably right. At least this will show people that the government is to be respected."

"I don't think they're opening up the fort for it. They want to keep it quiet, sort of. Riel says he doesn't want it to be a spectacle. He said it should be a solemn occasion."

Julien pondered. "You know, I listened to Scott say daily how he wanted to kill Riel with his bare hands. There is no talking to some-one like that. Maybe it's good to not make it a spectacle—it could rile up the Canadians more, and we don't need that."

The next day, the fort buzzed. Julien went quietly about his work, intending to sneak away when the time came so he could witness the execution. He had to see it. Last night, he dreamed of Norbert again. He woke up sweating. His talks with Mare at home had helped, but now that he was surrounded by angry men, it was easy to forget her teachings. He had to feel better once he saw Scott was dead.

He made his way to the far corner of the fort near the river, where the execution would be. He found the area empty, but the back doorway through the fort wall was open. He went through and found a small crowd of men gathered around Scott, who was bound, kneeling in the snow. The ground was still frozen, but the top layer of mud had started to soften. Julien stood near the door. He could see and hear everything clearly.

"This is cold-blooded murder!" Scott shouted as a cloth was tied around his head to cover his eyes.

The firing squad of six men raised their muskets. Riel gave them a nod, and they fired. The blasts echoed off the fort's walls. Scott fell in the snow face down, groaning. Some of the shots must have missed, because he was still alive. The squad looked at each other, not sure what to do. Scott's groans grew louder, so one of the men, François Guillemette, stepped forward, withdrew a revolver from his belt, and shot Scott in the head. The dirty snow around him turned red. It looked like the bloom of blood that had formed under Norbert's head when Scott and his cronies attacked him. Julien thought it was fitting for Scott's stain to match Norbert's, but seeing Scott lifeless in the blood-soaked snow didn't bring the comfort he thought it would. His death had been too quick. Too kind. Norbert had suffered for days. There was no fairness in it.

Henri had been right. He didn't feel any better.

CHAPTER 18

Marienne

May 1870

"The crocuses will be good now," Mare said.

Marienne pounded dough on the table. Mare sat at one end, cutting the flattened dough with a cup to make circles for biscuits. They were making a large batch, to last for a few days. Marienne hated having to make biscuits every day.

"Are you saying we'll need to go pick some soon?" Marienne asked.

Mare kept working without looking up. "My hands are getting stiff and I have none left. Poultice made from crocus is the only thing that helps. Many of my other medicines are getting low too. I didn't have much to begin with after that drought a couple years ago. This year we should make a long trip into the bush. It's bad luck to be low on medicines."

Marienne sprinkled more flour on the table and slapped the ball of dough down. The table shook, causing Mare to slip and end up with a misshapen circle.

"Ah ben, be careful," Mare said.

"The girls should be here helping with this, instead of playing tea party at the Wakefield place." Marienne wiped her brow, leaving a smudge of flour above her eye.

"I can still make biscuits just fine."

"You just complained about your aching hands!"

Mare sighed through her nose. "Why are you so testy? And don't say it's because you're tired of making biscuits. This mood is coming from somewhere else."

Marienne sat down. She suddenly felt very tired. She was irritated with everything lately. She understood in the abstract that it was good for the girls to go to the Wakefield house, but it still bothered her. Charlotte had grown full of pride. Suzette had changed, too, although she didn't act as haughty as Charlotte. Julien was already gone out of the house, probably for good, and Charlotte was on her way. Marienne wanted Fredie and Suzette to stay as they were. She wasn't ready for her two youngest to grow up yet.

The division between Clément and Julien had nearly split her, too. Things had mended between them, but her husband liked to pick at healing scabs, and he'd probably pick at Julien. He couldn't help himself. So maybe it was good that Julien lived at the fort. He came home to visit more often than before, especially to see Mare, bringing tales of all the important government people running things, Bishop Taché advising them, and, of course, the great man himself, Riel. Julien was clearly awed by him, and Marienne supposed some hero worship was harmless, but if she or anyone else said anything against Riel, Julien lost his temper. She worried about unwavering allegiance like that. Her son, who always had an easy laugh and got along with everyone, now had calcified opinions. Clément said it was part of growing up, and maybe that was true. But it still nagged at her.

Things in Red River had calmed down. After Norbert's death and the execution of Thomas Scott, the rest of the Canadians in prison were released on the promise they would abide the government. Most of them had opted to return to Ontario, and life resumed. Everyone she knew was relieved.

"We almost had a civil war," Denise had whispered to her at church. "Can you imagine? I shudder when I think about how close we came. Thank the Lord it's over."

Marienne had agreed. "But it wouldn't have lasted long, surely. We had the law on our side, and better numbers."

"Not everyone saw it that way," Denise said and paused. "*Sees* it that way. There's still plenty of talk, but it's underground now. Better to not stir up trouble, eh?"

Marienne could see the wisdom of that. She'd lost sleep also, these last few months.

She resumed flattening the dough, but more gently this time. "I'm not testy. Just tired after everything this winter. I'm ready for spring to get here."

Callum pulled into their yard, bringing Charlotte and Suzette home. Marienne and Mare both looked up at the sound.

Charlotte and Suzette burst in, all rosy and excited, followed by Callum. That had become the routine: after seeing them home, he came inside for some tea and a visit. Charlotte put on her usual display, performing as the dutiful daughter—serving everyone, anticipating when a cup needed refilling, cleaning up after everyone without complaint. Marienne was reminded of her younger self, showing off for Clément's family. The same rhythms bound them all together. New faces, the same story.

"Mare and I were just discussing a medicine trip," said Marienne, "since the crocuses are ready to be collected."

"When?" Charlotte asked, her eyes darted to Callum quickly, then back at Marienne.

"A week or so, most likely. Give the sun a chance to dry those forest trails."

"For how long?" Charlotte sounded almost panicked.

Marienne shrugged. "What do you think, Mare? Three weeks? Four?"

Mare looked at Charlotte, then to Callum. "Depends on what we find. If we time it right and stay a little longer, we can harvest several medicines, maybe even some berries."

"Berries!" Charlotte exclaimed. "Berries aren't ready until summer. We'll be gone half the season!"

"Some time in the bush will be good for all of us. Too much excitement here lately." Marienne kept her tone light.

"But what about the French lessons? Alyce will fall behind." Charlotte looked at Suzette, her eyes pleading.

Suzette turned to Callum. "Won't your family be busy for the summer?" she asked. "Mrs. Wakefield said something about returning home for a visit? Would you all go?"

"What?" Charlotte practically screeched.

Callum shifted in his seat. "Mother and Alyce have talked about it, and Father agreed. No dates have been set, though."

"Alyce has said nothing of this," said Charlotte. "It's not like her to stay quiet about something big like a trip. I can't believe it!"

"Maybe Callum will stay behind and still need lessons?" Suzette said, trying to be helpful.

Marienne and Charlotte locked eyes. Marienne spoke before Charlotte could reply. "Your father would never allow you to visit Callum unchaperoned."

"What if Julien came home to stay with me? That should be all right, shouldn't it?"

"Absolutely not. And Julien can't just leave the fort, he has responsibilities there."

"But what about the garden, or the animals?" Charlotte asked. "Someone needs to stay behind."

"You don't need to worry about that," Marienne snapped. "The garden will grow whether you're there to watch it or not, and I don't want to hear any more about it!"

Tension filled the room. Everyone avoided looking at Charlotte.

Callum cleared his throat. "I should get home. Thank you for the tea."

"No, please stay," Charlotte pleaded.

He gave a half smile and let himself out. When the door clicked behind him, Charlotte whirled on her mother.

"How could you?" she cried. "You arranged this whole conversation to make me look bad!"

"Charlotte, not everything is about you," Marienne said. "You need to calm down. Go find something useful to do—some sewing should settle you down. Or maybe some scrubbing."

"This is so unfair!" Charlotte stamped out of the room.

Marienne sighed. She wiped her hands on her apron and nodded at Suzette. "Finish with the dough before it dries out." She washed her hands in the basin.

"All that over some puny crocuses," Mare said, and sipped her tea.

Marienne went upstairs and found Charlotte sitting on the edge of her bed with her head in her hands. The bed creaked as she sat down beside her. Charlotte didn't look up.

"Charlotte, why are you so upset?" she asked in a steady voice. "You know you can't stay here alone, and you know you can't go visiting Callum on your own. Your father wouldn't allow it, and the talk would be unbearable. Do you want that?"

Charlotte faced her mother. "But why, though? I'm grown up! Why shouldn't I stay here? If I were a wife, no one would say anything about my husband leaving me alone."

"If you were a wife, you'd be with your husband, not left behind."

"But Papaa leaves you behind. He's away on a trip now."

"Not when we were young. You'll understand when you get married." She patted Charlotte's knee. "Uncle Robert and Aunt Denise and your cousins will watch over the farm. There's no reason to do anything different."

Charlotte's shoulders slumped. She started to say something, then reconsidered.

Marienne examined her daughter. Her cheeks had a ruddiness to them that no one else in the family had. "I know you have feelings for that boy. Are you sure that's wise?"

"What do you mean?"

"He's handsome and his family has money. I know he seems charming to you, and I admit he is friendly and seems like a good man. But if you pin all of your hopes on him, you'll be disappointed."

"Why?"

"Because men like that have big ambitions. Ambitions that will take him away from you. It may seem like you have his attention now, but he will outgrow you. And his family will never approve of you, not really."

Charlotte's face fell. "Mamaa, you can be so cruel."

"I just don't want you to be disappointed and hurt."

Charlotte started to cry. "I think you're too late there."

CHAPTER 19

Charlotte

June 1870

Charlotte stepped deeper into the forest. Twigs snapped underfoot.

Her family had been camped in the forest for three weeks, and she was tired of it. They'd arrived just as the crocus season was ending, and Mare was disappointed with their harvest. The few scraggly crocuses they found were sub-par by most standards, and certainly well below hers. "We should have come earlier," she'd complained yesterday.

"You said you wanted to get other medicines," Papaa replied. "We came at exactly the right time for that."

Mare scowled in response.

Charlotte felt bad because she'd begged Papaa to delay the trip. She knew she could cajole him, and he indulged her. She wanted to be home, not miles away digging in the forest for roots. But the delay had led to nothing. She had seen Callum only once before they left, so the result was a bad harvest and Mare being huffy about it.

She carried an empty birchbark basket. She should have been focused on the low-growing plants at her feet, but her head kept turning to the west, to Red River, to Point Douglas, where Callum was. Her mother and Mare called to her from the forest depth, excited at what they found, but Charlotte couldn't share their enthusiasm—she didn't want to be there in the first place.

She wondered if Callum missed her. She thought about him most of the time, but he seemed indifferent to her sometimes. Other times he was warm. She didn't know what to think. He was always polite and, when he shone his whole attention on her, it was as if she was the only person around. She had no experience of any of this, but she felt yearnings. Would Callum ever want to marry her? She could live in that huge house with its many stoves and endless rooms. Could such a thing be possible? She didn't dare speak of it out loud to anyone, not even Suzette. She didn't want the teasing that would follow, and also thought talking about it might make it not happen. If it was just a hope in her head, it would stay on the cusp of possibility. Once spoken, it could disappear. So she kept it to herself.

The mosquitoes were waiting in the forest shade. She swatted them from her face, but the cloud of them followed her as she walked. For once, she was glad to be wearing long sleeves, even if it was hot.

Her mind circled back to the last time Callum had accompanied her and Suzette home. It was the week after Callum had mentioned Alyce's trip to Toronto and she'd had her awkward outburst. They'd stopped near the riverbank to watch as a steamship floated past. Steamships had been arriving more frequently but were still rare enough to be remarkable. People always stopped to gawk. Her father didn't like the ships, since their appearance meant less work for him and his cart. "Soon the carts will disappear with the buffalo, and then what will we do?" he'd say.

She, Suzette, and Callum stood on the shore and waved at the boat as it passed; black smoke belched from the smokestack in the rear of the ship. People on the deck waved back. Once it was gone, Suzette wandered away to pick burdock, and Charlotte and Callum sat on the grass enjoying the afternoon breeze.

"Papaa says things are changing too fast," Charlotte said.

"My father says they're not changing fast enough," Callum chuckled. "Like that boat, for instance. Father thinks there should be one every week, maybe even more. And he thinks the railway needs to come here, the sooner the better. He's angry they haven't started building it yet."

"The railway! Here? I can't even imagine it."

"That's why we came here. Father feels like he missed out on all the major growth in Toronto. He thinks he can really make something here, where everything is just getting started."

"What do you mean, 'getting started'? The settlement has been here since before my grandfather's time, my people even longer, and Mare's longer yet. It's not like this land was empty."

"Well, the development and growth into a city is what I mean. When he heard about the sale of Rupert's Land, that's when he made plans to move here."

Charlotte scoffed. "I don't know who Rupert is or why he thinks this was his land. It wasn't. It isn't."

Callum turned to face her. "Well, it belongs to Canada now, so Rupert doesn't matter anymore."

She faced him. "How nice it must be to decide something is yours and then just take it. How do I get to be like Rupert? There are lots of things I'd like to have. Think he'd share?"

Callum laughed. "Oh, Charlotte, you say the most amusing things."

Charlotte grew angry at the turn in conversation, but as soon as he laughed and smiled at her like that, her anger dissipated. He leaned forward and touched her cheek. He looked at her for a long moment. She didn't know if she should say anything. She sat frozen, afraid to move.

Suzette emerged from the tall weeds, holding her right arm up. "I've got thistles stuck in my hand!"

Charlotte quickly stood and attended to her sister. "You have to be careful when picking burdock. You know that." She was embarrassed and hoped Suzette hadn't seen the intensity between her and Callum.

"We should get home," Suzette said. "My hand is swelling."

They rode home. Charlotte kept trying to catch Callum's eye, but he looked forward, and when they arrived at her house, he helped her down but didn't place his hand on her back as usual.

"Are you coming inside for tea?" she asked.

"We dallied too long on the shore," he said. "I should get back." He rode off with a friendly wave, but Charlotte felt cold watching him go.

She'd replayed that moment on the shore so many times that she wasn't sure if it had even happened. All she wanted to do was return home and see if it could be captured again. It surely wasn't even possible, since Alyce and Mrs. Wakefield were away in Toronto. She'd have no reason to go to their house, and there was no way her parents would allow it anyway. She was stuck.

She found her mother and Mare in a small depression in the forest floor. She remembered being a child and coming on these trips to Lac du Bois. She'd roam free with her child-sized birchbark basket and fill it with fat, juicy blueberries. She ate more than she picked and couldn't understand how Mare always knew she'd eaten so much, not realizing her purple-stained mouth and fingers gave her away. They'd laugh and sit in the pine needles to eat their fill.

"Ma bibiche! Isit!" her mother waved her over. "Look what we found."

They sat in a patch of conical mushrooms that looked like eggs poking through the soil. "Shaggy manes!" Excited, Charlotte rushed in and filled her basket. Finding a large patch like that was rare, a gift. Each mushroom made a hollow sound as it fell into the basket and rolled around.

"Remember when you were little and we found these mushrooms by a clearing, and you fell asleep in the middle of them? You didn't even realize when a bear came by and took a nap beside you!" Mare said.

Charlotte laughed. She'd heard this story many times but had no memory of it. It had become legend in their family, though, and with each telling, the bear got closer and bigger, until Charlotte was practically sleeping in its lap.

"That's the time when we found the fire lily, right, Mare?"

"Mmm," she nodded. "You almost picked it, but I stopped you. You pick it, and the whole plant dies, it doesn't come back. They're special and should be left alone."

"It's a plant of protection," her mother said.

"Yes, and it must be protected back. They're the first flowers to come back after a fire. They pop up in the scorched soil in big patches. When you see them like that, it looks like a lake of fire."

Charlotte had never seen a patch like that; she'd only ever seen single flowers. No clusters. But where there was one, there were usually more scattered about, hidden in plain sight. She'd love to see a field full of them, but then checked herself. That could only happen after destruction, and it was bad luck to wish for something like that.

That evening, by the fire, Charlotte turned to her beadwork. The beads glinted in the firelight, and it gave her an idea. She thought about the fire lily, how they were hidden and special, yet fragile. She looked at the partly finished shelf valance she was working on. Her father had wanted a good supply for his next trip to St. Paul, and to keep things moving, she'd settled on two designs and made only those. It made things easier; Suzette's skills had improved, so she did more of the rote beadwork, in addition to the hemming and trimming using the sewing machine. She sat beside Charlotte now, sewing the hem by hand.

"This is so much better using the sewing machine," Suzette said. "It's a waste of time to do it this way."

"We didn't even have a machine before, and now you can't live without it," their father said, irritated. "You're getting spoiled! Be quiet and help your sister. We still have to work, even in the bush."

Suzette sighed and returned to stitching, but dragged each stitch out, to make a point.

Charlotte held up the valance at arm's length and really looked at it. It was pretty, colourful, everything it should be, but it didn't have any life. The way the firelight danced across the beads showed her how it *could* have life. She didn't want to waste the work she'd already done, so she decided to not rip any stitches out. She would add to the design instead. She had some orange and yellow beads and a small supply of gold ones. She held the small glass jar of gold beads and swirled them around in the light. They sparkled. The full image of what she wanted to create sprang forth. She would add fire lilies. Each lily would get one of the gold beads in the centre. The current design was perfectly even and structured, which is what made it pleasant to look at, but lifeless. The lilies would offset that structure, make it slightly askew—but more interesting. She tore off a length of thread and set to work. It was the first time she'd been excited to bead in a long time. She was so absorbed, she forgot all about Callum.

∞

"Ma bibiche, these are extraordinary!" Clément held up the new valances and admired them. The family was home from their bush trip, all gathered in the sitting room.

Charlotte basked in her father's praise. He passed the valances to her mother, and she looked at them closely.

"You've outdone yourself, Charlotte," she said.

Mare patted her hand. "You should be proud of this work, it sings," she said. Charlotte was humbled. That was the highest praise Mare gave.

She *was* proud of herself. It had taken twice as long to make them, but they turned out better than she imagined. She'd ended up with a pair of valances, each a mirror image of the other. She had a matching set of shelves on the wall on either side of her bed, and she would hang them there.

"I can't wait to take these to St. Paul!" her father said.

Charlotte's stomach dropped. "I'd like to keep these, at least for a while."

"Ah ben, what? No, these are worth something; we can't have them wasted here at home."

"I'll make more! I need these as a pattern to work from."

He thought about it. "All right, all right. But I leave soon, so you better have at least one pair ready by then."

She said she would. Mare sat beside her and untied the pouch she always wore at her waist.

"Here, it's time for you to have this," Mare handed the pouch to Charlotte. The leather was soft and faded nearly white. It was smoother than the velvet of the valances. She opened it and pulled out Mare's ulu knife.

"Mare?"

Mare nodded, urging her to take it. "This is something that gets passed from mother to daughter. My mother got it from her grand-mother, who came from the far north, where these tools are common. The women in my family have cared for it and kept it safe and sharp all these years. I removed it from my mother's body when she and my whole village died from the weeping-sore sickness, brought to us by a black-robed priest from the fort. Not Fort Garry, but York Factory, where the ships come to take all the furs away. I ended up there after everyone died. I hated it there, but I couldn't survive in the bush on my own. That's where they splashed their water on my head and changed my name. Isabelle Saulteaux, they called me, named after what they called my people. But that is not my name. And that is not the name of my people. My name is Nimkii, and I'm Anishinaabe. But the priest said it was a sin to use my name. Now I'm Mare, which suits me fine, and I'll answer to nothing else."

Charlotte was stunned. Mare had never spoken so much, and never about anything so personal. She was afraid to say anything, in case it spooked her back into silence.

"My own daughter was not worthy of this knife," Mare continued. "It could have gone to your mother, but I chose to keep it. If no one was worthy of the knife, I would be buried with it. But now it has a new home. You must promise to wear it always and care for it as it should be tended to. You must think of it as a living thing. If it's damaged, terrible things will befall you. If it's lost, even worse things will happen. Are you worthy of it?"

"Yes," Charlotte whispered. She held the knife in her palm, like a baby bird fallen from its nest. She looked at it with awe and saw her distorted reflection in its shiny surface.

"All right then, it's yours now," Mare said. "You're responsible for it."

Her father grinned at her, and Suzette did too. Fredie clapped his hands. Her mother had glistening eyes. Charlotte had to look away from her, or she would cry too.

That night, she lay in bed staring at the ceiling. Her valances were in place above her bed. From that perspective, the fire lilies looked like flaming fleurs-de-lis. She knew she'd created something more than a product to sell. It was art. It said something. She held the ulu pouch in her hand. She could feel the sharp edge even through the leather. She placed it on her chest, above her heart. It rose and fell with her breathing. She imagined the knife expanding and contracting with her heartbeat. It was part of her now.

CHAPTER 20

Clément

July 1870

Clément was surprised when Pierre rode up.

They hadn't seen much of each other lately, with Pierre living at the fort. Clément watched his brother and saw someone new. The man standing before him held his head high and his shoulders back, as if he was braced and ready for whatever came his way. Clément felt like a slouch in comparison. He wiped dust from the front of his trousers.

"So, you went to the bush, eh?" Pierre patted his horse's flank.

Clément nodded. "It was good to be in the bush again. You know, I think I found a good spot for that winter hunting cabin we talked about."

"I'd forgotten about that. Where?"

"Remember where the good blueberries grow, near that spring along the deer trail? There's a nice spot there with good light. No big rocks, but enough smaller ones to make a chimney. I'd like to get started soon. It might not be all the way ready for this winter, but I could have a good start on it. What do you think? Would you come help?"

Pierre looked into the distance, thinking. "I know the spot. There's a marshy patch nearby, good place to find moose."

"Yes, yes. So? Want to help or what?"

"I think building a cabin is a good thing. But I don't know if I can help you build it."

"Why not?"

"I don't want to be too far away right now."

"Well, shouldn't all this business be over? We're a province of Canada now, aren't we? And we're getting to keep our land, so now the hard part is over, isn't it?"

Pierre shook his head. "Yes, all that is true, but not everything is settled yet. There's a lot more to come. People from Canada will take a census, see how many people are here, things like that. There's talk of future elections, and the Orangemen still aren't happy. And more settlers will be coming—a lot of them."

Clément scoffed. "I thought the whole point of this was to get things back to normal, maybe even with more opportunities for all of us. Now you're saying that's not happening?"

"Well . . . I'm just saying I don't think things are over yet and I want to stay close."

"Does Julien feel the same way?"

"Yes."

Clément ran his hands through his hair. "Of course. It'll take a lot longer to build the cabin now."

"Maybe I can help, in the fall. Even if it's just for a short time."

"So I guess that means no going to St. Paul either."

"Not this time, but next time I will. Things will have calmed down by then. Is there even enough freighting work, with those steamships coming?"

"There's less, but enough for now. It was a smaller group that went this spring; it wasn't the same." Clément sighed. "You might as well come in and eat. Marienne made her stew."

Later that evening, after Pierre had gone home, the women cleaned in the kitchen and Clément stretched his legs in the sitting room, smoking his pipe. Things were not going the way he wanted, at least not fast enough. He could see, now, that all of the vigilance and work by Riel and his men had been worth it. There was a structure now, and voices like his would be heard. All of that was promising. But shouldn't that mean growth and opportunity also? Where was that? He felt like he always had to scramble to find something new to trade. Every time he thought things were stable, something happened to upend everything. Now that they had a system going for Charlotte's beadwork, demand was drying up there, too. Collins said tourists were still coming, hungry for "Indian" things, and the floral beadwork of the Métis fit that bill nicely. It was just Indian enough to be exotic, though the patterns were familiar enough to be recognizable. But Collins said people wanted unique pieces, not something they saw in their friend's house.

So now he had a problem. A few problems, actually. No one to help at the cabin, no one to go carting with, and no fresh inventory to sell.

He decided Fredie would go on the cart—to hell with what Marienne wanted. It was time for the boy to grow up—he was too soft. At that age, Clément had been already guiding the carts on the buffalo hunts and had even shot one. Marienne could argue all she wanted, but Fredie would go. And he'd help build the cabin, too. Fredie would get a real education.

But Clément still needed new inventory. He took a long pull on his pipe and blew the smoke out in a cloud. The room grew hazy. Then he remembered Charlotte's new project, the one she started when they were camping in the bush. She'd been quiet lately, hadn't asked about the Wakefields. Something held her attention. This was a good development. It meant she was focused on work. He got up and checked the wall pocket where she kept her supplies. Inside were needles, thread, beads, all her supplies, but no works in progress. He looked at the staircase. Maybe he'd find something up there. He climbed the stairs.

It was warm upstairs and the low ceiling made it feel even more close. He went to the small window and opened it to let some air in. The wood screeched as the sash scraped the frame. He propped it open with a small block of wood. Cool evening air rushed in.

The girls' bed was made neatly, the covers pulled across tight. That's when he saw them.

Above Charlotte's bed were the two valances he remembered. They were exactly what he was looking for. He took them down and tucked them under his arm. He practically leaped down the stairs, he was so pleased. But in his haste, he knocked his forehead on the low ceiling.

"Tabernac!" That's what he got for stealing, he thought.

In the morning, a scream woke the house.

He sat up. Marienne was already up and out of bed. He could hear her thudding up the stairs, calling out. He sighed. So bibiche had discovered her valances were gone. He'd expected her to notice when she went to bed, but in the dark, she must not have seen what was absent. He'd convinced himself maybe she had noticed but didn't care. That was wishful thinking, he realized. He dressed and prepared to face her fury.

When he opened the bedroom door, Charlotte was waiting for him. "What have you done with them? Those are mine!"

"Calm down, ma bibiche. I'm taking them to St. Paul, as a sample."

"No!"

"You'll get them back. I just need to show them something different; people want something new. We need to update our stock."

"But those were special, they're not for sale. I don't want to replicate these over and over like we have with the others. These were for me only—one of a kind."

"You can make something else, then, something close to these. The merchant won't know any different."

Charlotte glared at him. "You can't take them! You can't!"

"I don't understand why you're so upset. I said you'll get them back. Now stop this and settle down. I won't hear any more about it."

Marienne stood behind Charlotte, looking torn. She usually tried to show a united front with him when it came to discipline, but this was different.

"Clément, maybe you could—"

He raised his hand to silence her. "I leave for St. Paul tomorrow, and these are coming with me." He looked at Marienne. "And so is Fredie."

"What? We need to talk about this!" she cried.

Fredie was behind Marienne, and he pushed forward, jumping up and down, whooping. Marienne looked at Fredie, then her husband, then turned and went into the kitchen. Charlotte followed her. Marienne filled the kettle with water and slammed it on the stove, and Charlotte slammed the tin cups on the table. Fredie hugged him and grinned. Clément went back into the bedroom and closed the door with a soft click. He sat on the bed and slumped. He didn't like conflict, especially with his children. Now everyone in the house was cross with him, except for Fredie.

CHAPTER 21

Julien

August–September 1870

It was the rainiest August Julien could remember. He thought of the drought from a couple of years ago. It was nearly the end of the month, and now they were experiencing the opposite. The roads were a muddy mess. It seemed like the whole world was a mess.

In July, Red River became a province in Canada—a little rectangle called Manitoba. Nearly everyone celebrated—at last, some progress and recognition. There were still rumblings from the Canadian faction, but the loudest ones—Schultz and Boulton and their men—had gone to Ontario to join the rest of the Orangemen. They drummed up hatred of Riel, saying he'd murdered Thomas Scott, and the newspapers ate it up. The headlines called Riel a savage, a new Napoleon, and said he should be executed in response. Julien had learned to read French. His English was still weak, but he understood the gist of the headlines. He wondered how much of it was sensational, and how much captured real sentiment. Martin said it was nothing to worry about; he'd seen worse. "Let them spew all they want. They're just mad they didn't get their way," he'd said. Julien agreed, but a bad feeling nagged him all the same. Each headline brought back images of Norbert's split skull.

The summer had been busy, but he'd managed to spend some time helping at home. Charlotte seemed irritated by his presence, probably because she had to share a bed with Suzette again. Fredie was upbeat as usual, full of his adventures on his first carting trip. "All the carts rumbled along together!" he'd said. "And Papaa let me talk to Mr. Collins and show him our new items. Just like all the other men!" As he talked, Julien could see the man Fredie would become: his jaw was a little sharper, his brow a bit thicker. His dark eyes were deep-set. He'd be handsome with an intense gaze. Julien remembered the excitement of his first cart trip, spending time with his father and the other men, sleeping under the stars with a sense of adventure and a touch of danger. It was nice to see that thrill carry on in Fredie.

Business in Red River had returned to normal, with a few changes, of course, since the Hudson's Bay Company was no longer in charge, and a new lieutenant governor named Archibald was coming to take over leadership. Julien wasn't sure what that meant for Riel or the government that was already in place, but Uncle Pierre said he expected a smooth transition. He said their new provincial status wouldn't change daily life. But with the shrieking headlines, Julien wasn't sure. He asked Martin what he thought.

"I think Pierre is right," he said. "Riel will step aside when Archibald comes, and then there will be an election. After that, no one can complain."

Julien was scheduled to patrol outside the fort that day, so he got his horse ready and rode down Main Street. The rain was light, a steady drizzle. Just enough to make everything wet and reduce visibility. A rider approached, his horse kicking up mud as it galloped toward him. Julien moved forward to intercept him once he recognized Edward, a scout in Florian's crew. When Edward stopped in front of him, Julien saw he was soaked from the rain and perspiration.

Edward wiped his brow. "We have to get Riel out now! They're coming!"

"Who's coming?"

Edward was breathing heavily and he took a gulp of air before speaking. "The soldiers from Canada—a thousand of them, maybe more."

"How do you know they're here for Riel? Aren't they escorting the new lieutenant governor?" Julien didn't understand what was happening.

The man shook his head. "Archibald is not with them. We've been tracking them since they crossed Lake Superior and arrived at Fort William. They're being led by a Colonel Wolseley. They want to hang Riel. They'll be here soon—we don't have much time."

They both rode fast back to the fort. They found Riel in the administration building, eating breakfast at his desk. Edward explained what was happening. Alarmed, Riel stood. "Julien, go find Florian," he said.

Julien raced outside and shouted Florian's name. His voice alerted others and soon a small crowd followed him. He explained the news to them in snippets, and the others dispersed to all areas of the fort, shouting for Florian. He found Uncle Pierre leaving the barracks. "Uncle! We need to find Florian. Riel needs him right away. A thousand soldiers are coming!"

Pierre didn't hesitate. "He's with the horses, come on!"

When they got to Florian and told him the news, he sent Pierre to gather the patrol. He grabbed Julien by the arm. "Let's go!" he said, and they ran back to Riel.

They found him wearing his coat and pulling on fresh moccasins. A satchel with some clothing and papers poking out sat on the floor beside him.

"We need to go, now!" Florian shouted.

By then, Pierre had arrived with a group of patrolmen. Riel looked each one in the eye before speaking.

"It's me they're after. We need to abandon the fort so they don't have an excuse to raze it. But they'll want to hang you too, Florian. Pierre, all the capitaines are at risk. You need to protect yourselves; we're no match for a thousand soldiers with muskets and cannons."

Pierre protested. "But what about you? We need to protect you!"

"Florian, you cross the Assiniboine and go west, but not too far,"

Riel said. "A scout will find you when it's safe. We need to move in small groups. Most of the men should go to their homes and resume their lives. They'll be harder to pick out once they're integrated again. Pierre, Julien, ride with me. Florian, get the scouts ready."

Julien, Pierre, and Riel rushed outside to the horses while Florian and the patrolmen ran in the other direction. At the stable, they each hopped onto a horse, and before Julien's foot was hooked into the stirrup, they raced out the rear of the fort toward the ferry to St. Boniface. He looked back to see men leaving the fort in all directions.

Luckily, they didn't need to wait for the ferry. Julien wished there had been a pontoon bridge over the Red River like there was on the Assiniboine side. The St. Boniface ferry had improved in the last year; it was larger and had a steam engine instead of a rope pulley to move across the water. When they got to the St. Boniface side, Julien told the ferry operator not to return to the fort side for a while. "Now would be a good time to do some maintenance," he said.

"Good idea," Pierre said. "Take your time with that."

They rode to St. Boniface Cathedral, which faced the fort. Bishop Taché, who had been part of the delegation to Ottawa and had helped during the talks to create Manitoba, met them on the steps.

"They promised amnesty to all who'd been part of the provisional government," the bishop said, "including the trial of Thomas Scott."

"It appears we've been deceived," Riel said.

From the steps, they could clearly see the invading troops in their red uniforms march along the empty, muddy streets and enter the abandoned fort.

"I think they expected a big reception," Pierre said. "They won't be satisfied without some bloodshed. We need to warn people that there's trouble ahead."

They watched as their flag was lowered and replaced with the Union Jack. A trumpet played "God Save the Queen," which echoed faintly across the river.

"So that's that," said Pierre. Riel was silent.

"Sir, we should move you," Julien said. "It won't be long before they start searching for you and Florian and the other leaders. They'll probably come here first." He gestured to the church behind them.

"They won't disturb the sanctity of the church," the bishop said.

He seemed certain of it, but Julien wondered how he could be so sure.

"I think Julien is right," Pierre said, nodding. "St. Joe's is a good place. It's across the Medicine Line and their reach doesn't extend to the United States."

Riel agreed, and they set off south. They stopped to escape the rain at a small cabin on the outskirts of St. Vital hidden by a stand of thin birch trees. They ushered Riel inside while Julien tended to the horses. He didn't know whose cabin it was, but he could hear overlapping voices talking quickly. He went inside and found two men he didn't recognize talking with Pierre and Riel.

"We'll stay here for now and move on when it gets dark," one of the men said.

Julien removed his wet outerwear and draped it over a chair to dry out by the fire. Riel's frock coat sat on another chair. A while later, a scout, James, rode up and Pierre welcomed him inside.

"Quickly, come and sit down," Riel said. "Tell us what you saw."

"Well, they marched into town like peacocks," James said. "No one greeted them. A few people came out to gawk, but not many. The colonel seemed disappointed, like he expected cheers or something. They were quite agitated to find the fort empty and were quick to take down our flag."

"We watched from St. Boniface," said Pierre.

"They expected to find you and hang you right there in the courtyard of the fort, sir," James said. "They've declared martial law and have put a five-thousand-dollar bounty on your head and that of anyone involved in the execution of Thomas Scott."

Riel nodded. "So they've seized on that as an excuse to kill me."

Pierre grunted. "If it wasn't that, they'd find some other reason. We need to keep you safe."

"I don't understand why so many of them came," Julien said.

"They said it was to escort Archibald through 'hostile' Sioux territory, along the trapping line from Lake Superior," James said. "They followed the Dawson Road from there."

Julien scoffed. "Everyone knows the Sioux are not in those forests at this time of year. And Archibald wasn't with them, so that's not even true."

"Sir, perhaps it's time to head to St. Joe's?" Pierre said.

Riel nodded. "I can monitor things from there."

"I think it's best if different men accompany you," James said. He looked at Pierre. "You're too recognizable together. New riders are on their way—they weren't far behind me. You and Julien should go home and lay low."

"Tell people I've gone west," Riel said to Julien and Pierre. "We'll keep them guessing."

"The last I heard," James said, "the soldiers were raiding the stores in the fort. They were already getting rowdy and I doubt they'll be content to stay put."

Julien wished he could do something. He thought about going to Main Street to see for himself how the soldiers were behaving, but thought better of it. He could be caught and questioned, and he wasn't sure how strong he would be if they beat him—he worried he would end up like Norbert, and he couldn't do that to his family. So he would try to resume his old life, but it would be flat, dull.

∞

The violence against the Métis community began after the soldiers' arrival. Pierre arrived with the news. "The soldier complement has two parts: trained soldiers and untrained volunteers, mostly Orangemen," he said. "They've been drinking the Main Street saloons dry, and now with no drink to keep them busy, they're causing trouble."

"What kind of trouble? How bad?" Julien asked.

"First they started harassing Métis on the streets, but it's gotten worse. They shot a man's horse while he was on it and beat him nearly to death when he fell to the ground."

"No!" Julien gasped.

"Yes, Boucher said he saw it himself. There have been many other beatings, and they're attacking women in the worst ways." He looked Julien in the eyes. "The worst. It's bad."

"Something has to be done about those savages! Shouldn't soldiers know better?"

"That's the thing. The real soldiers don't care and let the volunteers run wild. It's disgusting."

In early September, Archibald arrived and set up a police constabulary, made up of the volunteer portion of the Wolseley troops. But Wolseley himself didn't stay long and he returned to Ontario with his soldiers, leaving the volunteer portion behind. "Maybe things will calm down now," Pierre had said. "There's talk of a census and election, and Riel is still involved, even in exile." But the opposite happened. The mercenaries, now a constabulary, were emboldened.

There was no one to turn to for help. Red River wasn't the home Julien remembered.

CHAPTER 22

Marienne

January 1871

"You know Papaa is right. Don't go to Winnipeg, it's not safe," Julien said to Marienne, gripping her by the shoulder a little too firmly.

Her son and Pierre sat at the table, covered in blood and bruises. The pair had burst into the house cold and exhausted, with frozen blood crusted on their faces. Marienne had shrieked when she saw them and immediately set the water to boil on the stove. She filled a basin with warm water and dabbed her son's face, loosening the frozen blood. He winced as she pressed the cloth to his jaw. Mare poured tea for everyone and examined Julien's hands.

"I'd say you boys need something stronger than tea, but I think you've already had your fill," Clément said, frowning.

Pierre and Julien sipped their tea and, as they relaxed, the story of what happened came out.

"We were at the Emmerling Hotel," Pierre began. "Minding our business."

"You've been spending too much time there, in the drink," Clément said, angry.

"Let them talk," Marienne said.

"It was quiet all afternoon," Pierre continued. "Then the door banged open and four of those Wolseley mercenaries stumbled in. They were loud, like they were on a stage. We ignored them and kept playing cards."

"They sat down next to us, even though there were lots of empty tables," Julien said. "They bumped into me, and Uncle Pierre told them to be careful, in a friendly way."

"They called us half-breeds and told us to mind our business," Pierre said.

"We ignored them and kept on," said Julien. "But you could tell they were spoiling for a fight. So we decided to go home."

"That was the right thing to do," Marienne said, wringing out the cloth.

Pierre held his cup out for more tea. "We walked toward the river, past a couple of tipis on the bank, near the ferry crossing. There were two Cree men sitting outside next to the fire. One was drumming."

Julien shook his head. "Then we heard the mercenaries from the hotel shout out to 'quit it with those tom-toms.' They crowded around the fire, near the drummer, who ignored them and continued with his drumming. They told him to take his Swamp music and leave, it didn't belong there." Julien took a breath and paused. "The drummer didn't stop and ignored the men. One of them kicked at the fire, trying to stamp it out. Another reached for the drum. The two Cree men stood and calmly stared them down. The loudest mercenary shoved the drummer in the chest. 'You need to stop that noise.' His voice was like a growl.

"They called them dirty Swampies and other horrible things. Then the mercenary swung a wide punch, hitting the Cree on the side of the face. That's when it all went crazy."

"Julien went to help the Cree men. I called after him but he ran. He reached the nearest mercenary and punched him. The man hit back. Then Julien punched and punched and punched," Pierre said.

"Oh no!" Marienne gasped.

"Pierre pulled me away and we sank into the snow. He rubbed snow in my face. He said we had to leave, this wasn't our fight."

"It wasn't," Pierre whispered.

"We walked away, then we heard a gunshot."

"No!" said Mare, covering her mouth.

"One of the mercenaries was holding his revolver, aimed at the drummer, who lay bleeding in the snow," Julien continued. "But then a woman cried from inside the tipi. The other Cree man ran inside and came out carrying the limp body of a small child, around five years old."

Silent tears rolled down Mare's cheek.

"I wanted to call the constabulary," Julien said. "But Pierre said no."

"The ones who did this are the constabulary!" Pierre said. "It's them who did the shooting. They'd find a way to blame us. So we ran."

"That was smart," Clément said. "Trust me, the facts wouldn't matter."

"But it's not right. It's not right," Julien said.

"It isn't," Pierre said, "but there's nothing we can do about it."

Marienne wiped Julien's brow.

Mare took Julien's hands in hers. "Your hands will become stiff in damp weather like mine do, once they heal," she said. "Good thing I gathered more crocus last summer. You'll need it."

Suzette and Charlotte, followed by Fredie, came in from outside, bringing a gust of cold air with them.

"Julien! Your face!" Suzette rushed forward.

Fredie followed his sisters, looking concerned. Charlotte tried to keep her face calm.

"Charlotte, fetch Mare's medicines," Marienne said. She ran to the cupboard without removing her coat.

"This is why I hate going to Winnipeg," Clément said. "It's dangerous there now. No one goes until we absolutely need supplies, and when that happens, I'll go alone."

Charlotte looked distressed. "So we still can't go to Winnipeg at all? Not even with a chaperone?"

Marienne shook her head. "Not with this kind of thing happening. It's getting worse."

"But, Mamaa—"

"Think, girl! You know what can happen, I shouldn't have to tell you! Remember what happened to Sarah last year? Not everyone gets away."

Charlotte looked at the floor and said nothing.

Marienne's ears rang. She felt a sense of dread that could turn to panic. Something had to be done. They couldn't live like this. No one could. She looked at her husband.

"How bad do you think it will get?" she asked him.

Clément frowned. He looked like he wanted to give a good answer but had no idea what that would be. "This never should have happened in the first place," he said. "I don't know how bad it will get but it's not good now, so we have to be prepared. We have to be smart about what we do, how we behave."

Pierre nodded. "I don't think we've seen the worst of it yet. Those mercenaries are parading up and down the streets of Winnipeg, marching in full gear. Every afternoon they do this. The attention has gone to those men's heads. They're the source of this reign of terror, but their ideas are spreading and now we're hearing our neighbours, people who've lived beside us all this time, talking like they do."

"It's not good," Julien said. "We should have done more to help the Cree. Those men just shot their guns into their tipi without any thought. It was monstrous. I can't stop thinking about that little child."

No one said anything. After a few moments, Marienne spoke up. "Maybe we should leave."

Everyone stared at her.

"Leave?" said Clément. "And go where?"

"We can't leave!" Charlotte cried out. "We can't!"

"I already feel like a coward," Julien said quietly. "I'm not going to run away like a dog."

Mare eased into a chair at the head of the table.

"I've seen worse than this," Mare said. She paused to make sure she commanded everyone's attention. "Some of you have heard this story, and some of you haven't. I don't like to talk about it, but it's important that you know. Marienne, pour me some tea."

Marienne did as she was told and sank into a chair next to Mare. Mare took a slurp from the scalding tea and leaned back in her chair.

"I was a young girl when my whole family died, younger than Fredie," she said. She nodded at him and he sat a little straighter. "It was a bad season with little game, and winter was coming. We moved around a lot, looking for food, and ended up in the northern forests, much farther than we'd normally go, close to the sea. I'd never been that far north before. We didn't find much. It was as if the forests were dead. One of my uncles said he'd go to the nearby fort and get some food; he could speak their language and was sure he'd find help. A few days later, he returned with a white man in a long black dress. I know now he was a priest, but it was my first time seeing a man like that, and I didn't know what he was. My father had managed to kill a goose and we all ate that night. I remember how that priest ate his fill, his fingers and face greasy. He smiled at me a lot. I stayed close to my mother. The priest told stories of an undead man who wanted people to eat his flesh and drink his blood. Like a wendigo."

"Maman, that's sacrilege," Clément whispered. Mare gave him a hard stare and his eyes slid away.

"His stories gave me bad dreams. We'd been starving, and stories of the wendigo were whispered around the fire all season. When the priest came and said we should worship the wendigo, it was too much to understand. He left after a few days, and that's when people started getting sick, including me. Soon everyone had weeping sores all over their bodies. People moaned in their beds. My mother cared for them as best she could, but she fell ill too. I had horrible fever dreams and don't remember much from that time. I just remember waking up to a silent camp and finding everyone dead: my mother, my father, everyone. The sores had festered and they stank. I couldn't bury them in the good way. I didn't have the strength. I was starving. I found a water skin and drained it. There were dregs of fish stew in the pot above the fire and I licked it clean. I made tea from pine needles and devoured the scraggly red clovers I found nearby. It was the sweetest nectar I ever tasted . . .

"I covered the dead with blankets and pine boughs and hid in the tipi at night. Wolves came and dragged the body of my young cousin away. I knew I had to leave—that wolf would return and want fresh meat instead of carrion. I couldn't take down the birch-bark tipi and carry it, so I had to leave it all behind. From my mother's belt, I removed the pouch that held her ulu knife and tied it to mine. I gathered what I could carry and went north."

Marienne looked at Charlotte, who was rubbing the ulu pouch that now hung on her belt. When Mare had first given it to Charlotte, Marienne had been disappointed that it hadn't gone to her, as daughter-in-law. But she saw the wisdom in giving it to Charlotte. It was at home with her.

Mare continued. "I tried to survive as long as I could, but when the snow came, I had no choice but to go to the fort. I saw a different priest there, and he's the one who splashed water on my head and gave me a new name. I took his medicine to make him happy, but the ceremony had no meaning for me. I had to learn their language and their ways and become a whole new person. I did all that to survive. If I have to, I can do it again.

"Those soldier boys will go home soon. Either they will want to go home on their own, or whoever is paying to feed them will get tired of it. We stay here and wait it out."

The room was silent. Marienne took a deep breath. No wonder Mare never liked to talk about her past, and why she acted so strangely around the church. She attended dutifully, but always wore an expression like she'd encountered a bad smell. Marienne looked at Mare with awed respect.

Clément broke the silence. "So we stay and see what happens. Things should go back to normal soon. Maybe we're worrying too much."

Marienne didn't think things would go back to normal. Their old life was forever changed. Maybe things would settle down, but would they ever really feel safe again? She kept these thoughts to herself. Everyone was agitated enough already; she didn't need to add to it. Julien opened his mouth to argue, but he also stayed silent. Charlotte seemed relieved. Fredie and Suzette looked wide-eyed from person to person. The future was uncertain and unsettling.

Later that night, in bed, Marienne couldn't sleep. Clément snored softly beside her. She tried to breathe slow and steady but sleep wouldn't come. Instead, she calculated. She counted the number of years they'd lived on their lot. How many months it took to build the house, how many times Clément had to reconnect the beams until he got it perfect. Without nails, they had to adapt and build with precision, so the joints fit exactly, and they ended up with a sturdier home because of it. The number of furs they had to sell to afford glass windows and the cast iron stove. How much credit her husband had amassed for the sewing machine. She counted the dry goods and preserved meat they had in their cold storage beside the house. How many stitches she'd sewn to make their clothes. Her life was a series of accounts.

She wondered what she could pack quickly if she had to. What was absolutely essential? Was anything really essential? As long as they had themselves, what did they actually need? She imagined packing and unpacking a satchel, each time adding and discarding something different until she was satisfied with what she'd put in there. She considered having it already packed and ready to go, hanging on a hook on the back of the bedroom door, but decided against it, since the things she'd pack were things she used every day. But having it figured out in her mind was comforting.

In the morning, she found Pierre asleep in a chair next to the kitchen stove, the warmest part of the house. She worked quietly around him, letting him sleep. She made tea and sat at the table sipping it. She liked this time in the morning before everyone else was up. She could stare out the window and think. She needed it after her restless night.

The stairs creaked under someone's feet, and Marienne was surprised to see her elder daughter descend. Usually, Charlotte stayed in bed the longest. To avoid chores, Marienne thought. She poured her daughter a cup of tea and the two sat together. A dog barked in the distance.

"Mamaa, please can I go visit Alyce again?"

"Charlotte, you're not a child anymore, surely you understand how the world works."

"But maybe things aren't that bad. Point Douglas is safe, and I'd certainly be safe at her house."

"It's not about their house, Charlotte. It's getting there and back that's the issue. Especially now, when it still gets dark so early."

"I could go with Julien and Uncle. They go almost every day."

Marienne spoke a little more sternly than she needed to, but she was exasperated. "After what happened yesterday? Why would you suggest that? And don't tell me it's because you miss Alyce so much. It's very clear that it's her brother you really want to see."

Charlotte's face went red. "I've hardly been there! Alyce and her mother were in Toronto all summer and then they extended their trip into the fall. They've only been back a short time."

Marienne reached for Charlotte's hand. "I think maybe Alyce has new friends now, and might even find a husband soon, with all these new people arriving. She might have outgrown your friendship."

"How can you say that? Besides, how will I know if I can never visit? Things have been so dull around here. Nothing happened for New Year's, even. Please!"

Marienne felt bad that the Christmas and New Year's celebrations had been much more subdued than the previous year. They had gone to Midnight Mass in St. Norbert instead of St. Boniface, and their réveillon feast and gift exchange were small.

"You want excitement? Go then! But don't come crying when you get attacked or snatched away."

Pierre stirred at their raised voices. "Eh? Who's been attacked?"

"Charlotte, if she gets her way." Marienne grimaced.

"Fine! I'll just go get some snow, then! We'll need it to wash the dirty dishes that never end." Charlotte got up and grabbed a blanket from a hook by the door, wrapped it around her shoulders, and went outside.

Marienne sighed and cooked breakfast.

Charlotte spent her time on outdoor chores. She tended the dogs and the horses, but Marienne wasn't sure what else she'd been up to. She shouldn't have been so sharp with her that morning, but her anxiety had gotten the better of her. Charlotte's life had been relatively easy. In her eighteen years, she hadn't experienced any real conflict or serious hardship. There had been droughts, bad crops, floods—but all of that was to be expected. She could sleep in her bed and not worry about who would come knocking in the night, unlike Mare. Even when times were tough, they managed to find food. Charlotte didn't realize she was living in an easy time. Marienne wondered if she'd been too soft on her children. But wasn't that a parent's duty? To make the lives of their children better and easier than theirs had been? What was the point otherwise?

But now she wasn't sure. Julien was headstrong and idealistic. Admirable qualities, but risky ones to indulge. Charlotte was spoiled but didn't realize it. A dangerous combination. Suzette seemed more pragmatic, but she was still girlish, at fourteen. And little Fredie, at nearly ten, was turning into a scholar. He still followed his older siblings like a puppy. What would the future turn him into?

Clément would tell her she was worrying for nothing. So what if their children had an easier time than they did? That was a good thing. Sometimes she agreed, but now all she could do was worry. "Worrying doesn't help, so why do it?" he'd say with a shrug.

"Someone has to plan ahead or we'd all starve," she'd retort. The same dance, all the time. She was tired of it.

Julien winced every time he ate. He stuck to soups and soft bread. Marienne kept herself busy by helping Suzette sort their worn-out clothes to salvage the fabric for braided rugs.

Fredie sat beside her, watching. She put him to work, too, tearing the fabric into strips. He eagerly ripped it up, smiling with satisfaction as the threads tore along the grain. Suzette wove the pieces tightly into an evenly shaped oval. She was pleased with the result, especially when her father complimented her work. "Looks like we'll have some new items to sell in St. Paul!" he'd said. Suzette beamed. She and Fredie then went to the neighbours' to collect scrap fabric to make more rugs. It was good to see them excited about something.

Each day, Marienne assigned extra chores to Charlotte. She had her scrub every surface in the house, remove every dish to wash the cupboard, then wash all the dishes, too. Sometimes she made her do a chore twice. Charlotte fumed but didn't complain.

"Maybe you should go a little easier on her," Mare said. "She's young. She doesn't want to be trapped in the house, and the one thing that made her feel special is gone. It's understandable why she's upset."

She knew Mare was right, but agreeing with her felt like giving in. She just had to have control of something, and if that was Charlotte, then so be it.

"It's to do with that boy, more than anything else," Marienne said.

"Of course it is. He's handsome and represents everything that's new and exciting. It would be strange if she weren't drawn to him. She's been daydreaming about being his wife since the day she met him."

"Well, that will never happen. Callum Wakefield is not the type of man to marry a girl like Charlotte. She's beautiful, clever, and would make anyone a good wife. But she is not from his circle and nothing can change that."

"Are you sure? Lots of white men marry Métis women or even Indian women. Like me." She gave Marienne a pointed look.

Marienne looked away, embarrassed. "I'm worried that she'll be hurt or humiliated, or both. Charlotte is not that strong. She won't recover from that."

"I understand you wanting to save her from that, but she needs to decide some things for herself. Maybe getting bruised will help her grow. We all need to learn that the world isn't fair."

Like waking up in the wilderness and finding your whole family dead. Marienne understood why her mother-in-law could be so harsh in her opinions and why she saw things in absolutes.

"I guess I can't really protect her at all," Marienne said.

"Things will turn out the way they will. We help where we can and that's it."

CHAPTER 23

Charlotte

April 1871

The drudgery was worse than ever.

Charlotte knew she was being punished for daring to wish for something more than their small farm. Everyone was trying to thwart her. First her father, when he stole the valances—her art pieces—that he'd never returned, as she expected. He clearly didn't care about her at all. Now her mother was keeping her trapped in the house doing double the work. All to keep her safe, she said. But Charlotte knew that was a lie. It was to keep her head focused downward, not up.

How dangerous could Winnipeg really be if the daily troop marches were called "ladies' parades"? Alyce was probably there every day picking out suitors. Especially now that the weather had broken and the smell of spring was in the air. She probably had many fine new dresses from Toronto that she'd be eager to show off. Charlotte should be there, too. She wondered if Sarah or Hyacinthe were at those parades. They probably were. Maybe it was good she was trapped in the house, so she didn't have to hear them boast of their adventures.

The carousel of days spun by, each blending into the other. It felt as if a lot of time had passed, yet no time had passed. As if she existed outside of time. Eventually, the days grew warmer, the snow melted, and she decided to pay Sarah a visit. She knew Sarah's brother Thomas delivered hay to the fort. If she timed it right, they could join him and then visit Alyce. She considered just leaving the house without permission, but decided against it and asked her mother, who looked at her, frowned, then said, "Fine, but be home before dark."

When she got to Sarah's, she found her clearing away old stubble from the garden.

"It's too nice a day to spend it working," Charlotte said. "Why don't we go visit Alyce? Aren't you bored after being cooped up all winter? Isn't your brother supposed to deliver hay to the fort?"

"I could use a break," Sarah said, rubbing her lower back. "Thomas should be leaving soon."

"Maybe we can ride back with him, too."

Sarah removed the smock that protected her dress and they left.

Thomas dropped them off near the fort and they walked the rest of the way to Point Douglas, which wasn't far. At the house, Mrs. Wakefield met them after they were let inside. "I'm sorry you came all this way, but Alyce isn't home. She's having tea with Miss Bannatyne. With so many new people arriving from Ontario, her social calendar is quite full."

Charlotte tried to hide her disappointment. "Of course."

Sarah examined the room, barely looking at Mrs. Wakefield. Her eyes flitted from object to object. Charlotte understood her fascination, since she'd been wide-eyed herself the first time she visited. There was so much to look at. It was strange to see someone collect so many *things.*

"It's like being inside the rectory," Sarah whispered to her in Michif.

Mrs. Wakefield frowned. "What was that, dear?"

"Sarah was just admiring all your fine things."

"Oh! We brought back so many *objets* from our trip." She dragged out the French pronunciation in an almost comical way. She stood and pointed to a large oval frame on the wall behind her. "This one is the latest thing. It's made from human hair."

Sarah made a face and Charlotte nudged her to stop. Inside the frame was what looked like dried flowers pinned to a canvas. They moved to get a closer look. Indeed, the intricate shapes were made from twisted and braided strands of hair of different hues. A few dried flowers were mixed in for colour and to add to the illusion that it was all dried flowers. Charlotte imagined the hours it would take to painstakingly form each shape. The details were rich.

"That's very odd," Sarah frowned, still speaking in Michif.

"It's not much different from quillwork or tufting," Charlotte whispered back in Michif.

"But this is hair from people. Whose hair is it? What is this supposed to be, a trophy? Like the antlers on the wall over there? Only the English would display something so macabre."

"Amazing, isn't it?" Mrs. Wakefield gushed. "But that's nothing compared to the real prize." She led them into the dining room where a fireplace was flanked by a pair of shelves topped by porcelain figurines. "Look at this beadwork I picked up in St. Paul. I got it for a song! Made by a real Indian woman in Montana somewhere. Everyone has these valances now, but these are special, they're like nothing anyone else has."

Charlotte froze. There, on Mrs. Wakefield's wall, hung her shelf valances, the ones her father had stolen to sell in St. Paul. They looked garish up there, buried among all the other trinkets and art hanging on the walls. It was all lifeless. The entire display was a cimetière. Sarah was right, they were all trophies for Mrs. Wakefield. She was as proud of her objets as if she'd made them herself.

"That looks like something you'd make," Sarah said, in English.

"Charlotte? Oh no, this was made by a real Indian," said Mrs. Wakefield. "Someone with an artist's eye. It's far superior to the utilitarian pieces you girls make."

Charlotte opened her mouth to speak but Mrs. Wakefield had more to say: "No one can dispute your craftsmanship, of course, you're very skilled—but this is something else entirely."

Charlotte said nothing. She felt too shocked—and a little ashamed—to be angry. She should feel proud to see her work displayed, but the insults killed that. Mrs. Wakefield saw her as a talentless drone with no original thoughts. Even with evidence, Mrs. Wakefield couldn't see her as special or exceptional. She never would.

Sarah turned to Mrs. Wakefield. "Madame, I'm looking for some domestic work. Perhaps you could use a maid to keep all your treasures clean?"

Mrs. Wakefield tilted her head. "We are doing so much more entertaining now, we could really use the extra help," she said, smiling. She turned to Charlotte. "But dear, Alyce has her own friends now, and learning French isn't as important as before, so we won't need your services anymore." She patted Charlotte on the arm.

"What?"

"There's no role for you," Mrs. Wakefield said. "I just don't know how you'll fit here with us."

Charlotte was stunned. "I'm not sure what you mean."

"Your little language lessons were fun, and it was good for Alyce to have a companion. But I think the time for that is over. We won't need you to visit anymore."

Charlotte's head buzzed. She understood the words Mrs. Wakefield said, but the meaning didn't sink in. This was what her mother had warned her about: how people like the Wakefields seemed friendly at first, but they would never see her as anything more than a half-breed. She wasn't a real person to them and never would be. Of course, this would happen when Sarah was there as a witness. She would never live down the humiliation.

"I don't understand."

"I think I was quite clear. There's no role for you here." She gestured to the window. "There's plenty of daylight left, so you girls can make your own way home."

And so she was dismissed from the Wakefield home. Charlotte tightened her shawl around her shoulders like a shield and hurried out of the house. Sarah didn't follow—she must be discussing the arrangements for her new employment. Charlotte didn't wait; she had to get away from that house. With each step her humiliation gave way to anger. *There's no role for you here.* What kind of nonsense-speak was that? Did everyone in Ontario talk with such a weird affect? Who did she think she was? Standing there with a smile that never reached her eyes.

Charlotte's outrage grew. She pounded her anger into the ground, feeling the vibrations in her bones. She fell into a rhythm:

There's no role for you here.
There's no role for you here.
There's no role for you here.

She filled her lungs with fresh air. She wanted to cry but refused. No one would catch her shedding one pathetic tear, especially Sarah.

She passed through the growing neighbourhood of Point Douglas, barely noticing the clang of hammers and sawing wood of the rising houses. Already Point Douglas Common, the grassland everyone used as pasture, was shrinking. She barely recognized the area compared to the summer before. The air was full of dust from carts hauling lumber and bricks along the dirt roads.

Workers whistled at her as she walked by. She gripped her shawl tighter, wishing to be covered as much as possible. She was angry but also scared. The place was full of strangers now—as if it wasn't hers anymore. Maybe it never was.

But it was clear now that Mrs. Wakefield, and probably Alyce too, would never see her as a real person. She'd be a curiosity, like a trained dog. It didn't matter what she did or how she shaved off parts of herself to fit in their mould. It would never happen. The realization was freeing, in a way. She could give up trying to be something she was not. There was no point.

CHAPTER 23 • Charlotte

The future she'd imagined for herself, married to Callum and living his luxurious life, faded like vapour. What a child she had been! Thinking that she could be accepted by people like the Wakefields. All those stolen moments with Callum—what were they really about? Was she a trophy in his collection, like his mother's parlour of curios? Was he laughing at her? How could she have been so naïve? She didn't think she could survive the shame. She'd have to stick to St. Norbert and keep her head down. Work was all she was good for. She had to accept it. Nothing in her life would improve or change; she was trapped forever in her small orbit. She'd have to marry Henri or some other man her father thought would take her. She had no real worth, no value.

She arrived at Main Street in time to see the "ladies' parade." A small crowd lined both sides of the street, the majority of women and girls waving gloved hands and handkerchiefs. She stood to watch. The men marched along the dirt road, their steps in formation. They did look smart up there, all moving together. But after weeks of daily drills, they *should* look smart, she supposed. She refused to be impressed.

"There you are!" Sarah arrived next to her, out of breath. "Why didn't you wait for me?"

"I wanted to leave and didn't want to intrude on your conversation with Mrs. Wakefield."

Charlotte hoped Sarah wouldn't notice the turmoil she felt inside. When Sarah spotted a weakness, she was quick to exploit it. But Sarah could also be self-absorbed. She was probably too happy about her own good fortune to notice anything odd about Charlotte.

"It's strange she didn't offer you a job, too," Sarah said. "I bet she will need more than one maid. I'll see if I can get her to hire you later on, maybe."

Charlotte was repulsed by the idea. "You don't need to do that, I'm busy already."

Sarah shrugged. "So this is the big parade! Some of them look quite handsome—look at the one on the end!" She pointed and Charlotte mumbled agreement, uninterested. She didn't want to look at these invading men and see them as handsome prospects. She looked at their faces. Which ones had shot at the Cree family? Had the Cree man and child died? Nothing was mentioned in the newspaper about it—Julien had checked. If he and Uncle Pierre hadn't been there to witness it, no one would have known about the shooting. She wanted to spit at the soldiers' feet.

She examined the crowd. People seemed to enjoy the display. She hoped to see some scowls or at least looks of boredom, but there were few. Sarah was enthralled with the spectacle and cheered along with the other watchers. Charlotte was glad she hadn't been offered a job as a maid; the indignity would have been too much.

Looking at the young women smiling coyly at the marchers, Charlotte noticed how different they seemed from herself and Sarah. They acted bashful, but proudly stood along the road like they belonged there, like the whole town was meant for them only. She realized why she'd been banned from the Wakefield home. Mrs. Wakefield didn't want her around Callum, in case he did get the idea to take her as a wife. Which meant that if Mrs. Wakefield thought it was a possibility, then maybe there was something more behind Callum's attention. She was a threat. So perhaps she wasn't powerless after all.

She noticed Julien's friend, Martin, across the street, watching the parade. He looked a little shabby, his hair not combed back neatly as usual, and his shoulders hunched. He had the same vacant look Julien did. Charlotte waved and he nodded in response, making his way toward her.

"Is Julien with you?" he asked when he arrived.

Charlotte shook her head and introduced him to Sarah, who smiled and gave him her full attention, the parade now ignored.

"You really shouldn't be out here alone," he said.

"Everyone seems to be having a nice time, enjoying the show," Sarah said.

"It's nice and safe for some people here, but not for us," he said. "Are you going back to St. Norbert? I think I should go with you, and we should leave soon."

"Why are you being so cautious? Look around, it's fine." Charlotte gestured at the crowded street.

"When this is over," he said, "only the unsavoury types will be left, and you don't want to attract their attention, trust me."

He gripped Charlotte by the arm to lead her away. She tried to shake loose, not liking how firm his grip was.

"Is everything all right, Charlotte?"

She turned to see Callum in front of her, looking concerned. She was surprised to see him; she'd looked for him in the crowd.

"We were just at your house," Sarah said. "Your mother hired me as a maid."

Callum seemed surprised by this but recovered quickly. "Well, I guess we'll be seeing quite a bit of you, then." He smiled and looked at Charlotte, as if she'd been hired, too.

"Your mother said I wouldn't be needed there anymore," said Charlotte, "since Alyce has new friends and French is no longer important for her." She gave him a flat look.

This time, he couldn't cover his surprise. "But Alyce has been asking about you," he said. "She wanted to send an invitation when she and Mother returned from their trip. I wondered why she never did."

Sarah eyed them both. "Why didn't you send your own invitation, then?"

Callum sputtered, "Well, that wouldn't be proper now, would it?"

"No, not at all," Martin sounded angry and looked at Callum with suspicion. "Besides, aren't you busy setting up your business? A bank, isn't it?"

Callum looked uncomfortable. "We've decided on land speculation now; it's much more lucrative. Too many regulations with a bank."

"I can imagine. And I expect you'll find a lot of land to speculate on, eh? It must be easy for you, with the rules changing all the time."

"Well, yes, of course. Lots of opportunity here."

"For some."

Charlotte held her breath. Martin looked tense, as if he was about to strike Callum. His eyes were full of disgust. She wanted to say something to smooth things over but couldn't think of anything.

"There's room for all of us to succeed," Callum said weakly.

Martin scoffed.

"You don't sound so sure of that," Charlotte said. "I don't think you believe that yourself."

Martin grabbed her arm and Sarah's and led them away, although much more gently this time. Charlotte looked back at Callum, who looked away with his head down.

They took the secondary trails home, away from the river, walking quickly. Martin said it was better to not be hemmed in on one side by the river if bad men came upon them. Charlotte didn't like being away from the main road. She felt safer around people, but Martin's reasoning made sense. The afternoon was warm, so the long walk was pleasant enough, but Charlotte was uneasy. Too many strong emotions in a short time left her impatient and testy. She wanted to lash out at someone or something but had no outlet. She didn't want to go home, but she had nowhere else to go. She felt trapped and hopeless.

"So that's why you've been so quiet about your visits with Alyce," Sarah said. "You've been keeping secrets."

"No, I haven't!"

"Your feelings for Callum are plain to see. You've been working on getting a husband this whole time. A rich one, too."

Charlotte's face grew hot. She avoided looking at Sarah and Martin. "Suzette was with me on every visit. Nothing inappropriate happened."

"I'm sure."

"All the more reason to be glad to be rid of them," Martin said. "Those people are trouble. Callum and his father have been sniffing around the fort and have been around for every development. Their hands are in everything. You can bet they're orchestrating things in their favour. All of those rich men have each other's backs."

They continued walking, and Sarah turned her interrogation on Martin, asking about his family, where he went to school. Sarah had to probe into people's lives, even when they didn't want it. Martin gave distracted short answers, his attention on the trail ahead.

When they reached the edge of St. Norbert, they saw a pair of well-dressed men walking up the roadway to a river lot house.

"What are those men doing at the Belcourt place?" Sarah said.

"Let's hang back for a bit—I want to see what's going on," said Martin.

They stood by some birch trees, watching. The men knocked on the door and were welcomed inside.

"Who do you think they are? It looked like they were carrying papers," said Charlotte.

"I've heard something about this," Martin said. "They're doing a census. Possibly some redistricting or something—at least that's what I heard."

"Redistricting? What does that mean?" Charlotte's voice rose in frustration.

"Kiyam, I'm sure it's nothing," Sarah said, trying to smooth things over. "Everything's been sorted out; a census makes sense. Canada would need to know exactly how many people are here. It can't be more than that."

"I need to go see Pierre," Martin said. "His house is close, right?"

Charlotte nodded and pointed. "Julien is probably with him; he's been there a lot lately. Practically lives there."

"Good, they need to know about this. Charlotte, if they come to your house, tell Julien to let me know." Martin hurried off.

"Do you think he's right, that there's more to it?" Sarah asked.

"At this point, I wouldn't be surprised."

They reached the turn-off to Sarah's house. They hugged, then Charlotte walked the rest of the way home alone, her head full. She felt jangly, like a violin string that was about to snap. The humiliation was still there, and she wished she could have thrown some insults back in Mrs. Wakefield's face. At the very least, she should know that it was Charlotte's beadwork she displayed so proudly. But she would never believe it. Was recognition so important? Why? Because she needed to be seen. She didn't want to be invisible anymore.

The next step for her was marriage, but she didn't really want it. She'd imagined marrying Callum, of course, but if she was honest with herself, she didn't want to belong to anyone. She wanted to be her own person, but that was impossible. So if she had to marry someone, a life of comfort with Callum was the best she could hope for. Seeing him after such a long absence helped her realize the fantasy was silly. He was as handsome as before, but there was no foundation there, nothing to build on. He'd been the prince in a fairy story. She hadn't seen him as he really was. It was time to stop her childish thinking. No longer would she let someone else hold power over her. She would determine her fate, no one else.

CHAPTER 24

Clément

June 1872

"I'm going to have to sell the cows," Clément told Marienne. "We need money."

They were standing in their hay field behind the house, in the fragrant grass. Marienne broke off a strand and twirled it in her fingers. "Are you sure? There must be something else we could do. We need those cows."

Clément shook his head. "Those steamships are ruining the freighting business, plus that new Winnipeg company has monopolized any business that was left. And they refuse to hire any of us to work for them. They hire newcomers only."

Marienne dropped the piece of grass. "They're squeezing us out of our own home." She broke off another strand and crushed it.

Clément looked north to the neighbouring houses. "Philip said they're going west," he pointed to a small whitewashed house in the distance.

"Them too? So many are going west, or south. Denise said her neighbours, the McKays, are going to Montana. It's not surprising, after what happened to their daughter."

Clément nodded. Marienne wouldn't speak of it directly, but everyone knew what had happened to the girl. She'd been walking home when a group of "police" came upon her. It was daylight, not far from the road. They took her into the trees, and their attack was brutal. They beat her so badly that her face had permanent damage. They did other unspeakable indignities as well. Clément remembered seeing the family at church in the weeks after the attack—the girl, the same age as Suzette, spoke to no one and wouldn't let go of her mother's hand. He wasn't surprised they were leaving.

"Maybe we should think about moving somewhere else, making a fresh start," Marienne said.

Clément spun to face her. "Why are you bringing that up again? And where would we go? I built this house. Look at what we have here: the garden, the horses. No, we stay."

"But you like the roaming life. You always said the carting trips are when you're happiest."

"And you said you wanted to stay in one place, put down roots. Now you want to rip those roots out."

"I'm thinking about what's best for us. I don't feel safe here anymore, and what kind of future will our children have? We have to think about what's best for them."

"Things have to get better soon; they can't stay like this forever. It will turn around. We'll find other ways to make money—there's always a way."

Marienne didn't say anything for a moment, then said, "All right. Sell one cow and we'll see what happens."

∞

"They're calling it scrip," Pierre said. "It's a new system for land allotments." He sat at the kitchen table with Clément, Marienne, Mare, and Julien.

"It comes in either land or money," Julien explained. "Martin told me you can get eighty, one hundred sixty, or two hundred forty acres or the same amount in dollars."

"How do you know which amount you get?" Clément asked.

Julien held up his hands. "No one seems to know. Martin says you have to go to the Dominion Lands Office to find out."

"So we need to get this scrip so we can stay on the land?" Marienne asked.

"That's what they say," Pierre said. "Or you can take the money instead and buy different land. There's supposed to be 1.4 million acres set aside for us."

"Million!" Marienne said. "Surely some of that must include the river lots we're already on."

"That only makes sense," Clément said.

"The only problem is the office is in the fort."

They all went quiet.

Marienne was the first to break the silence. "I don't want you going there alone," she said to Clément. "That's the nest of those Orangistes troops. You need to go as a group. Talk to the neighbours, see what they're doing. It's safer if there are more of you."

"But not too many," said Mare. "They'll think you're invading the fort again."

"Well, we don't have much choice," Clément said.

"It sounds like the system is confusing on purpose." Marienne frowned.

"Scrip. *Scrip.*" Mare said, like she was tasting the word. "Sounds a lot like *scrap.*"

∞

A group from St. Norbert decided to visit the office together, thinking they'd be safer that way. Clément took Julien and Fredie with him, leaving the women at home. Between Julien and Fredie, maybe he could understand the English documents better. Pierre joined them.

A long line of Métis men stood outside the fort's gates, which were being blocked by soldiers. They were too far back in the line to hear clearly, but it was obvious the soldiers were harassing the Métis for sport.

"Again with this," Pierre shook his head. At last, the line began to move and they were allowed inside. The guards, who perhaps recognized Julien and Pierre as being part of Riel's resistance, spat at them as they walked past.

"Be glad it was not worse. Ignore them," Clément said.

Julien's jaw pulsed and Clément worried that he'd lose his temper. But Julien stayed calm. Fredie looked from one man to the next, as if he was trying to gauge how he should behave. The boy was always excited to visit Winnipeg or the fort, but things were so different now, it probably wasn't the same for him.

An English man with a curled moustache and round spectacles waited for them at the desk. Guards stood at either side. Clément stepped forward. The clerk asked for his name and where he'd "resided." Clément asked what that meant and Julien said it meant where he'd lived. So Clément listed all the places he'd lived, including on the plains in his youth, the buffalo trail, everywhere he could remember.

"So you've had no permanent domicile in any location previous to the transfer?" the man asked, looking up from his papers.

"What the hell is a "domicile"?" Clément asked in Michif. Fredie shrugged his shoulders and Pierre looked confused.

"Damned if I know," Julien said. "Maybe he means mayzoon?"

"Speak English, please," the clerk said, frowning.

"I live in St. Norbert now," Clément said, guessing.

"Have you accepted the commutation of your Indian title?"

Here, all of them were lost. Fredie looked like he might cry. After confused looks among them, Clément shrugged. The clerk sighed and marked something on the page. He handed Clément a paper and told him to make his mark where he pointed and handed Clément his pen. He held it awkwardly in his hand, his fingers stiff. He marked an X and handed the pen and page back. The clerk wrote some more and handed him a paper where all he could recognize were the words "Dominion of Canada" at the top. The process was repeated for Pierre.

When they left, Clément said, "I didn't understand any of that." He felt like he'd been swindled but couldn't say how.

"It was confusing on purpose, just like Mamaa said," Julien said, angry. "None of this makes any sense and they're using their fancy talk to make it harder than it needs to be. I heard a lot of language like that at the fort, and it's tiring to listen to."

The guards gave them stern looks as they walked out of the office. Outside, men in suits called to all who left. One of them was Callum Wakefield. Clément waved at him in greeting, and he came right over.

"Well, if it isn't the Rougeaus," Callum said. "How nice to see you again." He held out his hand to Clément, who shook it warmly.

"How's business?" Clément asked.

"It's going well. I'm glad I saw you today. My father and I, our company, we're helping people manage their scrip. You have a lot to think about, and we can make things easier for you. You can have cash for that scrip, then you can buy the land of your choice, no need to worry about anything, we'll take care of everything for you."

Julien stepped in between them. "We could have gotten cash in there. We want the land," Julien said. "This doesn't concern you, Wakefield. Go bother someone else."

"Of course, of course," said Callum. "But remember, the offer stands. Come find us when you're ready."

They walked away and were approached by a couple of other men like Callum, looking to get their scrip.

"This is all one big racket," Pierre said. "And we're stuck in it."

When they got home, Clément told Marienne what it was like. "That Wakefield boy was waiting like a vulture to take scrip from people. There were lots more just like him. This whole thing feels wrong."

"We should have had a treaty," Marienne said, "not this piece-by-piece thing."

"This *is* our treaty."

"But we're not being treated like a people, like the nation we are. We've been split apart. Too many families are already drifting away. How long before we've all been blown off like seeds on the wind?"

∞

Clément fed the dogs with Fredie. "These shyins need to stay in shape, we can't have them getting fat and lazy all summer. We'll have the slowest carioles in Red River next winter if we're not careful."

"Let's hitch them to the little wagon; they always like that," Fredie said.

They harnessed the dogs, who yipped in delight when they saw the wagon come out. Fredie was in charge of the dogs' care now that he was older and thrived with the responsibility. He was eleven now, as tall as Clément's shoulders, and getting taller every week, it seemed. He was awkward and tripped like his feet were too big for his body. Clément was glad to see Fredie grow up. He would be an asset to their farm and might even find new ways to make money.

They let the dogs run ahead, the empty wagon rumbling along behind them. Clément and Fredie followed; Fredie whistled so they wouldn't go too far.

"St. Norbert feels so empty," Fredie said. They passed the Pelletier house, which stood lifeless, their once-lush garden gone to weed. They'd left last summer, saying they were going south, to Pembina, to live with family. "I miss them. Sometimes I think I see Madame Pelletier in the garden, but there's no one there."

"I miss them too," Clément said. "But it's not surprising they left, after those Orangistes beat William almost to death. It's sad."

"It's wrong. It's *all* wrong."

Clément put his arm around Fredie. "I think those dogs have run enough. Let's go home."

Fredie whistled and the dogs looped the wagon around and headed back. "When are we going to St. Paul again?"

"Probably not for a while. There isn't much work anymore."

Fredie looked disappointed. "What about going on the hunt? I heard the Flammands are going this summer."

Clément shook his head. "I don't think there's much to be gained by that. We'd probably have to go as far as Montana to find a herd, and any we find will be small. It's not worth the effort. Besides, I think it's better to stay close to home for now."

The dogs returned panting, their pink tongues lolling. They walked back home and they turned onto their lane as a small carriage pulled by a single horse pulled up. "Father Ritchot!" Fredie called and ran to meet him.

Clément wondered why the priest was visiting. "Father, it's good to see you," he said, as the priest climbed down from the carriage, smoothing the front of his cassock.

Father Ritchot smiled and patted him on the arm. He also bowed to Fredie and shook his hand.

"I want to talk to you about something," the priest said.

Clément invited him inside. They sat at the table, and the rest of the family joined them. Mare sat in her usual seat and Marienne busied herself making tea. Suzette and Charlotte sat next to Mare, while Julien leaned in the doorway. Marienne seemed a bit flustered by the priest's unexpected visit. Mare watched the bearded man with narrowed eyes.

"As you know, more settlers arrive all the time, and things are changing fast," the priest said. "We don't want to lose the community we've built here, so the church has been working to encourage settlers from Quebec to come, to balance out the new immigrants from Ontario. We want to ensure the French heritage is secure here."

"But isn't French protected? Isn't it an official language?" asked Marienne, as she placed a cup of tea in front of him.

He nodded. "Yes, but we think these steps are necessary, for the good of the community."

"What does this have to do with us?" Clément asked.

"The government has said there will be allotments for Métis children, so they'll get scrip too."

Charlotte leaned forward. "All children, girls and boys?"

"Yes, and it's a good time to stake claims for the children's allotments. The church is buying scrip to make new settlements south of here, along the Sale, Rat, and Roseau rivers."

"How many people are doing this?" Julien asked.

"Quite a few, from several different parishes. The Quebec settlers will join them too."

"We were expecting neighbours from Quebec for a while, but they never came," said Marienne.

"I think the events of the last couple of years have kept them away. All the uncertainty. But that's all been cleared away now, and we have an opportunity here." The priest gestured for more tea.

Julien sat down at the table. "We're supposed to have the right of first selection when it comes to land allotments, and our first choice is the lot we're on now."

The priest frowned. "Some of the families have already sold their lots to the church, to help us maintain our parishes."

Clément frowned. "It doesn't make sense to sell our lot here to the church and then start over somewhere else. This land suits us, we've worked it for years."

The priest sipped his tea. "You've heard the stories of cruelty and violence from the soldiers and the other Canadians. Some of them are squatting in Métis homes after they've removed the family first. It's happened in St. Vital and St. Boniface, and other areas. It won't be long before they make their way here."

Julien fumed. "They ransacked one house in St. Boniface and then used it as a latrine."

Marienne looked at Clément. "I told you things are getting worse."

"All the more reason to consider it," the priest said. "There's no guarantee you'll get to keep this lot. The rules have changed again, and you need to show habitation on this lot in July 1869. Not many people can do that."

"Our house has been here since Julien and Charlotte were small, and Suzette was a toddler. Everyone knows that." Marienne strained to keep the panic out of her voice, but she ended up sounding shrill.

"You don't have patent from the Hudson's Bay Company, so they may not recognize your title."

"But we did have patent!" Clément said.

The priest shook his head. "Your settlement here is à la façon du pays. But the church is here to help you." He finished his tea and then left for the next house.

"His mouth is full of sugar," Mare said. "We need to be careful there."

∞

Clément and Julien took their horses south to see what Father Ritchot was talking about. When they got to the Rivière Sale, Julien pointed out where he camped when he was working at la barrière. "That seems so long ago now," he said.

They found stakes in the ground marking out lots in the same seigneurial fashion as in St. Norbert and the other parishes. The landscape was similar to their own property, but with a few more trees and willows. It wouldn't take much to clear the land for gardens and crops. Clément crouched and sifted a handful of soil. It was dry, but workable.

"You could stake a claim here, build a life," he said to Julien.

"It looks like someone's marking a claim over there." Julien pointed to a couple of men in the distance. They were using surveyor's chains, but not in a way that matched the other stakes.

"It looks all wrong," Clément said.

"They're doing a grid system. It's the same thing as Petite Pointe des Chênes all over again. Nothing ever changes."

Clément didn't like hearing Julien sound so defeated. His son was in his prime and should be starting his own life. He remembered how he and Henri talked about the big freighting empire they were going to build. It used to make him smile, the dreams of boys. It used to be easy to goad him into a race or competition of any kind. That was all gone. Now he'd soured on nearly everything and it took nothing to raise his anger. Clément had hoped that this ride to explore the new communities would give him something to look forward to. He had to stop looking backward all the time. The past was a trap that would swallow him.

"Canadians think they can pick whatever land they want," Julien said. "They're going to cut us in half again. We're half-breeds but we shouldn't have half-rights."

"Maybe. But frying in your own grease isn't going to help anything," Clément said. "I'm tired of you moping around. All the drink, doing nothing to help your family. I won't listen to it anymore, and you're not welcome at home unless you turn yourself around. Go live with Pierre if you want, but don't bring this to our door anymore."

Julien stared at him. Clément wanted to hit or shake him. He'd never hit his children and didn't want to start now. But the feeling was there.

When they got home, Julien rode off without a word. Clément didn't know what to think, but since he hadn't packed any belongings, he figured he'd come back eventually.

"What happened?" Marienne asked.

"I told him he needed to smarten up and stop it with his moping. It's time for him to figure his life out. I guess he's not ready to hear that."

"Better to let him burn some anger off," she said.

"Let's hope anger is all he burns."

CHAPTER 25

Julien

August 1872

"I'm going west," Pierre said, and he played his cards—a winning hand. "You can come with me."

Julien folded and tossed his cards down. "Ah ben! You have cards up your sleeve or what?"

They were at Pierre's small log cabin. They'd been playing cards all afternoon, draining Pierre's stash of rum that he'd saved since Christmas. They used an empty crate as a table, which wobbled on the uneven dirt floor. Julien's head felt cloudy from the rum. He squinted in the dim cabin light.

"Where in the west?" Julien asked. "South of the line?"

"Some people are settling along the South Saskatchewan River. The country's nice there, lots of game, rolling hills."

"People from here?"

Pierre nodded. "Some. A few others too. But mostly people like us. Maybe out there, with some freedom, we can find a reason to jig again, eh?"

"I can't remember the last time I jigged. Or raced. Or did anything fun like that."

"That used to be your whole world."

"It is easy to be proud about winning a horse race when you don't know anything about the world." He gulped down the last of his rum. It burned his stomach and curdled there. Suddenly, he didn't want any more. He dropped the cup on the floor, where it landed with a soft thud.

"Hey, watch that. I only have two cups."

"You'll get new cups when you start your new life. You'll have new everything."

"Why do you sound so mad about that?"

Julien didn't have an answer. He stood up from his seat too fast, and the room shrank and expanded. He needed some air and to feel the sun on his face. As he stumbled out the door, the light stung his eyes, so he shaded them with his hand.

"Come back to the game," Pierre called from inside.

Julien waved him off and went to the riverbank. He fell-sat in the grass and rested his arms on his bent knees. He watched the water flow past. A fallen tree drifted by and got hung up on some bramble on the shore. It splashed in the current, tugging but not breaking free. He was that dead tree: caught up and going nowhere. He was tired of thrashing. He wanted to be unrestrained, but without a destination. Maybe he should float along with Pierre and go west. It was one decision he wouldn't have to make; Pierre could take care of everything. He was tired of thinking, remembering, and feeling useless. He went to the log to unsnag it. It would be a relief to watch it flow away, going all the way north through Lake Winnipeg and out to sea in Hudson Bay. As he waded into the water, his foot slipped on the muddy bottom and he fell in chest deep. The current was strong, and he felt himself being pulled away from the shore. When sober, Julien could swim well enough, but in his state, he couldn't control his limbs, he was like a limp octopus.

"Grab my hand!" Pierre had waded in and reached for him. Julien managed to make his way toward Pierre's outstretched hand and eventually grabbed hold. Pierre hauled him onto the shore where he lay in the grass, coughing.

"What the hell were you doing in the water?"

Julien sputtered. "A log was caught on the branch there; I wanted to free it."

"A log? That's enough drink for you, you can't handle it."

It was not like Pierre hadn't drunk as much as he had. Who was he to judge? But Julien didn't have the energy to argue. "I need to go home," he said.

"That's probably a good idea." Pierre went inside and slammed the door.

He lay on the ground until his clothes were mostly dry, then readied Julienne for the ride home. The once-bright ribbons tied to the saddle had faded and their ends were frayed. When was the last time he'd gotten new ribbons? It seemed pointless to dress his horse when there was no one to decorate for. Julienne nickered, as if chiding him for letting her get so shabby. "All right already," he said as he patted her neck.

Near home, he came across Charlotte and slowed down to match her stride.

"You look awful," she said.

He offered to help her up, to give her a ride, but she held her hand in front of her nose.

"You smell as bad as you look. When's the last time you washed your clothes—or even yourself?"

He shrugged, irritated. Now she was judging him too. "You don't look much better," he said. "Look at all that dust on your dress. Where've you been? Rolling around with Wakefield?"

Charlotte gave him a dirty look. "That's a mean thing to say."

"Relax, you know I'd never question your sacred virtue."

"Now you're being condescending. No, I wasn't with Callum. I haven't even seen any of them in months, as you well know. I was with Sarah."

"So you're getting information on Wakefield from her, then, since you can't get it direct."

"Sarah's my friend. I can't visit my friends now?"

"Don't get all worked up. Why is everybody fighting with me today?"

"Hmm, I wonder what the reason could be. You've been in a sulk for a long time now, growling at everyone. Why don't you figure yourself out—go away for a while or something. Maybe make some money."

"Funny you mention that. Pierre says he's going west to Saskatchewan. Wants me to go with him."

"Saskatchewan? Are you going? What's even out there, other than more forts?"

"There's a group of people going, quite a few. And it's mostly open country, that's what's good about it. None of the bullshit that's going on here. Florian's already gone there."

"I thought he was in exile with the rest of those government people."

Julien felt a twinge at that. With all the people he'd admired now scattered and gone, Red River seemed lifeless. It wasn't even Red River anymore, it was Manitoba now, and Winnipeg was growing. It was going to officially become a city. But to him, it was still empty.

"Some of them have been back in secret, you know," he said.

"And sometimes not so secretly," Charlotte said. "Riel walked around openly when those Irish Fenians wanted the Americans to invade last year. Raised a militia ready to fight them in no time. I'm surprised you didn't join them."

"I didn't learn about it until after," Julien snapped. "It happened so fast. But even with Canada's betrayal, he still protected this place."

"As soon as Archibald got what he wanted, though, Riel was back in exile."

"That five-thousand-dollar bounty is still on his head. He was here openly and no one turned him in, not even the English. I think that says something."

Charlotte looked up as a flock of geese honked overhead, heading south.

"When is Uncle Pierre leaving?"

"He said soon. He wants to get as far as he can before the snow. Maybe winter in Qu'Appelle, or wherever he ends up. He said it would be easier with someone else on the trail."

"You better decide soon. And if you go, Mamaa won't like it."

When they got home, Julien went to bed and woke the next day with a blistering headache. He couldn't stay in the house, with all the noise and cooking smells. He dunked his head in the rain barrel outside and washed up as best he could, pouring bucket after bucket over himself until he felt like a person again. He put on fresh clothes and decided to go see Henri, who'd settled back into his home life, putting all his energy into the farm. Henri was outside, pitching hay. He looked older, a lot like his father, with lines around his eyes.

"You've heard about the scrip for Métis children? The allotments? What are you going to do?" Julien asked.

Henri leaned his rake against the barn wall and wiped his hands on his trousers. "Father Ritchot came by. There's a lot of pressure to sell and go to these new locations."

"He came to see us, too. I went to see the ones along the Sale. A lot of stakes, but no building yet."

"My family is thinking about Roseau. We want to be further away from Winnipeg. Nothing good is happening there, and it will only get worse."

Julien agreed. "Uncle Pierre is going west, to Saskatchewan."

Henri didn't seem surprised. "I've heard that from a few people. I think there's a pretty big group going, some from St. Vital, some from St. Boniface. It's not a bad idea, but I want to be close to home. My parents won't leave, and I want to be there to help them."

Henri had always been loyal to his family, so Julien wasn't surprised. His sister Claudette would probably end up a spinster, so he'd have to take care of her, too. Henri would never put his own wants first.

"I'm thinking of going with him," Julien said.

Henri looked at him. "Your father won't like that. Why don't you join us in Roseau? We could be neighbours again, and a fresh start could only be a good thing. With people coming from Quebec, it will be easy to hide among them."

"What do you mean, hide? Like give up who you are? Speak only French and put away your sash? What good is that? Besides, the Quebec people will look down on us just like the English do."

"Not all the way. We go to the same churches and can speak the same language. It wouldn't be giving up so much."

"So that's why the priests are so interested in us moving there— they want us to become French only, nothing else."

"That's not fair. They're trying to help us keep what we have."

Julien felt his bile rise. Coming to see Henri had been a mistake. He should have known Henri would be too soft to stand for something. In the end, the Canadian soldiers didn't need to work so hard to split up the Métis—they could do it on their own. It was easy. How could their community be so fragile? It had always been so strong. And if it was so easy to fracture his people, shouldn't it be just as easy to do the same thing to another group? Perhaps he should turn things around and break up the Canadians. Why should his people be the only ones suffering? There was enough to go around.

He left Henri's place feeling more restless than before. No way would he put his sash away. Never. He might feel aimless, but at least he knew that much. He rode his horse hard, needing to feel the wind in his hair. He breathed hard, leaning into it. His headache faded and his mind cleared. He wouldn't take any more indignity. If the only way to stay in Red River was to bury his nature, what was the point? He couldn't do it. Wouldn't do it. His only choice was to go west. Perhaps then he could find some peace. But how long would it last? How long before the tentacles of Canada reached across the whole plains? He'd have to go west as far as west would go, and then what? Eventually he'd be right back where he started. South of the line probably wouldn't be any better, since destruction was happening there, too. North? How long before the same thing happened there? Maybe it was happening already. The continent was large, open, and should represent freedom, but instead it felt like a prison. He had nowhere and nothing. Exhausted, he slowed his horse and went home.

His father was smoking his pipe at the kitchen table. He inhaled deep and blew out a cloud that lingered. "So you going with him, or what?"

"Uncle Pierre told you?"

"Well, are you or not?" He put his pipe down and looked at him.

He wanted to say yes, but the words were stuck. Instead, he shrugged and looked away. "I don't want to go and I don't want to stay. Henri says they're going to Roseau."

"Why don't you do that? Could be a good thing."

"I don't want to think about it anymore. There's nothing ahead of me."

"You have to do something. I thought when you helped build the winter cabin, you'd turn this around, but no. All this playing cards and guzzling rum is making you act like what all those English accuse us of being. I don't want to be ashamed of you—but you're making it hard. Why don't you go shovel the muck out of the stables? Some hard work should fix you right up."

Julien grumbled but did as he was told. Shovelling shit was his life, no reason to expect anything different. And now he was smelly again. He shouldn't have bothered putting on clean clothes.

The corner of the barn held their saddles and equipment. He grabbed a brush and groomed Julienne, brushing her coat until it shone. As a child, he used to watch his father groom the horses alone in the barn, sneaking glances through the cracks between the boards. His father's face had a serene blankness in those moments. Julien used to wish he could make his father look like that when they were together, but he never could. He came close sometimes when they raced carioles, or sat by the fire on a carting trip, but not quite. His father had said it was his time to relax, and now Julien understood. The repetitive motion was just what he needed; it helped him think.

His reverie was interrupted by shouting outside.

"I told you, I never sold my land! Take your papers away, I will not touch them!"

His father's voice carried all the way to the barn. Julien dropped the brush and emerged from the barn to see his father standing in the lane, arguing with two men in black suits. One had a waxed mustache, and the other was clean-shaven, which was a shame, because a beard would have disguised the fact that the man had practically no chin. Their clothes looked expensive and their shoes shone, which was nearly impossible on these roads, where even the most delicate step raised a little cloud of dirt. The chinless man held a surveyor's chain, the long links folded up like an accordion and tucked under his arm. One link dangled loose and swung as the man gestured.

Julien knew what that chain meant. Even if his father hadn't been yelling, he knew those men meant no good. He ran over to them.

"What's going on?" he asked.

"These men say this land is theirs, they bought it. But I never sold it! Julien, go get the scrip from the house."

Julien ran inside to the kitchen table. His mother and Mare were shelling peas. He swept their bowls aside, knocking one over.

"Ah ben! Watch what you're doing!" his mother said, gathering the spilled peas. Julien lifted the centre board of the table, revealing a compartment underneath, where his father kept important papers and other valuables. He'd built the table so that when the cover was in place, it just looked like a regular seam between boards, with no hint of what was below. Julien rustled through the small pile of papers and found the scrip certificate. He snatched it and slammed the board back into place.

"What's all that yelling outside?" Mare asked.

"The same thing that happened two years ago," said Julien, "only now we have no Riel or anyone else."

He rushed out the door. His mother and Mare went with him, followed quickly by Charlotte, Suzette, and Fredie. When he reached his father and the men, he shoved the scrip certificate in their faces. "Here's our proof that this is our land. See, it says 'Dominion of Canada' right at the top."

The men barely glanced at it. "That paper means nothing. This one is the official document—notarized and authorized. We have every right to measure this land however we desire to."

"How can that be?" Clément asked, his voice rising. "We went to the lands office. This is what they gave us!"

"Disputes between actual settlers like us and squatters like you will need to be handled by the local militia. Is that what you want?"

His father sagged. Julien could see he felt beaten. He'd never have that serene look on his face ever again. The man with the moustache gestured toward Charlotte and Suzette. "Perhaps we can make another arrangement," he laughed.

His mother stared in shock. Suzette and Charlotte made sounds of disgust. Julien's vision darkened and he lost all sense. Time seemed to slow down. He seized the chain from the man's arm, unfolded a length, and swung it wide like he was roping a calf. The men took a couple of steps backward.

"Come now, we're just talking here," the man with the moustache said.

Julien tilted his head to the side, swung the chain in an arc, and cracked it against the man's head. He fell back into the dirt with a yelp, clutching his face. At least now he'd have some proper dust on him, Julien thought.

"You barbarians!" the other man cried. "You all need to be put down like dogs."

He knelt down to check on his friend and help him up. The skin on the man's cheek had split and was bleeding heavily. He held his hand to his face and the blood seeped through his fingers. His waxed moustache hadn't moved, though, its curl still perfect. He moaned in pain and sputtered, as if he was trying to talk, but it was unintelligible.

Clément snapped into action. "Fredie, run to the Flammands, tell them to get Pierre, now!" Fredie ran at full speed without looking back.

The two men shuffled their way to the covered carriage that waited on the road. With its leather seats and oilcloth cover, it looked as out of place as the men's shiny shoes.

"You'll pay for this!" the chinless man shouted.

They climbed in awkwardly and rode away, fast.

Once the carriage was out of view, the family rushed to Julien.

"How did they have papers like that?" Marienne asked. "They can't be real, can they?"

"I remember Martin saying there are public lists of allottees—all the names of every Métis, from their census. The land speculators get someone to come in and pretend to be a person from the list, and they steal scrip," Julien said. "It's easy, they just get someone to mark an X and the lands office signs it all away."

His heart was still racing, but he no longer felt blind rage. His breathing was returning to normal. The rush of violence brought clarity for him—he had a purpose again.

"I heard something about this," Charlotte said, talking fast. "Sarah said she heard Mr. Wakefield say the lands office has fixed it so that no one can investigate fraud. You can't even report it. She didn't really understand what it meant, but now it makes sense. That's what Callum meant when he said land speculation was a better business. 'Fewer regulations' he said."

"More like no regulations," Clément glowered. "They can make more money, faster. Off of us."

"You think the Wakefields were part of these men showing up here?" Marienne asked, looking at Charlotte.

"It's possible," she said.

"I wouldn't be surprised," Julien said. "We all saw Callum at the fort, waiting outside the land office like a buzzard. Everyone I talked to said he approached them, too."

His father held him by the shoulders, locking eyes with him. "They will come after you for this. They'll probably kill you."

Julien nodded and hung his head. "I have no choice now—I have to go west."

"You have to go tonight. You can't wait. And don't stop until your horse won't go anymore. The constables may chase you. Your path only has one direction now. Son, this has sealed your fate."

Julien embraced his father and held him tight. "I know. I know what I've done comes with a cost." He let go of his father and looked at his mother, his sisters—*This may be the last time I ever see them.* "I guess I just decided it was worth the price."

CHAPTER 26

Marienne

September 1872

Marienne hung Julien's blanket on the line to dry. After he'd left, she washed the sheets and blankets. She wanted things clean, fresh. The blanket snapped in the wind, hitting her in the face. It smelled clean, but wrong. Julien's scent was gone, just like he was, and in her heart, Marienne knew she would never see her son again. She kept thinking she heard his footsteps on the stairs or heard him whistling at his horse. Sometimes she thought she caught glimpses of him, but as a small child, sneaking around corners. She knew his thoughts when he was small. She realized she didn't really know him now, as a man. Now she'd never get the chance.

Every day since the chain slap, Marienne and the rest of the family had been tense, jumping at every horse and wagon that rode past, fully expecting soldiers to swarm their house and force them out. But days went by and nothing happened. Denise had visited to check on them, since the news had spread quickly.

"Don't worry," she'd said. "No one is saying anything about where Julien and Pierre have gone. Everyone is acting as though they'd never existed. But no one is really asking."

"Doesn't that seem strange?" Marienne asked.

"No stranger than any of the other goings-on lately. Nothing makes sense anymore."

When they were starting to relax and pick up their regular rhythms, Charlotte shattered things anew. She was in the sitting room with Marienne and Mare, sewing. Clément was resting in his chair with his eyes closed, but still awake.

"Papaa, I've found work as a dressmaker."

Clément's eyes remained closed. "That's good, ma bibiche. See, that sewing machine was a good investment."

"Sarah told me about a new dress shop in Winnipeg, and how the owner was looking for help. So I went with her last week when she went to work at the Wakefields' and met with the shop owner, Mrs. Lambton. She said she'd hire me and I can board there, above the shop. I'll also do some housekeeping in exchange for lodging."

His eyes snapped open. Charlotte sat tall with her shoulders back, braced for an angry lecture. Marienne set her embroidery down and looked at Charlotte, her expression stern. She was struck by how much Charlotte resembled Mare.

"You snuck off to Winnipeg?" Marienne said, her voice shrill. "You know it's not safe there. You cannot take that job; I won't allow it." She had already lost her oldest, and now her second was going too? What would be next?

"Please, Mamaa. With so many new people there, I can blend in. It's a good opportunity and we need the money." She looked at her father. "Let me take it."

"I thought you'd be making moccasins for someone by now," Clément said. "Henri, or even that Wakefield boy, although there's no way I'd approve."

Charlotte bristled. "How could you think I'd consider Callum after what his family has done, and not just to us. Besides, I'm not something to barter away. If you love me like you say you do, you'll let me do this."

"But you *should* be getting married, not getting started on the spinster's life already," said Clément. "You know you'd have your choice of suitors. Even an English husband, if you could find a good one."

Marienne wondered about this. Charlotte had mooned over Callum, but she had soured on him before the land and scrip business. She'd tried to ask Charlotte about it, but her daughter had changed the subject.

"I'll go with or without your permission, but I'd rather have it," Charlotte said now.

Marienne panicked. "It's impossible! Why would you want to go there of all places? You're not going, that's final."

Charlotte glared at her. She pulled a length of thread from the spool and cut it with the ulu in mid-air, while maintaining eye contact with Marienne. But in her anger and haste, she sliced the base of her thumb. She yelped in pain and dropped the knife. When it hit the floor, the knife's wooden handle broke off. Charlotte squeezed her wounded hand, trying to staunch the bleeding, but some dripped to the floor and onto the knife.

Mare gasped and looked like she would fall off her chair. Marienne leapt to Charlotte. "Let me see," she reached for Charlotte's hand. A clean slice revealed a purplish layer beneath the skin's surface. She wrapped her hand around Charlotte's. "It's deep, we need to clean it, follow me." She led her to the kitchen and cleaned it as best she could.

"Ow!" Charlotte hissed at the sting.

Marienne bound Charlotte's hand with a clean strip of cloth, tight. "Keep your hand raised, so it doesn't swell too badly." Charlotte nodded.

They returned to the sitting room to find Mare on the floor whispering to the knife. Clément knelt beside her like he wanted to help but was afraid to speak.

"All this friction in the house is what caused the knife to break," Mare said, her voice strained.

"Maman," Clément placed his hand on his mother's back, "the knife was old, older than your mother and her mother—that handle was going to break at some point. It just needs to be repaired."

She whirled on him. "You don't understand! It's the worst kind of luck for this knife to break. The worst! That's what my mother told me, and she made me swear to protect it. And I failed." She cried softly.

Marienne couldn't think of a single time she'd seen Mare weep. Mare, who had always been outwardly calm to the point of being stoic, was now falling apart. It was unsettling. It made her want to leap into action and find a way to make everyone feel better. But she had no idea how, and if she were honest with herself, she was too tired to even try. Let Clément tend to his mother. Let him take up the slack for once.

Charlotte was rigid and seemed afraid to go to Mare or to touch the knife. As if it were alive and hungry for more.

"Charlotte, go upstairs and rest," Marienne said, "I'll bring you some willow tea. Suzette, go put the kettle on. Fredie, help her get the willow."

Suzette and Fredie looked at her.

"Now, please."

They ran to the kitchen.

She turned to Mare and Clément, who were still on the floor. "Get a hold of yourselves. It's a knife, nothing more, and it can be repaired. Get up."

Clément rose and helped Mare up. They stood like a pair of scolded children.

"Marienne—" Clément began, but she cut him off.

"Clément, go see if you can re-attach the handle. Mare, sit down and we'll bring you some tea. Everything will be fine, you'll see. Charlotte is not taking that job. She stays here, and next week we are going to get the ginseng like we always do. It should be a good harvest with the weather we had, and the coughing season will be here soon, so we'll need all we can get. And now we'll also need it for Charlotte's hand."

Clément looked stunned, then did as he was told. Mare, who

would normally offer some quip or withering glance, kept her head down and sank back in her chair. Suzette came in with tea for Mare and Fredie followed behind with a cup for Charlotte. He climbed the stairs slowly, being careful not to spill. Marienne left the house and went to the river. She could see light from a lantern in the barn, where Clément was rummaging around, trying to fix the knife. She sat on her favourite stump by the river and watched the moonlight dance on the water. She wished Julien could have seen her just now. He would have said she was almost as good a soldier as he'd been. She wondered where he was now. Was he sitting by a fire looking up at the moon, too? Did he miss his home, did he wish he was with his family? She wasn't prepared for the ache of his loss. It was like he'd died. She was numb.

∞

For the next few days, the family was careful around her, trying to gauge her mood. She kind of liked them being wary of her. It was nice. She should be unpredictable more often. Charlotte couldn't do much of the housework, with her bandaged hand, but for once, she didn't seem happy about skipping work. Marienne supposed it was a mixture of pain and disappointment about the dressmaker job. Marienne shrugged; Charlotte would get over it. The sooner she learned those lessons, the better.

The family packed up their cart and went to the forests near Lac Manitobah, where she remembered picking ginseng as a girl. It was a special spot she told no one else about, not even Denise, who had long forgotten about it. She was right about the season being a good one for harvesting and tried to cheer Mare up by saying so. Mare didn't brighten, but did at least reply dryly, which was better than her silence.

"The jiisens ojiibikan is good, like I said, see?" said Marienne.

"It's thin, but not too bad."

And so tensions eased up. They were having a meal break and

enjoying the sunny afternoon when Charlotte spoke up. "I haven't seen any fire lilies around, not one."

"They're better in July," Marienne replied.

Mare perked up. "There should still be a few somewhere."

"The forest is big. They probably aren't in this spot." Marienne was dismissive.

Charlotte and Mare didn't seem satisfied with that answer.

"Still, it's strange," Clément said. "We should have seen at least one."

"I wish we'd find one," said Charlotte. "It's not right to be in bush like this and not find any. It's a bad omen."

Charlotte rubbed her bandaged hand. Marienne watched her daughter with narrowed eyes.

That night, Marienne and Clément stayed up by the fire after everyone else had gone to sleep. She couldn't remember the last time they'd had a real talk. "I think we should let bibiche go to that job," he said. "She will only become more miserable than she already is if she stays. You've heard her talk about omens, she's sounding like Mare. She needs a change—it will be better for her."

Marienne couldn't argue with that but tried anyway. "I just don't like it. Soon Winnipeg will be like the big cities of Ontario and Quebec. Those new buildings that are going up are too tall and they block out the sun. I heard one of them will be taller than the cathedral. Can you imagine? What kind of place will it be then?"

"Maybe it won't be a place for us anymore. Maybe it will. This land is our home, but we're not tied to one piece of it. It's good to remember that. We should be glad that we're not penned in on a reserve like the Cree and the others."

Marienne was surprised to hear her husband talk like this. "What are you saying? Do you want to follow Julien and Pierre?"

"I don't know. I know you miss Julien; I miss him too. But if we follow him, we could be putting him at risk."

"You're right. It's safer to leave him be for now. Maybe we can find him again one day."

"Nothing is forever, Marienne, you know this. Charlotte will be all right. We raised her well. And Fredie and Suzette will find their way too."

That night, Marienne had a restful sleep. She felt the glimmer of being at peace with Julien and Charlotte leaving. Things would be all right; they would work out the way they always did.

∞

She saw the smoke in the distance and she knew.

It was late afternoon and they were almost home from their harvesting trip. "Look!" Marienne pointed ahead. "That's our place."

Clément snapped the reins to spur the horses on, but pulling the loaded cart, they couldn't go much faster. Marienne wanted to leap down and run, anxious to see what she feared.

"Maybe it isn't our place, maybe someone is burning hay."

"A hay fire doesn't look like that. Go faster."

Their property came into view. Or what was left of it.

Where their house should be was a pile of smoking rubble. The only things standing were the cast iron stove where the kitchen used to be, and the stone chimney. The air was hot and acrid, and the horses reared back. Clément pulled them to a stop and Mare wailed.

Clément climbed down and ran to the pile of rubble. Marienne followed and went cold. Some beams had fallen down but were burnt only part way. She could still see the grooves where Clément had planed them smooth. Memories of building the house rushed forward: Charlotte and Julien stripping bark off logs, sheltering in tents during rainstorms, Suzette waddling about and scared when a skinny coyote hung around, sniffing their fire. How Mare had chased it away by yelling at it in her language. Julien beside her throwing rocks at it. How they dug the well and used a gravity system for the first few years, until she insisted on erecting a pulley like Denise and Robert had. Filling the bucket with bottles of milk and squares of butter and lowering it down the well to keep them cool. She looked to the well now—it still stood, untouched by the fire. She went to it and raised the bucket, but the butter she'd left behind was gone. At least they wouldn't need to drink river water, which was now full of pollution from the steamships.

Clément poked around the fallen beams, looking for anything that survived the fire. Suzette and Charlotte skirted the edge, lifting the odd scrap to examine it before tossing it back down. Mare went to what used to be the kitchen and sifted in the rubble. She picked up the copper tea kettle, which was black with soot, but held its shape.

"I think we can save it," she said.

"I found the sewing machine!" Suzette called, kicking over some rubble. "Can we fix it?"

"We'll try," Clément called back. "Dig it out."

Suzette and Charlotte started to clear the rubble away when Fredie screamed.

He'd gone to the dog pen. Marienne left the well and ran to him, and the others followed. What they found there was worse than the house. All the dogs had been shot dead. They lay piled up like old rags. Their fur was matted with dried blood and a cloud of flies buzzed around them. Fredie sank to his knees and cried. His whole body shook with each sob.

"Why the dogs?" he cried. "What did they ever do to anyone?"

Marienne knelt beside him and held him, trying to absorb his pain and sorrow.

"It was those men," Clément said, his voice shaking. "They couldn't get Julien, so they took it out on us."

"Thank goodness we still have the horses and the cart," Marienne said, trying to sound positive.

"What's in that cart is all that's left of us, now," Charlotte said, wiping her eyes. "There's nothing else."

"Why would those men need to destroy our house and ruin us when they can use paper and systems to take it from us?" Suzette said. "They had the papers in their hands. Why do this?"

"It's revenge for Julien," Charlotte said. "Men like that take insults to the extreme. If we'd been here, they would have killed us instead of the dogs."

"Charlotte!" Marienne scolded. "You're scaring Fredie and Suzette!"

"Tell me it isn't true, then."

Clément shook his head. "Bibiche is right. They probably were watching us and waited until we were gone, but it's good that we were away for this. If they didn't kill us, they would have made us watch as they burned the house and killed the dogs. They probably took the cows. And they would have beaten us. Or worse."

He glanced at Charlotte and Suzette, then Marienne. She took his meaning.

Mare pointed behind them. "The barn still stands."

They made their way toward it. "I wonder why they left it?" Marienne said.

"They'll probably find it useful when they take the land," Clément said. "Our house was useless to them, so it would have to come down anyway, no doubt."

Inside the barn was dim, but they could see that everything in there seemed untouched, including their old pad saddles and farm tools.

"Oh!" Charlotte breathed.

On the workbench, something shiny caught the light. She went to it and lifted the ulu knife, with its new handle. She held it up for all to see and Mare covered her mouth. Marienne looked at Clément, who looked sick.

"I hadn't fixed it yet," he said. "I don't know how that's possible."

Charlotte gingerly handled the knife and said, "Mare, this should go back to you."

"No," said Mare, turning it over in her hands. "Your blood paid for it. It belongs to you without question now. Take it."

Charlotte opened the pouch that still hung from her belt, and placed the knife inside as if she was afraid to touch it. She patted the pouch once the drawstring was tight and took a deep breath, accepting that it was hers.

Marienne didn't understand. The knife should still be broken. Who fixed it? Mare would say the little people protected it and brought it back to life, but Marienne didn't want to hear that. There had to be a reason, but the others didn't want to discuss it. She pushed the thought aside, but it nagged her.

"We should make camp for tonight," she said, "but we can't stay here long. Those men may come back."

Clément agreed. They moved the cart near the barn. Fredie tended to the horses, seeming to find some comfort in that.

"We can't leave until we bury the dogs," Fredie said.

No one argued with him, because the dogs were special to all of them. They were work animals, but also close companions. It would be a sign of disrespect to leave them to rot in the sun, no matter how satisfying it would be to leave a mess for the invaders.

They huddled together in the barn that night. "Is this a good idea, all of us being together in one spot like this?" Suzette asked.

"For tonight it should be fine, but I'll keep watch," Clément said, hugging her.

No one slept. Marienne was next to Charlotte.

"You should take that dressmaker job after all, if you still want to," she said.

Charlotte was surprised. "Are you sure? I thought this would make you even more against it."

"We have no home anymore. You have a promise of lodging and a way to earn money. That's more important. And you're right; you can blend in there, more than any of us can. It's the right thing."

Charlotte cried. "Maarsi, Mamaa."

"You only have one dress now, but you can make more in your shop, eh?" Marienne wiped a tear. "And you have your beading supplies; it's good you kept them with you."

"But our wall pockets are gone! Everything is gone!"

"You'll make more, for the next réveillon, maybe."

"I can't even think about that now," Charlotte said. "I can't imagine ever being happy again."

Mare sat up to join them. "Be careful there, bibiche," she said. "Don't fall into dark thinking. Hopeless thoughts are always lurking, and they get bold in times like these. Don't invite them in."

"Yes, Mare," Charlotte said, her voice subdued.

"And when you get to Winnipeg, be even more careful," Mare said. "It has grown too big. There's no quiet place anymore to hear the wind in the leaves, the birds singing. It's all noise to stop you from thinking. This place isn't Red River anymore, it's Dead River."

Everyone went silent at that. Marienne tried to sleep, but her thoughts turned round and round. She didn't think she'd slept at all until the sunlight startled her awake. Clément was already up and packing all he could salvage into the cart. She joined him.

"Where will we go?" she asked.

"We can go to Pierre's place for a few days, maybe. Then we have to figure something out. We can't stay, though, that's for sure."

"I wish there was time to see Denise one more time."

"It's probably better if she doesn't know where we've gone, at least for now. We can send word later, when we know it's safe. This doesn't mean we're gone forever—who knows what the future holds. Maybe things will turn around. Maybe not for us, but for Fredie and Suzette. Their futures could still be bright."

"Let's worry about right now before we start dreaming big about the future."

She found Fredie digging a grave for the dogs, using all his force to stab the spade into the hard ground. "Let me help you," she said and found a pick to help break the ground up.

"I should bury this, too," Fredie said, pointing at the sash around his waist.

"Don't say that. Never be ashamed of who you are." She put the pick down and looked at him. "We are like the sash, woven together from different peoples and traditions, making something new, beautiful, and strong. You should wear your saencheur flayshii proudly. Always honour who you are and where you come from, no matter what anyone says."

Fredie looked embarrassed. He continued digging, more slowly this time, and Marienne resumed with the pick. Others came to help, and soon they were able to bury the dogs. Fredie cried when the last shovelful of dirt fell on them. Marienne wanted to rip the arms off the men who made her baby cry.

Exhausted, they sat in the shade of a large elm tree. "How are we going to get Charlotte safely to Winnipeg?" Marienne asked.

Clément was about to answer, but Charlotte interrupted. "I can go to Sarah's, then travel to the city with her when she goes to work at the Wakefields'."

"We'll drop you there on our way."

"On our way to where?" Marienne asked.

Mare spoke up. "I want to go home, to the bush. It's the best place to heal and start over. The smell of tamarack and pine will do wonders. We should go to the winter cabin."

Marienne thought about it. It made sense. The cabin was built well enough to survive the winter, but they'd have to do some work to make it livable. It would be cramped, but it was better than nothing. And no one would come looking for them there. They could start over and be truly free. "What about the children's scrip? Should we try for that? Join Henri's family in Roseau?"

Clément scoffed. "That scrip is probably long gone. You saw how easy it is to get fake documents. Probably Henri's will disappear, too. We'll all have to go to the bush, or west like Julien and Pierre."

"So it's decided, then," Mare said. "We go to Pierre's and salvage anything he left there, then go to the cabin."

They set off. When they got to Sarah's place, Charlotte hugged everyone and tried to keep from crying. Marienne stayed strong to keep Charlotte from falling apart. "Be strong, Charlotte, and keep hope."

Charlotte wiped her eyes with her sleeve. "Why? It's killing us. I don't ever want to cling to hope again. Hope is disappointment. Hope is death."

Marienne grasped her hand. "You're too young to have such feelings."

Mare interrupted. "She might as well learn early."

Marienne shot her a sharp look. She yanked the end of Fredie's sash. "Look at the yarn." She tore off one strand. "Alone it can break, but woven together it's strong—strong enough to carry heavy weight. You're going off alone now, but you're never really alone. Our strands are with you. Do you understand? There is happiness in this life. There is love to be found in this world. Home is not just on this land. You carry it in you."

Charlotte took her words in and nodded once. Then she made her way up the road to Sarah's place. She turned and waved good-bye, her hand limp.

As they rode away, Marienne wondered what kind of life they could have in the bush, with no school, no church, no community. They'd be reduced to living like animals, scraping by. Her mind returned to all she'd learned as a child, how they'd survived without access to a fort store, when they'd done nearly everything using tools they could make themselves. She remembered how to pound bulrushes to make flour; the galettes made from them weren't bad. In fact, she could taste them still. She smiled.

After staying at Pierre's place, they decided to stop at Petite Pointe des Chênes and stay with the Fletts before continuing on. They could relay word of their fate there, and the news would travel. She wanted to laugh at the irony of going to the place where this all started, when Florian rode up that spring day to tell them about the surveyors, worried they'd measure their home, divide it up, and take it away. *Despite everything, that is what they have done.*

She looked back to the home she'd known for the last dozen years. She realized their choices were just a mirage. Not much was really up to them, in the end. They'd survive, or they wouldn't. All they could do was try.

CHAPTER 27

Charlotte

April 1873

Charlotte's foot bobbed up and down on the sewing machine's treadle.

Starting work at the dressmaker shop on Main Street and settling into her new lodgings above the shop hadn't been easy. She wanted to be excited about living in such a buzzing, growing place, but all she could think about was the sound of the river and the night sky she used to stare at through her bedroom window. Now that window was gone, the room was gone, and it seemed like the sky was gone too. She could see it from her new room, but the window was small and the view was blocked by a neighbouring building. She could only see a small slice, and it seemed like a different sky altogether. She felt the same way about the river. There were no trees along the shore here, only grasses and sparse shrubs. Chunks of soil broke off and fell into the water, especially during the spring melt. Erosion was swift when there was nothing left to anchor the earth in place.

"Charlotte, the silk we've ordered has arrived," said Mrs. Rosalie Lambton, the owner of Lambton's, where Charlotte now worked. Everything about Mrs. Lambton was brisk: her English accent was clipped and her movements were efficient. She could manage several tasks at once and make it seem effortless. But when she spoke with a customer, she exuded a helpful calm and gave them her undivided attention. She was a widow from London who'd always craved adventure, so when her husband died and left her with an inheritance, she came to "the newest part of the newest country" and settled in Winnipeg. She was a formidable woman disguised by a gentle exterior. "Finish up here, but I want you to sort the silk soon."

Charlotte paused her sewing to look up. "Yes, ma'am."

She waited until Mrs. Lambton walked away before resuming her stitching. Once interrupted, the rhythm she had with the foot treadle and feeding the fabric through the machine was lost. She wished she could keep her focus on the machine like Suzette always could. It took a few moments to find it again, which made her anxious, because Mrs. Lambton expected her to work quickly. Normally she could work at that pace, but the better she performed, the more Mrs. Lambton expected. She found herself longing for the old chores she did at home, which she used to find such a burden. Scrubbing laundry or hauling buckets seemed like pleasant pastimes now. She could only imagine what her mother would say about that.

In the back room, Charlotte found the crates of silk. The bolts were wrapped in a rough cotton, similar to flour sacking. She carefully ripped the stitches so she could keep the cotton for herself, rough as it was. The silk was wrapped around flat bolts, instead of the usual round ones. She ran her hand across the smooth surface, relishing the sensation. This silk came from France, even though good silk was available from the United States. Mrs. Lambton insisted on French silk for her best customers. "People want their fashions from the old world, not the new," she'd said. "New world fashion is unsure of itself. Maybe one day the trends will flow the other way, but not anytime soon."

Charlotte could see the wisdom in that. Fashion in Red River was certainly years behind anything in Europe, plus there wasn't access to the same fabrics and other materials, so local fashion would never set trends. How could it?

The silk was in soft colours: white, ash pink, robin's egg blue, and a pale yellow. Such light colours were unusual, and frankly impractical, for Red River. Dresses usually came in a blend of darker colours that would better hide stained hems. Charlotte shrugged; Rosalie Lambton must know what she was doing, buying colours like that—she hadn't erred yet. The white was particularly striking. She'd never seen such crisp, pristine white, ever. It had to be for trims and accents; no one could possibly want a dress that was full white. Such a dress could only be worn once, if that.

Life at the shop kept her busy, which was a good thing because it gave her little time to dwell on her loneliness. This was another irony she hadn't expected: missing her family. Now that they were gone, she wished she could hear Suzette and Fredie argue, or even her mother's scolding. Sarah stopped by when she could, but her visits were few. It was easy to disappear into the city's crowds, but Sarah, with her dark skin and hair, stood out, and the reign of terror they'd lived through after Wolseley and his soldiers arrived had left its mark. Her people had become subdued, smaller. But they had survived. Whenever Charlotte did venture out, she'd catch the eye of someone she knew from St. Norbert and they'd give each other a slight nod of acknowledgement, but nothing else. Those moments were small comforts, which she tallied up and savoured.

She saw Martin once, and he'd said he was going west to join Julien. More and more people left when their homes were swallowed up by new immigrants. She'd thought maybe Sarah and Martin would marry, since they seemed to have formed a connection, but it didn't take. Sarah mentioned how disappointed she was, and Charlotte assured her she'd find a good husband soon. She suggested Henri as a possibility, but Sarah waved that idea away. "Hyacinthe has had her eye on him since we were small. Let her have him."

Charlotte still looked for Callum on the streets, but only saw him once. She learned through Sarah that his family had set up their business in one of the new brick buildings on Main Street, not far from their Point Douglas home. The dress shop was at the opposite end of the thoroughfare, so the chances of seeing him were few. But a few months ago, when the winter was deep, she saw him walking with some men, engrossed in conversation. He wore his felt coat with the brass buttons on the martingale that she'd been so fascinated by at Midnight Mass all those years ago. Now the streets were full of men in coats like that. But those buttons drew her eye again, and they gave her an idea—she could incorporate a martingale like that at the top of a bustle on the back of a dress. It would securely hold the gathered fabric in place and add structure. In the shop, she had access to all kinds of scrap fabric, plus plain cotton they used to test new designs. She sketched out her idea by lamplight in the wee hours and collected spare fabric that was nice enough for an everyday dress but inexpensive enough to not be missed. She worked on her idea before bed. She sacrificed sleep for it. Between her shop hours and the housework, she had little energy left. But the idea had hold of her, and she turned it over in her mind as she worked.

She also fulfilled one of her dreams: she bought a pair of heeled lace-up English boots. It took four months to save up the money. Although the leather was soft, the boots were uncomfortable, hard to walk in, and completely impractical for the muddy streets. But they clicked on the floor when she walked, and she loved them. She packed her moccasins away.

She wore her hair up the way Alyce did—no more long braids down her back. She blended in well with the new immigrants until she spoke and her French accent came through. She tried to suppress it, but it was impossible.

When she lay in her bed at night, she watched for the moon to pass through her tiny sliver of sky, and she planned her future. She knew it wouldn't be in Red River. There was nothing for her here, even if Winnipeg were becoming more cosmopolitan every day. She was too well-known as Métis, and that stigma would hold her back. She'd always be a half-person here. She decided her future was east,

Toronto, she thought at first, but soon realized she'd stand out there, too. She didn't want to be surrounded by a bunch of French-hating Orangemen. So she settled on Montreal. She'd stick out less there, and her French, taught by nuns, was good. She could easily drop the Michif. In fact, she'd worked hard to not blend languages in one sentence as so many other people did. If the conversation was in French, she spoke only French. She was rigid about it.

Her plan was to save every penny, stay in the dress shop and, when she had enough savings, buy a train ticket and leave for good. The idea gave her comfort. She played the scenario over each night. She couldn't fall asleep until she heard the train whistle in her mind. She knew the railroad to Winnipeg was being built and one day there would be a train station right on Main Street, but that was still years away and she didn't want to wait that long. She'd have to go by stagecoach to St. Paul and catch the train there. She considered the steamship instead, but passage to St. Paul from Winnipeg was too expensive. The stagecoach would do.

She was working on the sewing machine as usual, when Mrs. Lambton called her to the front of the shop. When she got there, she was shocked to see Alyce, Mrs. Wakefield, and a third woman who looked to be close to her own age, with blond hair that was almost white, and blue eyes. Her thin neck poked out from her dress and looked like a twig that would snap in a strong wind.

"Well, if it isn't Charlotte!" Mrs. Wakefield exclaimed, feigning excitement at seeing her, which Charlotte could clearly see was not genuine.

"Oh! Charlotte, how nice to see you," Alyce said. She seemed unsettled by Charlotte's presence, but soon remembered her manners. "This is Elissa, Callum's fiancée."

Charlotte stopped cold. Of course Callum would be engaged. It was actually surprising he wasn't already married. But perhaps he'd been too focused on business. Mrs. Wakefield probably went shopping for a bride for him along with all her trinkets on her yearly Toronto trip.

"How nice to make your acquaintance," Charlotte managed to keep her smile and tone bland. She was already learning from her employer. Elissa smiled and said hello.

"Charlotte, please take measurements for Elissa," Mrs. Lambton said. "We'll be preparing her bridal gown."

"Of course." Charlotte removed the measuring tape from around her neck. "Please, come this way."

The three followed Charlotte to a private area separated from the main shop where Elissa stood on a small platform in front of a trifold mirror. Charlotte took her measurements. She didn't realize she'd been holding her breath until her ribs hurt. She said as little as possible and avoided looking at Elissa's face. Charlotte was sure she wouldn't be able to hide her emotions if she had to look her in the eye. She focused on the task, noticing how small Elissa's wrists were and how pronounced her collarbone was. She measured everything, including the circumference of Elissa's arms, which were nearly as small as her wrists. Charlotte glanced at her own arms in comparison. Hers were bigger, with muscle from a lifetime of physical labour. Elissa's silhouette was perfectly suited to the new style of dresses, with their cinched corsets and snug sleeves. Even if Charlotte did nothing but sit on a settee all day, she'd never have arms as thin as Elissa's. One more example of how this world wasn't for her.

"Charlotte dear, it's so nice you've found a place for yourself, something apt," Mrs. Wakefield said, sweetly.

Charlotte gave a thin smile in response and continued measuring.

"I'm not surprised," Alyce said. "Charlotte was always so good at anything with a needle."

Charlotte sensed no malice in her comment and felt relieved. "Thank you, Alyce."

Mrs. Lambton came to collect the measurements and led the group away to her office where she went over the design proposals. Charlotte returned to her work on the sewing machine. After they were gone, she instructed, "Charlotte, put the white silk aside; I think we'll need all of it for this order."

"All of it?" Charlotte couldn't keep the surprise out of her voice.

Mrs. Lambton nodded. "This bride wants the latest thing, something that hasn't caught on here yet, and honestly, it might never catch on, but we can hope. She wants an all-white gown, with an extra-full bustle with an additional crinoline layer. The only embellishment will be in embroidery along the hem, cuffs, and neckline, also all in white—that's where your skills will come in."

Charlotte could imagine the dress. It would be stunning; the white silk would glow. "The bustle will be heavy with all that silk," she said. "There will need to be something done to keep it in place."

"I have some ideas about that; we'll also have trouble securing whalebone for a custom corset. It's become much more expensive, and even if we managed to find some at a good price, it will likely not arrive in time."

Charlotte had rarely worked with boning, having never encountered it until working at Lambton's. No one she knew wore a corset; it would restrict movement too much for daily chores, and no one wearing a corset could jump on a horse and shoot a buffalo. But the undergarment was necessary for the style of dresses people like Alyce and Elissa wore. Charlotte supposed that was the price for wearing something so beautiful—it turned the wearer into a decoration, an object. Charlotte had once tried on a corset and matching dress and found it hard to breathe. She also couldn't bend low enough to lace up her boots. Getting dressed in a garment like that was a two-person process, and she'd never have someone to help her, so she put the idea away.

"Perhaps we can find a substitute for the whalebone," Charlotte said. "We used the roots from black spruce trees as lashing for birch-bark baskets and canoes. It's sturdy and flexible. Maybe that could work?"

"This is why I took you on, Charlotte. You have such creative solutions! Please try using the spruce. If it works, it could be a new revenue stream for us."

Charlotte agreed to try, but then didn't know how she could do it. Harvesting the roots was best in spring and fall, and spring had already begun. Once harvested, the coils of roots had to be boiled for a whole day and then stripped of their bark. When would she have time for that? She wished she could ask for Mare's help. She probably would have a supply already, now that they were living in the bush, with spruce all around them. She felt another ache for her family.

She felt overwhelmed by all she had to do, but she managed to get it done. She practised the embroidery for the bridal gown on the test dress she'd been working on at night. She'd used the plain cotton that became soft as she worked with it. The weave was tight, and it held its shape well. As the dress came together, she decided it was nice enough to add to her small wardrobe. She found a sizeable supply of embroidery thread in vibrant orange that had been sitting untouched. As soon as she saw that orange, she knew what she would use it for. She stayed up late every night, working on it.

At last it was complete, and she was proud of the result. She'd lengthened the bodice so it went past the hips, with no horizontal waist seam. It made for a cleaner, longer look. The overskirt had a bustle, but much smaller, and gathered at the back, making the front smoother, more form-fitting. She'd been inspired by a priest's cassock, which gave a long, smooth silhouette. She'd also raised the shoulder seams and eliminated the puffed sleeves that were still popular. This was out of necessity; she didn't have enough fabric to create the extra volume. Instead, she thought of Callum's coat and how well it fit his frame, how elegant its cut was while still allowing free movement. She fastened everything at the back with a martingale, with buttons covered in the same fabric.

But the real achievement was in the embroidery. She'd used several colours to create a floral border along the hems, cuffs, and neckline. She used the orange to add fire lilies throughout the design, with two prominent ones on the martingale buttons. They were like two flaming eyes—the focal point of the gathered bustle. She'd managed to barter with Sarah for some spruce roots and made a corset for herself that had more give without losing structure.

She kept it on an old dressmaker form in her room so she could admire it from all angles. The unbleached cotton had darker flecks in it, giving the fabric a rich texture, like the sandy loam of the forest. She could smell the pines when she looked at it. The lilies dominated the design; all that orange should have looked garish, but it was alive with colour. At first glance, the embroidery looked like beadwork. She knew she'd created something special, like her valances that had ended up on Mrs. Wakefield's shelves. She wondered if they were still there.

"Charlotte, come join me for some tea," Mrs. Lambton called. She'd locked the shop door and pulled the shades down, closing business for the day. She usually ended her day at her desk with a cup of tea, but this was the first time she'd invited Charlotte to join.

Mrs. Lambton poured some into a porcelain cup and handed it to Charlotte.

"Thank you, Mrs. Lambton," Charlotte said. The cup rattled in the saucer as she held it.

"Call me Rosalie, and let's add a little something, shall we?" She produced a small flask decorated with silver filigree and poured generously into both cups. It burned Charlotte's throat. Rosalie laughed. "We'll make a sot out of you yet!"

Charlotte laughed along and took another sip, this time without grimacing.

"You remind me of myself, Charlotte. When I was your age, my father brokered a marriage for me to a cruel man. Thankfully, we had no children," she looked down. "I think he was unable, but of course, that could never be said aloud. The best thing that man ever did was die early."

Charlotte was rapt. She'd never heard a woman, other than Mare, speak so frankly. She looked at Rosalie anew. "I've never been betrothed to anyone. Maybe I never will be."

"That's not something to mourn. The only way to keep any kind of control of yourself is to never marry."

"Perhaps for someone like you, but not for someone like me."

"There is always a way, dear."

Charlotte didn't think she could disagree, so she downed the rest of her tea. Rosalie refilled it. Charlotte started to feel warm.

"If you could do anything, what would it be?" Rosalie raised her cup like she was toasting.

Charlotte looked around them. "Have a shop like this of my own, maybe."

Rosalie put her cup down with a clang and clapped her hands. "Yes! That's exactly what I hoped you would say. Charlotte, I'm going to show you everything there is to know. I could tell there was something different about you. You're not like those other Métis girls, you're one of the good ones."

Charlotte's face fell. She hid it by taking another gulp of tea. She'd thought Rosalie was different; she had such modern, even futuristic ideas, and was successful. Everything Charlotte wanted to be herself. But in the end, Rosalie was like everyone else, and saw her as a half-person. A useful one she could pamper like a pet, but always a half-person. She was stained with the kind of dirt that never rubs off. Well, let them think that, she thought. If they thought of her as a half-person, they wouldn't pay too much attention to her. She could be half-hidden and do as she pleased.

Maybe she *could* go somewhere like Quebec where she wouldn't have to hide at all.

"Why, thank you," she said, raising her cup for more. "You're one of the good ones, too."

Rosalie threw her head back and laughed, then filled their cups again, this time without any tea.

∞

Rosalie had given her an afternoon off, so Charlotte put on her new dress and walked down to Wakefield & Son. People ogled her as she walked along Main Street. She knew she stood out and held her head high. She walked the way Rosalie walked: with purpose. Ever since that first evening of tea, Charlotte had observed her closely. When alone, she practised Rosalie's speech patterns, and felt sure she'd shed some of her French accent. It would probably never disappear all the way, but a hint was rather enchanting, so she was satisfied with that.

They'd continued having tea every evening. Now that Rosalie saw Charlotte as her protégé, she was much less demanding on her time. Charlotte no longer had to clean, and she was allowed to focus on the embroidery and the other detail work where she excelled. Rosalie hired another girl, an English one from Kildonan, to do the other work. Charlotte enjoyed her new elevated status. It was easy to be charmed by Rosalie, but she was careful to not let her guard down all the way. Part of her wanted to prove to Rosalie that she was more than a half-person, but she could see that would be fruitless. Even a forward-thinker like her employer still held to old prejudices that she didn't even recognize. Her ideas of native peoples were as regressive as the other settlers' but to her that was "just common sense."

Charlotte learned what she could from Rosalie Lambton, and continued with her Montreal plan, which she kept to herself. Occasionally, Charlotte would casually ask Rosalie about which were the prominent dress shops in Toronto and Montreal, which she saw as both inspiration and competition. Armed with her new knowledge, Charlotte was confident she could find employment at one of them.

Ahead of her on the boarded sidewalk, she saw a family: a father, mother, daughter of about ten years, and two small boys. The mother and the girl both wore kerchiefs on their heads, tied under the chin. They spoke to each other in a language she didn't know. They seemed to be confused and the parents argued, gesturing at different buildings. She thought about her own family's trips to Main Street when she was younger. She'd been so impressed with the few buildings that made up the town then. It was a grand place full of wonders. Now those original buildings were dwarfed by the new; some had even been torn down to make way for something bigger.

When she opened the door to Wakefield & Son, a little bell signalled her arrival. She liked the sound and decided to suggest that Lambton's also get a bell. A low partition separated the entrance from a row of desks where men sat doing paperwork. The room was noisy, with lots of talking and the distant clack of a typewriter. She understood the reason for the bell; no one would notice her otherwise.

A young man with spectacles rose from the nearest desk and met her at the partition. "May I help you, miss?"

"I'm here to see Callum Wakefield," she said.

"I'm afraid you'll need an appointment."

"Is he not here?"

"Well, he is in the office today, yes, but he's very busy."

"Tell him Charlotte Rougeau is here to see him. I'll wait."

The man looked annoyed but disappeared through the desks. He returned a few minutes later and opened a little gate in the partition to let her through. "Right this way."

Callum rose to meet her when she arrived at his office. He urged her to sit down as he closed the door behind her. "Charlotte, it's a surprise to see you. What can I do for you today?"

He seemed unnerved by her presence. Good, she thought.

"I'm here to sell you my scrip."

"Your . . . scrip?" His eyes shifted about.

"Yes. I know that's your trade. I'm here to sell it at face value."

He noticed her empty hands. They were folded in her lap and she carried no pouch or satchel. He gave her a knowing look. "Well, I'm not sure that's possible . . . scrip has seen some different market rates. Most people are happy with half-value."

"Half-value? Happy? I think that's a mistake on your part. I'm not interested in half-value. As I said, I'm here to sell to *you* at full value. It's what I'm owed. It's only fair."

She levelled her gaze at him and held it until his eyes slid away. He was quiet for a few minutes. "Well, I suppose you're right. Let me see what I can do."

He went to the corner where a safe was. He turned the dial and cranked it open. Inside she could see stacks of bills and other papers. A lot of it looked like the scrip her father had. He grabbed a stack of bills and returned to the desk. "Scrip like yours is valued at one hundred sixty dollars, but I'll give you the higher value of two hundred forty. For your trouble."

Charlotte smiled. "Thank you."

He counted out the bills, put them in an envelope, and handed it to her. He dropped it in her hands as if he was afraid to touch her. She folded the envelope in half and put it in her dress pocket, which was deep. "You look lovely," he said, his eyes soft. "So different from the girl who tried to teach Alyce French."

"I'm sure Alyce has other distractions now. As do you."

He folded his hands on the desk. "Yes, well, we've all seen a lot of changes. Did you know they're naming a street after our family? Wakefield Way. Has a nice ring, doesn't it?"

"Charming. You've really done well for yourself here. You'll probably sit in the government next. Who knows what else they'll name after you—maybe a whole town."

He didn't acknowledge her sarcasm, but she sensed he'd picked up on it. "Well, it was nice to see you. Maybe we'll cross paths again."

"Not likely. However, your bride's dress is almost ready, so I'll probably see her soon."

He rose from his desk and said, "Thank you for stopping by."

He led her by the elbow out through the desks and to the little gate. He left her there and returned to his office without looking back.

She patted the envelope in her pocket and returned to the shop. She should feel cheapened after that exchange, but she didn't. She knew she had no scrip documents, and he knew it too, since his family had been redeeming fake scrip for years and grown even more rich from it. But Callum was a decent enough man to feel shame at what he'd done. She was proud for collecting what was hers. That money belonged to her.

∞

Elissa came to the shop for her final fitting. The wedding was to take place at the end of June, which was unusual. Charlotte was accustomed to winter weddings. In summer, most people were away or farming so having a wedding then wouldn't work. One more change that didn't make sense.

Elissa did look lovely in her bridal dress. The white embroidery on the white silk was subtle and gave the effect of lace trim. It added life to the fabric. Mrs. Wakefield held the hem of the overskirt and bent close to examine it. On most dresses she worked on, Charlotte used the same floral pattern as on her beadwork valances. She knew the pattern so well that she could do it with her eyes closed. But on this dress, she created a replica of her treasured valances, the ones with the fire lilies she'd been so proud of.

After peering at it for several minutes, Mrs. Wakefield looked at Charlotte with narrowed eyes.

"Sarah always insisted the beadwork on those valances in my dining room is actually yours," she said softly. "I said such a thing was impossible and that she shouldn't tell fibs. But now I wonder."

Elissa turned in front of the mirror, revealing the back of the dress with its voluminous bustle and train, held in place with a martingale and two large buttons covered in the same silk as the dress. Charlotte had embroidered a fire lily on each one, in the same orange as the ones on her own dress, which she was wearing.

Charlotte smiled. "Every artist has a signature. That one is mine."

∞

It was an early morning in June when Charlotte packed up her case with her beading supplies, spare dress, and other meagre items. Her money was tucked away in the hide pouch with her ulu knife, which she carried in her pocket. She knew the knife would keep it safe. She looked around the room one last time and her eyes fell on her old moccasins, which sat in the corner. She considered for a moment, then added them to her case.

She left a note for Rosalie, letting her know she'd gone to Montreal. Rosalie would be disappointed her protégé was gone, but Charlotte no longer worried about pleasing other people. After all she'd been through, she knew she'd have to put herself first, because no one else ever would. By the time her employer found the note, Charlotte would be out of her reach.

Charlotte did feel a twinge of guilt and wondered if she was doing the right thing. Perhaps Rosalie truly did want to mentor her and leave the shop to her one day. But was that likely? She could waste years and years there and end up nowhere. Besides, if Rosalie meant what she said about controlling one's own life, she should understand why Charlotte left.

She descended the back stairs and closed the door behind her with a soft click. Few people were on the street at that hour. She stood in the dirt road and looked up at the shop. She'd been there less than a year, but it felt like a lifetime. She turned and walked toward The Forks, where the Assiniboine and Red met, and climbed into the waiting stagecoach. She looked at the fort, then down Main Street, and felt nothing. She leaned back in her seat and waited for the coach to leave.

Fredie
Lac du Bois Forest, June 1873

Fredie walked through the tall grass, as he did every morning.

It was early. The sun hadn't warmed the air yet, and the ground was still wet with dew. He climbed a sand hill through the tamarack. Dried needles crunched underfoot, releasing a pleasant scent. His breath was heavy when he reached the top of the hill and sat on a fallen log, facing east. The climb had been his morning ritual ever since they arrived in the bush. That first night, he hadn't been able to sleep. Restless, he went outside in the thin pre-dawn light and saw a fox skirting the edge of their clearing. The fox froze and stared at him, and Fredie froze, too. It blinked slowly at him, then turned and sauntered into the forest. He followed.

The fox led him through the grass and then up the sand hill. It paused at the fallen log, hopped up on it and sat there for a moment, then went down the other side of the hill and disappeared. Fredie sat on the log and was struck by the view. It was autumn then, and the birch leaves had turned bright yellow, like a dying fire. The hill was high enough to show the tops of trees, the stretching forest, and a faint glint of Lac du Bois on the horizon. Elk bugled in the distance. Sitting there, he felt the presence of something bigger than himself, bigger than the whole world. He thought maybe it was God, or perhaps the Creator from Mare's teachings. Maybe the two were the same thing. All the time he'd spent in church, he'd never experienced a feeling like he did sitting on that log. He'd repeated the journey every morning since, hoping to catch that feeling again.

This morning, his thoughts turned again to their life in St. Norbert. He wondered about Julien and Charlotte, what their lives were like, what they were doing. Were they happy? Did they think of him? He even missed his private lessons with Father Courchene, knuckle-rapping and all.

He wouldn't let himself think about the dogs. But some nights they came to him in his dreams; their charred bodies in one horrific tangle. He woke up cold and sweaty. He worried he could never bring himself to care for dogs again. He hoped the pain would fade with time, and the appearance of the fox gave him hope.

He and his father worked every day to improve their cabin: patching gaps where cold air came through, building a plank floor so they didn't have to constantly smooth out the lumpy dirt that made the table and chairs wobble. Planing the lumber by hand took time—"This is tedious without a mill," his father complained—but Fredie didn't mind. The repetition was peaceful; everything fell away when he was absorbed in it. He felt like he was shedding his grief with each curl of wood he shaved off.

"Leave it to me, Papaa," he said. "I'll take care of it." With Julien gone, Fredie had become his father's right hand. They'd built furniture together, and Fredie found hammering the joints together satisfying. Soon their sparse cabin looked like a home again.

He returned from the hill and saw his mother was up and stoking the embers in their outdoor oven. He'd collected the stones for it from around their clearing.

"The cattails will be up soon," she said. "We can go to that slough where they grow good, get enough to make some flour, eh? You and Suzette are good at pounding them into powder."

"Maybe the blueberries will be good this year and we can add them to that flour," Fredie said.

She opened her arm to invite him in. "You're getting too tall for hugs like this," she said.

He bent down and rested his head on her shoulder, like when he was little. She laughed and squeezed him tight.

"You looking for your fox again, aen rinaar?"

Fredie winced at his childish nickname. "I think he's gone. We're probably too noisy for him."

He knew his pain and sense of loss wouldn't last forever. But he didn't really want it to fully disappear. It was his inheritance. He could wallow in it, or use it to become stronger. He thought about Mare finding her family dead and having to start a new life. He could do that too. It was time for him and Suzette to fill the space Julien, Charlotte, Pierre, and their whole community left behind. It was time to weave the threads of his life into something new.

She handed him the stick she was using to stoke the fire and gestured for him to take over. Smoke billowed and filled his eyes. He coughed and waved his hand in front of his face.

"Did I ever tell you what my father said about foxes?"

Fredie shook his head, still coughing.

"He said that when you come across a fox and it turns around and looks at you, you can ask it for something."

Fredie looked at her. "Really?"

She nodded. "When I was little, I used to look for foxes, hoping for a wish." She patted his arm and took the poker back. She stirred the logs and a small flame took hold and grew. "I think you should keep looking for that fox on the hill. One day, he'll be waiting for you."

Acknowledgements

I want to thank many people for their help and support in creating this book, especially Dave Williamson for reading and editing the manuscript and offering advice and encouragement. It was during his Creative Writing class and later working one-on-one when the idea for this book took hold. I can't thank him enough.

Thank you to Maria for being my first reader and always asking for more pages. She helped me figure out why some things weren't working and always kept me going.

And special thanks to Sean, for endless love, support, and urging me to do this in the first place. None of this could have happened without him.